T0165340

REVELATION WARS

Book I:
The Beginning

J. SCOTT BYERLEY

iUniverse, Inc.
New York   Bloomington

Revelation Wars
Book I: The Beginning

Copyright © 2009 J. Scott Byerley

This is a work of fiction. All of the characters, names, incidents, organizations, and dialogue in this novel are either the products of the author's imagination or are used fictitiously.

iUniverse books may be ordered through booksellers or by contacting:

iUniverse
1663 Liberty Drive
Bloomington, IN 47403
www.iuniverse.com
1-800-Authors (1-800-288-4677)

ISBN: 978-1-4401-5077-7 (pbk)
ISBN: 978-1-4401-5079-1 (cloth)
ISBN: 978-1-4401-5078-4 (ebook)

Printed in the United States of America

iUniverse rev. date: 7/17/09

CHAPTER 1

"It is in our lives and not our words that our religion must be read."

Thomas Jefferson

EARLY SUMMER, 2007

The archangel Michael gathered his angels in the tabernacle on their 600-acre ranch nestled in a valley amid the Sangre de Cristo Mountains of northeast New Mexico. When he took his place behind the pulpit he was indeed energized, and his ocean-blue eyes peered deep into the souls of the five seated angels. To those gathered, only God and the angels of God could direct the citizens of the world safely through Armageddon. They were honored to be in the presence of Michael, the great angel who sits closest to the throne of the Lord. With his willowy, shoulder-length black hair and his glowing aura, he was the personification of strength and beauty.

Michael welcomed them as always with a warm smile and then he kneeled down before the cross behind the altar and bowed his head quietly in prayer. His naked body was covered in lamb's blood. When he rose, the air lifted with him, every spec of dust electrified by his powerful radiance. Every angel sat mesmerized.

The sacrifice had energized Michael for the sermon at hand. Mystical smoke, flowing from the small fire, escaped through the stone chimney high above the altar where he stood. His shadow towered on the wall behind him, making him appear even more reverent as he dipped the silver cup into the lamb's open wound, filling it with blood.

Slowly, he drank from the cup; his eye's closed as he savored every drop. The lamb's blood, he felt, purified him; he felt born again, divine.

Knowing they were ready, he began, "The Beast, the Anti-Christ, the Red Dragon of ten horns and seven heads, has risen in America, the new Babylon," he said. "Yes, Babylon, the filthy city of the whore, Jezebel, who polluted with her fornication and her proselytizing! Just look at what America has become – a nation of slaves to money and modern technology! Children grow up brainwashed, believing technology is the key to the future. Technology, spreading like an evil malignancy, we know, is nothing more than the beating drum of the Beast, calling his followers to the abyss. It is the portal to darkness.

"The goal of the Beast is to conquer the souls and minds of all who will listen and then take part in the Beast's slaughter of all that is sacred and holy. Already he has amassed an army of followers who have been deceived by his message lauding the so-called technological revolution, a revolution to which he has so self-righteously dubbed himself the founding father. The Beast must be stopped or the great deterioration, the loss of our souls to his world of sin, will continue, until we are powerless to stop him! We must intervene for the sake of God! This gift we will give our Father. We shall set the sacrifice, the glorious lamb, at his hand, and the sun shall break through the darkness and the glory of God will reign again, on Earth, and in heaven, as it is meant to be!

"We are at war! The Antichrist is alive and breathing fire into Babylon! Soon the seventh angel will join us and our mission will be revealed in the last revelation.

"Behold, the coming of the Lamb, the return of Christ our savior, is at hand!"

CHAPTER 2

AUGUST, 2007

Jimmy Davidson was in a deep sleep when the doorbell started ringing in the distance. He tried to ignore it, but the ringing didn't stop. He wanted more sleep. Actually, he wanted to sleep all day rather than have to deal with the trip that was ahead of him. He couldn't believe that whoever was at the door would not just go away. The visitor was persistent as hell, and it put Jimmy in a foul mood.

When he opened the door and saw their eager eyes, saw the Bibles clutched in their hands, he wanted to slam the door in their faces, hoping they would take the hint. "Sorry to wake you; I'm Brother Carroll and this is Brother Donte," said the first man, a chubby fellow in a cheap white button-down shirt and solid blue polyester tie. "Could we just have a few moments of your time to share with you the glory of the coming of the Lord?"

"Are you kidding me?" Jimmy answered.

"I'm sorry," Brother Carroll said, eyes bulging.

"Can't you guys take a hint?" Jimmy began to close his door.

Brother Carroll grabbed hold of the door, his cheeks puffing red. "There's no time for sleep in the face of Armageddon, my friend. Save yourself before it's too late. We'll pray for you!"

"Come back here again and I'll have you both arrested for trespassing!" Jimmy said before slamming the door shut. He stood behind the door for a few minutes and then peered through the side window to make sure they'd left.

At that moment the phone started ringing. "Jesus Christ!" Jimmy said. "It's Grand Central around here."

"Hello," he answered, more indignantly than he otherwise would.

"Today's the big day, huh?" the caller asked.

"That's right, Chase. Today's it. We're blowing this town this afternoon. Should be a nice drive."

"Yeah, right. So have you thought about what I asked you?" Chase said.

"Yeah, I have, and I'm sorry, but I just don't think the time is right for that just now. I'm just not sure I'm the personal injury type, you know."

"No, I don't know. What is the personal injury type? Is that what you think of me? Your brother's just a personal injury lawyer type of asshole?"

"No, of course not! I just haven't figured out what I'm going to do yet, Chase."

"All right, but I'm keeping the offer open. I'm not such a bad guy, you know," Chase said. "All I've ever wanted for you is your happiness, and I just think you might be happy with PI work if you tried it. The money's good and it's always interesting. It's good work."

"Yeah, I'm sure it is, but it's never been about money for me."

"It's not all about money for me either, Jimmy," Chase countered. "I'm a little more than you give me credit for. Maybe I'm not as smart as the money I've made should indicate, but I'm not a jerk without a soul. But hey, you've always been the deep one. Look, you're my brother, man, and what's mine is yours, you know that. If you ever want to give this a shot, I've got your back. Just remember that!"

"You've always had my back," Jimmy said.

"Stay out of trouble, will ya?" Chase replied.

"I'm a prosecutor," Jimmy snapped. "What kind of trouble could I possibly get into?"

They laughed and as Jimmy hung up the phone, he checked the clock in the cramped kitchen and started to make some coffee. It was 8:30 in the goddamn morning. He was agitated; he couldn't get Brother Carroll and his sidekick Brother Donte out of his head. Not only did they screw up his sleep, they'd disturbed him with their words. *What was that all about? Why do people like that feel like it's their mission to go around freaking people out?*

Two hours later Jimmy pulled up in front of Susan's house and just sat there staring into space. This was the last thing he wanted to be doing today. Susan Montera and Jimmy were moving dangerously close to the end of the long and winding road of a rocky relationship. He loved her and he hated her, and at that moment there was very little in between. Jimmy sat there knowing that in three short days it was possible he would be single again, something he had yet to embrace.

Susan, a recent graduate of Kentucky's University of Louisville, was taking off for Los Angeles to attend grad school at UCLA. She wanted to be a psychiatrist, and Jimmy knew better than anyone that she certainly had the talent for it. She could pick his mind like no one else. In some ways, he felt like he was being released from an intensive therapy program. He felt like he was her experiment, as if she could change the things she didn't like and make him better. The problem was that her experiment had failed. He felt more worthless now than ever.

She opened the door with that familiar sweet little fuck-you smile and Jimmy sauntered inside with a grimace. He hated breakups, and he had seen his share in his 28 years. None, however, were as difficult to swallow as this one. Susan, half Mexican American and half American Indian, was very bossy and super smart. *Too smart for her own good.* Jimmy knew he wasn't perfect, but he also knew he couldn't go through the rest of his life feeling like a complete failure just because he couldn't live up to her ideological expectations of achievement.

Of course, there are two sides to every coin. And Susan would waste no time reminding Jimmy that she supported him while he was in law school so he could become someone, not so he could lose all his energy and ambition just because it turned out to be something different than he thought it would be. You make a commitment and you stick to it. That's the way it was for Susan. And she still hadn't given up on Jimmy; not yet, anyway.

When he stepped into Susan's place, with all the boxes stacked in the corner, the apartment looked almost empty. Jimmy took a seat on a suitcase while she disappeared into the bathroom, still getting ready for the road trip. He was going to escort her to LA in her car, then fly back after a few days, once she was situated. The big things, furniture, clothes and such, were already on their way to California.

Her father, Lake Montera, whom Susan relied on heavily, insisted he pay her moving expenses. He'd also offered to help her with her rent in LA until she finished with graduate school. Jimmy and Lake had always gotten along well. Lake, a real estate developer in Tucson, Arizona, built a successful business and had become a self-made multi-millionaire. Although you'd never really know it, because he came off like a down-home rancher or western cowboy type. He was rough around the edges and very protective of his family.

Susan was an only child. Jimmy, over the few years they'd dated, had become the son Lake never had. Lake would have loved nothing more than if Jimmy would marry Susan and come to work with him in Tucson. Every good developer worth his salt wants a lawyer he can trust.

At one time Jimmy was actually considering a move to Tucson, which was major for him, but then Susan decided she was going to attend UCLA. Their relationship had suffered mightily ever since she'd made that decision. Neither would admit it, but they were both feeling the pressure of marriage. Both their families and Jimmy's friends and cohorts kept pushing the idea. Everyone seemed in favor of it, but the one person who mattered: Jimmy. He just wasn't a fan of marriage. His parents had divorced when he was two, and he never had a great relationship with his father. He watched his mother struggle to raise him and his brother and he just felt that what he had seen of marriage did not sell him on the ultimate contract – till divorce or death do us part.

Jimmy was a Kentuckian, and while he had grown fond of Tucson on his visits there, LA was a different story altogether. Though he loved adventure and travel, Kentucky was a beautiful state with a lot of southern charm and he just couldn't see himself leaving his roots for a city like LA. Not that there's anything really wrong with LA, but it just wasn't his cup of tea. For one thing, he didn't have any job connections there and he didn't want to start out on the bottom of some law firm's pecking order; he just couldn't do that.

On the other hand, his older brother and his only sibling, Chase Davidson, a partner at Davidson, Huehn & Park, L.L.C., had been making numerous overtures to Jimmy about associating with the firm and making the switch to personal injury. If he took that position it would be a decision based solely on making great money and he'd just been unable to bring himself to do it.

That was something that had become a real bone of contention between Jimmy and Susan. When she met Jimmy, he was a second-year law school student who was full of ideas and talked about a future in politics and maybe even working at legal aid after a stint at the Commonwealth's Attorney's office. And the truth is, he had Susan's number as a tree hugger from the start. Besides, she was gorgeous, so he would have told her anything. They weren't necessarily out-and-out lies; they were just ideas of his that weren't very well thought out at the time. For some reason, she just had this opinion about lawyers – that they were in the most useless, vain occupation in the world, unless they tried to do something with it that would actually benefit mankind.

That all sounded great when Jimmy was running his mouth back in law school, but the reality was much different now that he had been involved in several trials of largely lower-tier criminals who all shared the similar misfortune of growing up in impoverished communities. As a prosecutor he had already met enough local politicians to conclude that they – at least the ones he'd met – weren't in it for the right reasons. In fact, lately, more often than not, his thoughts turned to leaving the practice of law altogether; he just wasn't sure what he wanted to do or what he was looking for from a career. That killed Susan. She couldn't understand that kind of reluctance and indecision. When she decided to move to LA and wanted him to go with her, he didn't like the idea at all and everything just seemed to boil to the surface from that point on in their relationship. Jimmy and Susan just seemed to be locked in one long, uninterrupted argument. The trouble was, aside from all their differences, in a very basic sense they still loved each other. It was a volcanic equation.

After an hour of piddling around, they were nearly ready to depart on what both knew could possibly be their last journey together.

Susan walked into the room with her dark brown hair pulled back in a ponytail. She threw Jimmy a sad look with her brown eyes and sat down Indian style on the floor beside him.

"I'm sure going to miss this place," she said.

"Something tells me you're going to adjust just fine," he snapped.

"What do you mean by that?"

"You're just that kind of person. You'll be fine."

"What kind of person?"

"You're always moving forward." Jimmy stood and extended a hand to lift her to her feet.

She shook her head. "What? Does that mean I can't reflect?"

"Of course not, Freuda, I'd never accuse you of that."

"I hate it when you call me that. It's insulting."

"To whom, you or Sigmund Freud?"

"Whatever."

They packed the last few boxes into her Honda Accord and they were off. It was a beautiful August day, a great day for driving. Jimmy had the trip all mapped out. They planned to take it slowly, to stop and see the sites along the way. Susan really wanted to stay at least one night in Taos, New Mexico, if they made good time. She also wanted to include Tucson on the itinerary, but Jimmy ruled it out since he didn't think their relationship was up for it at the moment.

Lake would mean no offense, but he would start asking them when the big date was going to be. That was the last thing they needed. Jimmy was pretty sure they were breaking up. He knew Susan wasn't going to give up without a fight, and as it always is in the end, people just seem to hang on longer than they should. Their sojourn to California was either going to be the end or a new beginning and neither was really sure which.

They were just past St. Louis when Susan started another assault to bring Jimmy into the light. Jimmy yawned. Outside the car the sun was fading into the horizon, and as Susan continued her rant, Jimmy wondered if their relationship was fading away with the sun. He also wondered why she insisted on talking about it so much. He just wanted to try to enjoy their time together, but she just wouldn't let it go.

"So have you figured out what you're going to do?" she finally asked.

"Do we really have to talk about this right now? Let's just enjoy the ride."

"I think we *need* to talk about it."

"No, I think you *want* to talk about it."

"Well, what's wrong with trying to figure things out? I want to know where you stand. I want to know where *we* stand."

Jimmy broke into song, doing his best Jagger. "'You can't always get what you want. You can't always get what you want. But you can try sometime and you just might find, you'll get what you need. Oh yeah. You'll get what you need.'" He tried to move his mouth like Jagger, looking more like Mr. Ed.

"Seriously, Mick, are you just planning on taking me to LA, dropping me off and never seeing me again? I need to know."

"This isn't just about me," he shot back. "What do you want?"

"You know what I want," she said. "I want you to move to LA with me. I want us to have a fresh start in a new place."

"The only thing that would be different is the location, and I'm not sold on the location you've chosen."

"Maybe you're just not sold on me."

Jimmy just shook his head and was quiet. He was a prosecutor and he still could never win an argument with her. He was upset about the fact that she'd made her decision to attend graduate school at UCLA without much consultation with him. She just assumed he'd follow her there. She'd quickly point out that they had a great psychiatry program and that since he wasn't happy with his career in Louisville, he had more reasons to go than to stay. Jimmy didn't see it quite so simply. Moving to LA was more than a career shift; it was making a commitment he wasn't sure he was ready for.

If he followed her to LA, they may as well be married. And as much as he loved her, their constant bickering was wearing him out. He didn't want to tell her, but he needed some time away from her to figure out what he wanted. It's difficult to decide exactly what you want when someone keeps badgering you to make up your mind. He wanted a separation, maybe not for good, but at least for a short while to put things into perspective. He had a lot to think about and he wanted more space in which to do it. The truth was, he kept going back and forth about his career and his future and he wasn't sure where he'd be in a few months, so he wasn't going to lie just to pacify her and make her happy.

She wanted more than he was willing to give her. Yet, even though he felt like they were breaking up, he also felt deep down that doing so might be the biggest mistake of his life. He loved her. He was just mad at her because she was forcing him to analyze everything and he was tired of it. She could never accept the status quo; she always forced the issues. The only thing Jimmy knew for sure was that he was seeking salvation; he needed direction and he also needed a change.

They stopped over in Oklahoma City and spent the night. They were both exhausted. Jimmy was content to go to sleep and as soon as he hit the king-size bed it was lights out for him. Susan couldn't sleep. She lay awake beside him feeling she may have made the mistake of her life in deciding to attend grad school at UCLA. She'd been pushing Jimmy too hard and she knew it. He just wasn't ready and she could tell. She was scared that these last few days of travel would be their last together. She had a very bad feeling and it was making her sick to her stomach. She spent the better part of the night on the cool floor in the bathroom fighting back her nausea.

Jimmy slept through it all. She could sense that they were already separated in his mind and it was killing her. Always the devout Catholic, she prayed to St. Jude, the patron saint of hopeless causes, for an answer to her prayers. She prayed that Jimmy and she would find the light again and spend the rest of their lives together. She prayed that Jimmy would just wake up and tell her what she so desperately wanted to hear – that all he really needed was her and that everything else, including his career, was just details.

Exhausted from thinking and praying all night, Susan finally fell into bed beside Jimmy and went to sleep. The light was already coming in through the hotel window. She snuggled close. If only for a while, they were resting together, quietly, peacefully.

CHAPTER 3

Jane Tierney, a political news correspondent for GNN, Global News Network, waited with her cameraman, Uriel Galatan, in a hangar at Boston's Logan International Airport for Richard Novak to arrive. He was late, and she was growing nervous. The short notice had given her very little time to prepare for the interview. Plus, it was slated to last only 15 minutes, tough work when there are thousands of questions to be answered. Although she'd done lots of interviews with bigwigs in the past, this one was by far her biggest to date.

Richard Novak was one of the ten richest men in the world. He was a member of the .000001 percentile, one of the richest of the rich, and at only 53 years old he had already amassed a fortune larger than the GDP of some of America's longest standing foes, Cuba and North Korea, combined. He rarely granted interviews and he was known for being a tough assignment, always careful and noncommittal in his positions.

Jane was especially worried since most billionaires tend to surround themselves with yes-men, something that spelled danger for a correspondent such as Jane, known for brazenly throwing coals into the fire at every opportunity. The world didn't know much about Richard Novak, primarily because he kept a low profile and surrounded himself with a small circle of friends and advisors. Behind the scenes, though, he was known as one of the great philanthropists of modern times.

The fact of the matter was he had amassed billions, and given away billions. He supported medicine and made significant contributions to lick some of the greatest plagues known to man in the Common Era: AIDS, poverty, hunger, contaminated water and cancer. He even spent millions on promoting birth control and safe sex throughout the world. By all accounts, he was an extraordinary and fascinating man.

His great fortune was not a birthright; he'd earned it in the great techno-revolution, a process through which the world's globalized society is still evolving. He was the founder of Red Diadem Incorporated, most often referred to as RDI, and a media mogul who'd recently acquired GNN in a move that positioned him at the summit of the race to interactive TV, a major technological battleground and a new frontier for the major players in the world of cyber-technology.

Shortly before noon, a black limousine appeared on the asphalt tarmac slowing to a halt next to a glossy white Gulfstream G550, no ordinary private business jet. Known for its sleek design, its extra-large cabin and its superior technology, the G550 was easily one of the finest, most beautiful aircraft in the world. Jane looked at the shiny, white fuselage and shook her head admiringly. This was the modern day chariot of kings. When you'd reached the highest stratosphere of wealth and were able to travel in the luxury and comforts of a G550 at your leisure, you were one helluva powerful human being.

Still not sure how she'd been lucky enough to draw the assignment, Jane's stomach was tied in knots. For the first time in her life, she was having a hard time getting a grip on her emotions. Her biggest fear was that she was going to blow the interview and with it, her lofty ambitions. Only 34 years old, she'd been with GNN for just five years, having paid her dues at a WBC affiliate out of Washington, DC, for several spectacular years where she quickly mastered the art of the interview. She was always well prepared, and the heavyweight networks noticed right away that she was special. Although she hated the hours and the migraines, she loved being in the limelight of media coverage. GNN made her the right offer, and she took it – to anchor the afternoon news and handle the cream of special political assignments.

Richard Novak stepped out from the back of the limousine and immediately strode over to Jane with long, purposeful steps as she fidgeted with her hair that was blowing in the wind of the roaring jet engines. Suddenly it dawned on her that not only was this the interview of all interviews, but this man, Richard Novak, was a towering figure and pretty damn good-looking. Even the patches of grey at his temples were more stately than age-defining. Still, the most lucid epiphany of all was that the billionaire walking toward her was also her boss. At last she admitted to herself that she was not just nervous, she was frightened.

"Ms. Tierney, glad you could make it on such short notice," he said, extending his hand, and then walking her to the open jet door. Uriel followed closely, his equipment in tow.

It's a great honor to meet you, Mr. Novak," she said. "I have to be honest, though. I really hope I don't screw this up. I do like my job."

Richard looked down at her smiling, his dark brown eyes glistening. "I really hope you don't screw this up, too," he said.

"I'm sorry," she said, stepping up into the plane, "I'm just a little nervous."

He laughed. "I'm only kidding you. Relax, you'll be fine. Let's get settled and then whenever you're ready we can start the interview. I hope you don't mind about having to go along with me back to Seattle, but my son goes off to college next week at Stanford and I want to send him off properly. You know, I'm going to give him a swift kick in the ass and tell him not to come back until he's got his shit together."

Jane laughed aloud, like it was the funniest thing she'd ever heard. She wasn't one of the suck-ups who always laughs whenever Richard Novak says something mildly amusing, but she thought he was genuinely funny. A geek at heart, his charm struck a chord with her and she instantly felt more at ease.

She walked to a leather sofa and sat down, and with a nod Uriel quietly began setting up for the interview from a corner spot in the main cabin. Uriel knew he had to be ready to roll quickly, as Jane had a knack for starting an interview without ever giving the proper cues. In fact, her record for driving her cameramen crazy was well known. He was newly assigned to Jane, and he was doing his best to keep a low profile and blend into the scenery. She liked him because he was quiet, which allowed her to think. The last cameraman she'd had always made small talk, driving Jane to bring the matter up with her superiors and thereby forcing his reassignment.

She couldn't help it. It's not that she was a prima donna; it was the exact opposite, in fact. She knew she was good in front of a camera, but only if she was prepared, and for that she needed to be able to hear herself think. She really believed that if she was not fully prepared and in control, she could appear quite ordinary. Jane wanted to be more than just another pretty news face; she wanted her delivery, as much as her story, to be newsworthy.

"Would you like something to drink? Have you eaten?" Richard asked, taking a seat across from her.

At that moment they were interrupted by three men passing between them in dark suits, wearing earpieces, and very much resembling the Secret Service. All nodded at Richard as they walked by and disappeared into the next section of the plane. Richard seemed unfazed by their presence, but Jane's eyes followed them quizzically.

"Security," he said. "You can't be too careful these days."

Jane nodded. "Some water would be nice," she said, taking a moment to gaze around the lush interior. The G550 was trimmed out in mahogany and the furniture in the main cabin was all brown leather and very soft. Everything was polished to a sparkle and although she'd been in premium jets before, she'd never had a man as powerful, rich and charming as Richard Novak sitting in front of her. *Remember that I've got a job to do. I've got to get this right. This has to be perfect.* She was starting to get nervous again as she could hear the chant of positive encouragement in her own mind; she was freaking out.

"I'm just curious," she said, smiling. "Why did you request me, specifically, for this interview? You could have had anyone you wanted."

"I know that, that's why I picked you."

"Yes, but why?"

"Because of moments just like right now. You always ask the tough questions and you say what's on your mind. I like that."

"But most good reporters are just like that, so why me? You still haven't answered my question."

Richard smiled. "In my estimation, Jane, you are the best. And I always get the best because I can."

Jane blushed. That was not the answer she'd been looking for. She was surprised by his candidness. He was going to be one helluva interview. She'd struck gold.

"Why 15 minutes?" she asked. "This is a long flight."

"Sure it is, but I think it gets boring when someone talks about themselves for too long, don't you? I have some things to say, but I want people to have time to digest my words so their interest and curiosity about me are merely aroused. Let them learn about me gradually. As in all relationships, it's a process, and this is only the beginning. I assure you, this will be an interview you won't soon forget."

"We'll get started when we get up in the air," she said. "I hope you don't mind, but I want to get started while the questions are still fresh and before I get to know you better. Less small talk makes it easier for me to ask the tougher questions."

Richard laughed. "So you're going to make it tough on me, are you?"

She smiled. "Well, I was told the purpose of this assignment, excuse me, this interview, was because you wanted the world to get to know you more on a personal level. I want to get to know you along with the world and beginning promptly will help me focus and ask the right questions."

"I'm very impressed," he said. "You may not have been told, but I was planning on making an announcement at the end of the interview, so if you could set the stage for it, well, that would be great."

"Yes, and may I ask what that announcement will be so I know how to set the stage?" she inquired.

"Yes, you may ask, but you will have to wait to hear it along with the rest of the world." He smiled, knowing her interest was piqued.

The plane started down the runway and everyone braced briefly for the lift-off. The Gulfstream was smooth and they barely noticed as the pilot ascended to 30,000 feet. Jane gathered her thoughts. Uriel quickly shut a few of the windows behind Richard, adjusting the lighting.

"Are you ready?" she asked.

Richard stood and checked his silver tie in a mirror and sat back down across from Jane. "Yes, I'm as ready as I'll ever be, Ms. Jane Tierney," he said.

She smiled nervously. "Good, then let's get started. Anytime you need to take a break, please just say so; we're in no hurry."

He nodded, and she began. "Welcome ladies and gentlemen. I am here today with an extraordinary gentleman, Richard Novak. I'm sure most of you are aware that he is one of the founding fathers of the great technological era. He is also a man the world has yet to really meet. It's often the case that we are affected by great citizens of our time, great philanthropists such as Mr. Novak, without ever getting an up-close look at who they really are. Today, we're going to spend a little time with Mr. Novak and hopefully answer some of your questions about who this remarkable man really is. What is his vision for the technological revolution? How does he see his current position in the world? How does he see his future taking shape with RDI? I'm also told that at the end of the interview Mr. Novak plans to make an announcement that is sure to cause considerable buzz.

"Mr. Novak, first I want to say thanks for inviting me and our audience on board here with you for this interview."

"Thank you," he said. "It's a great pleasure to have you all here. Please Jane, call me Richard; I assure you I'm not as old as I may look."

"Yes, of course," she said, "and might I say that you do not appear old at all. In fact, for a man of such modest means, you have managed to take pretty good care of yourself."

Richard laughed playfully as Jane enjoyed the moment, before the interview began in earnest. To start things off, Jane decided to throw up a softball. "Richard, all kidding aside, you are obviously a man of great means. Can you share a little something about yourself that people probably don't know?"

"I would be very happy to do that," he said. "I just want people to know that outside of my corporate life at RDI, I am just an ordinary, very normal man. My wife, Marian, and I have been married for 22 years and we have a son, Jack, who is heading to college this spring. We live a normal life. I go to work every day at RDI. Yes, we have a lot of money and the accompanying privilege, but that is not who we are. We are human beings with passions and ordinary problems just like everyone else. We understand that with privilege comes great responsibility and that is something we take very seriously."

"I see, and isn't it true that you have devoted a great deal of your time and money to charitable causes around the world?" Jane asked. "Can you tell us why you are so inspired to put your money to such good use for your fellow citizens?"

"Thank you. Yes, actually I'm very pleased that you started out with that question, not because it gives me an opportunity to talk about myself, which I will, of course, but because it enables me to express my concerns about some wealthy members of society who seem to think it's okay to make a fortune and then hold onto every penny for their own use and enjoyment.

"Giving to causes I feel need my financial support is something I take very seriously. I have given over a billion dollars of my own money to fight AIDS in Africa. It's a significant amount of money and it has helped some. But let's be honest; this disease is a growing monster and even a billion dollars is like putting a Band-Aid on a grossly severed limb. These people need more help and they are desperate. I am here for them and for people all over the world, whether they are starving in an American ghetto or on the streets of Mozambique. I want to make a difference in the world, not just with my money, but with my leadership.

"Did you know that over 1.3 billion people in the world lack access to safe water? This is the most basic human necessity besides love. We look out into our lakes and oceans, and we see its abundance. Yet, there are entire countries with overused, contaminated and diminishing water supplies. I want the world to unite to help these people.

"I believe the richest in our society should give the most. And, as a great man by the name of Andrew Carnegie once said, in far more eloquent terms than I can now submit to you, 'I would be ashamed if I died with any money left in my pockets that I did not spend to help the citizens of the world.' Mark my words; I intend to spend every penny I've got on the causes I believe in. I intend to spend all of my energy encouraging others to do the same. But, do not be naive; these problems cannot be fixed easily just by someone throwing money at them. The bigger task is making sure that money gets put to proper use. That takes management. That takes organization. That, my friends, takes leadership."

When he stopped, Jane sat stunned. It took her a moment to catch her breath; she found herself completely caught up in his words and for a moment forgot about the fact that she was there to give an interview. "Wow, thank you, Mr. Novak; I'm sorry, Richard," she said. "Please expound on what you believe others, besides the very wealthy, can do.

Obviously, it's not only the wealthy who have a responsibility to make the world a better place."

"Glad you brought that up." Richard paused for a moment, as Jane cursed herself quietly, vowing no more softballs. "Let me just say that we cannot solve the problems in the world — disease, hunger, thirst, crime and poverty — with money and charitable contributions alone. That is not enough. People have to be committed to change. They have to be committed to helping their fellow man just as passionately as they feel when the battle drums sound, sending young men and women off to war in the name of peace, liberty and democracy.

"If we have chosen to be the great emancipators, if that is our job, then I wish to really open this debate. Why shouldn't we go to war against the greatest threats to our world: over-population, lack of adequate education and birth control, technological gaps between societies that allow one country to prosper while another is still fishing for dinners in contaminated waters. Waters contaminated, I might add, by waste from our factories and the pillaging of resources vital to their existence.

"And yes, maybe the greatest gap, the greatest problem in the world is economic, but as a tech-minded individual, I believe strongly that if we invest in these countries with technology and training, we can bring them into the new frontier, we can raise the level of opportunity for everyone and improve their quality of living to a level every man, woman and child is entitled to enjoy. The world needs so much, and we, with so much wealth, education, power, passion and means, have so much yet to give."

Jane smiled. "Won't critics just say these are not new ideas, that you're espousing on matters close to your heart? Isn't this just Wilsonianism?" she asked.

"Jane, I'll be honest with you and the audience. If I cared about what critics would say, I wouldn't be here and I wouldn't make a very effective leader or businessman, now would I?

"Woodrow Wilson was a visionary. There is no doubt about that, and while I agree with his belief in greater internationalism and cooperation within the global community, I do not necessarily believe the world needs to be conquered by our democracy. That's what you're asking me, isn't it?

"I'm a man of history and history has proven that Wilsonianism doesn't work. People will always resist change when they themselves have not decided that change is desired. You can't implement change with outside force. Look at Iraq; it's been almost five years since the war and it's still very much a failed experiment. Want more proof? Think of the British around the time of the American Revolution, and look at their experience in India, Africa and the Boer War."

"I hear what you're saying Richard, but these great changes you're talking about – isn't this just an example of yet another rich, white man in America experiencing Rudyard Kipling's *White Man's Burden?*"

"Well, I appreciate your concern that I'm just a man with a lot of money trying to exert my will upon the world, but I am not a missionary. My goal and the purpose of this discussion is to raise awareness of the great plagues in our society, and I believe we can help.

"Do I mean just wealthy, white Anglo-Saxon men and exclusively Americans? No, I'm talking about a unifying effort to make the world a better place. But, yes, someone, some country has to lead the way. Let me make this clear; I don't see myself as a "neocon." I'm not promoting ethnocentric demagoguery. I simply believe there's a lot we can give from our experience and with our technology. I'm not saying our way is best and the rest had better follow suit. But let me ask you this: Does that water you have beside you on the coffee table taste any better because you know it's been purified and is free of cancer-causing contaminants?"

Jane was in her rhythm now and she wasn't rattled by his attempt to bring the argument back to her. *Bring it on!* "You say you're not a missionary. Are you a man of faith? Does your faith guide you in making the determination that more needs to be done and that you can play an important role to that end?"

Richard's face turned red. "Am I a man of faith?" Richard reiterated, obviously annoyed. "I believe in mankind. And I have faith in our ability to make a difference in the world with our gifts. I'm a man who has been blessed and I feel it is my duty to give back." Then for the first time, he paused and studied her eyes, then took a deep breath. "Do you believe in the Bill of Rights?" he asked.

"Why yes, of course," she answered.

"And religious freedom?"

"Yes."

"And I do as well," he said. "However, I do not personally rest my faith in God; I rest my faith in man. This is not a one-size-fits-all world, and I have tried to be clear in my view of that. I'm a humanist. I believe in people."

"Richard, you also mentioned that we have 'chosen to be the great emancipators.' I'm sure everyone would like to know, were you referring to Iraq?"

"I was referring to Iraq and Afghanistan, the war on terror, and also to the most embarrassing and disappointing manner in which we dealt with the Bosnian conflict. My point is this: Changing leaders is one thing, changing hearts and lives is another. We have the greatest military in the world. We also have the greatest technology in the world. And our citizens have the greatest opportunities in the world.

"You want people to stop being terrorists, well then, give them a reason to live. I recognize that that may sound controversial, but it shouldn't. This, again, is a socio-economic problem. The cancer of the world is poverty and the fact that ordinary citizens, the lowest common denominators in every society, don't believe their lives have any great meaning and impact. People need to feel valued. People need to feel a sense of power. If you grow up in a village in Iraq, where are you going to get the power that validates your existence, and your suffering, and the suffering of your family? How are you going to justify the hardship of living in a world with little means and very little, if any, hope for any real future? Honestly, Jane, what do these people have to lose? They are so dangerous because they have absolutely nothing to lose!"

Sensing the need to wrap things up, Jane said, "So is it your belief then that with generosity such as yours we can change even the hearts and minds of terrorists?"

"You've missed the point," he said. "Am I not being clear? Am I not being deliberate? What I'm trying to say is that for every cause there is an effect, it is a scientific certainty. If you want to change the effect, you need to first alter the cause. And perhaps more clearly, if you want to change people, change the conditions of their lives. Then you can begin to change the things that attract them to suicide bombs and other heinous crimes because they will have more options – better options – available to them.

"There will always be terrorists. The world is never going to be a perfect place for everyone. I was not trying to suggest I could make it so, or offer a simple solution. These are difficult times that raise tough questions with multi-faceted answers. I am merely saying I'm prepared to use my money and my leadership abilities to raise the opportunities and quality of life for all people in the world and I want to encourage all Americans to join me."

"Richard, our time is almost up here. When we started I indicated that you were going to be making an announcement today. Would you care to take a moment now to share that with us?"

"Yes. Before we sign off, I wish to announce that I am planning on running for President of the United States in 2008. Please join me in this great endeavor, the highest of all endeavors, to make the world a better place for all people. I want to win *your* hearts and minds. I plan to win the presidency and to make you proud of the world you live in. Thank you."

"Cut," Jane said to Uriel, smiling in approval at Richard. "You are a very interesting man. I wish I could have asked you more questions; there's so much more to know. I had no idea where you were going when you started. You really surprised me."

"I'm sure I surprised almost everyone," he said.

"I'm sure you did," she said, her excitement visible in her broad smile.

CHAPTER 4

GNN.com

U.S. NEWS
Animals Massacred in Southwest

Friday, August 17, 2007 Posted 8:30 AM EDT

SANTA FE (GNN) – Strange attacks on livestock in Arizona and Oklahoma have devastated farmers and animal rights activists alike, bringing together a strange alliance, uniting to seek a breakthrough in the shocking string of crimes.

"I've worked for years to support my family, raising livestock for beef," Buck Pace said. "I have never seen anything like this before. It makes me sick. You can argue about what is cruelty, but farmers ain't cruel. We're ordinary people working to feed ordinary folks. We make our living off the land and God's creatures. These people must be deranged and sick! How could anyone cut the heart out of a cow, or decapitate a lamb, completely draining its blood from its carcass? I don't know if it's kids or or some kind of a cult, but I'm taking steps to protect my stock. They got 14 of my cows in one night. Down the road, I heard they killed several lambs, decapitated them right there on the spot. I mean these people are sick!"

Police departments across the Southwest are working with the FBI, following thousands of leads that have come in since the rampage began last week. To date, no arrests have been made, and investigators seem baffled by the scope and numbers of animals that have been killed.

Stay tuned to GNN for the latest developments.

CHAPTER 5

Jimmy woke up first and walked to Starbucks across the street and bought some coffee. He was ready to hit the road and anxious to get the day started. Originally, when he mapped out the trip to California, he thought when they were in Oklahoma City they should stop by and see the Oklahoma City National Memorial, located at the site of the 1995 bombing where the Alfred P. Murrah Federal Building in downtown Oklahoma City once stood. Now that he was there he wasn't so sure it was a good idea since they had a long way to go, and they weren't getting along very well. He knew the site would be haunting and emotionally draining; so many innocent lives were lost there.

A first-year law school student when the bombing occurred on April 19, 1995, Jimmy remembered hearing about it on the radio as he drove to class and recalled being in shock at what he was hearing. When he walked into class only a few people had heard about it, but the news spread like wildfire and everyone spent the rest of the afternoon glued to televisions as the nightmare unfolded before their eyes.

The horror was unimaginable; the prevailing thought was that it had to have been an act committed by foreign terrorists. No one thought for a moment that Americans could have inflicted so much pain and bloodshed on their own people. Everyone was angry and saddened when they found out about McVeigh and Nichols. To think that Americans would attempt to make a statement to the government by killing innocent U.S. citizens was preposterous.

While Jimmy will never forget the tragic events of September 11, 2001, that changed the world, it was the tragedy in Oklahoma City that had first inspired him to become a prosecutor. He may have been an idealist, but he wanted to put the bad guys away, to be the hand of justice tipping the scales in favor of the victims; he wanted revenge against anyone who would purposefully hurt innocent people of any race, creed or nationality.

Naturally, these qualities made Jimmy a fast-rising star in the Commonwealth's Attorney's office, but he was just tired of all of the deals and all the petty political wrangling that gets in the way of justice being served. He wanted to make a difference in the world and he still believed he could. He just wasn't sure where he belonged; he needed to find his place, his mission.

Susan was still in bed when Jimmy opened the hotel room door. She looked up at Jimmy with tired eyes and a weak smile. Jimmy could tell she'd stayed up late, but he was ready to go and he wasn't about to let the fact that she was a night owl slow him down.

"I hope you got me some coffee, too," she said.

"Of course," he answered.

"Oh my head hurts," she said, "I stayed up too late."

"Why?"

"Why did I stay up so late?"

"Yeah."

"I don't know, just wasn't tired after the long drive," she answered unconvincingly.

Jimmy knew better, but if she didn't want to talk about it that was fine with him. He knew her well enough to know it was probably going to come up later in the day anyway, whatever she was thinking about. After they both took showers they were back on the road again. Susan wanted to stop by the memorial, so Jimmy followed his directions to the Murrah Plaza and Memorial Overlook situated between Harvey and Robinson avenues in downtown Oklahoma City. Their hotel had been on Main Street, only a few blocks away, so it didn't take long before they were there.

They parked the car on Sixth Street and walked to the outdoor

Symbolic Memorial which sits on three acres, entering through the first of what are referred to as the *Gates of Time*. At this place the entrance notes the time of 9:01, and the exit notes the time of 9:03, memorializing the time of 9:02, the moment of the explosion. That moment in history brought destruction of the innocent and the chaos of the aftermath, raising questions that would never be fully answered, Jimmy thought.

There was a lot to see. It was all very moving and at the same time there was a very serene feeling to the place. The strangers they passed as they moved from one place to another were all quiet and respectful, and every face reflected the true meaning of the memorial; Americans must never let this happen again. That was the same lesson learned from 9/11 perhaps, but it struck Jimmy and Susan that the message of Oklahoma City was that we can never again let this happen at the hands of our own citizens.

Jimmy, as a prosecutor, had always believed that while America is a country built on freedom, the price of freedom is almost too much to bear when you see what those who abuse their freedom can do in a moment of madness. He saw the memorial as testament to the fact that sometimes even Americans do not understand how great their freedom really is and how lucky they are to have been born in this blessed country. This is America, where if you want to get a message through to a politician you write a letter, you protest, you exercise your rights as citizens to speak out and question the leadership. You do not, however, kill and maim innocent people and destroy the lives of all who knew and loved them. To do so is evil, pure and simple.

Jimmy and Susan sat for several moments in front of the reflecting pool listening to the flowing water and looking around at the peaceful surroundings.

"I just can't believe people could do this to other people. To take 168 lives is just so monstrous, so insane," said Susan.

"But they weren't insane," he said. "They were evil."

"You're right," she said. "Only an evil person could commit such a horrible crime. They were really brainwashed with their anti-American crap."

"They saw themselves as heroes in a new American revolution,"

Jimmy replied. "McVeigh thought he was a soldier. He never showed any remorse."

"Well, convincing yourself that you're a soldier is just a means of desensitizing the act, but any good shrink will tell you half their clients are soldiers of past wars," Susan said. "Soldiers are not without remorse; only sick, depraved, fame-seeking, disillusioned sickos are without remorse. Maybe McVeigh and Nichols weren't technically insane or sociopathic, but they were definitely living in another reality."

"Yeah, you're right, and the scary thing is that right now somewhere in this country there are probably some other freaks just like them organizing their followers," Jimmy said. "They're probably showering in the glory of their privilege in knowing what no one else can know — their mission, their justification for being in existence in the first place. As a prosecutor, let me tell you, I learned firsthand that people can rationalize anything. McVeigh did it. Nichols did it. Hell, even Hitler did it.

"The irony is that our country, which is founded on principles of freedom, just happens to be the ultimate breeding ground for these kinds of freaks, whether they're religious fanatics like David Koresh or people like McVeigh. Their freedom allowed them to become monsters and they seem to have one thing in common, that need to stand out, to be special. Some people just believe it's their destiny to be what they perceive as great. The problem is society offers little protection from those who appoint themselves judge and executioner."

"It's insanity really," said Susan. "It reminds me of Raskolnikov in Dostoevsky's *Crime and Punishment* — the young man, how he committed the murders, convinced that his victims didn't matter and didn't deserve to live. It was only afterward that he considered the consequences. And with McVeigh, you get the feeling the consequences never mattered to him because he committed the crime with the consequences in mind, only the consequences in reality were different than his ideological fantasy. Murderers can be rational and highly intelligent and calculating, but they're still not living in the same world as everyone else. Whatever their reasoning, it's always morally vacant logic."

"Well you're the one who wants to be a shrink — good luck!"

"Yeah, well maybe I can snap some of these fuckers back into reality!"

"I doubt it! You can't even fix me. Besides, they don't want to be snapped back into reality. They don't see shrinks until they're pleading an insanity defense at their criminal trials. Then some poor prosecutor like me gets to lose sleep at night trying to make sure they don't get away with it and that they get what they deserve."

"Lucky you."

"Well, I think I'm almost done with it," said Jimmy. "I've got to find something else. There's something better for me."

"What about me?"

"You already know what you want," he answered.

"No, you big jerk. I'm saying maybe you could choose me and move to California and find that something else in your career there."

"Susan, does it always have to come back to this? Every time we're talking it has to come back to you and me and California?"

"I'm sorry."

"Well, then please, stop! Christ, just stop!"

"I'm sorry," she said. "Take my hand."

When Jimmy looked at her she was starting to cry. She was an emotional person and he didn't want to let her go. The effect of the memorial was to make them appreciate what they had. Although they went in there glutted with everyday thoughts and the turmoil of their fast-paced, changing lives, they were leaving with a renewed appreciation for life and Jimmy knew he had to think about moving to California with Susan. He wanted to give the idea a fair chance. He wasn't about to tell her that though; she'd never let him think if he did.

Jimmy and Susan were holding hands as they walked back to the car. At that moment they didn't want to talk or fight, they just wanted to enjoy each other's company and to appreciate all they had just shared.

After several hours of driving, Susan wanted to talk about their relationship again. Jimmy was in no mood for it. He was the one driving and he wondered why they couldn't just continue enjoying their time together without seeking answers under a microscope. They were somewhere near Taos, New Mexico, surrounded on all sides by the Sangre de Cristo Mountains. The windows were rolled down, the fresh mountain air filling the vehicle. Jimmy just wanted to find a place in Taos, but Susan had changed her mind about Taos and wanted to see if they could make it to Santa Fe. He was sure it was just so she could have more time to torture him.

"I prayed for us last night, Jimmy," she said.

"Oh for God sakes, you did what?"

"I prayed for us."

"Why?"

"What do you mean, why? I pray. I believe in God."

"Why does everyone insist everything has to be perfect? There's this bright light, this energy out there looking out for all of us, guiding us, teaching us. It's bullshit!"

"It's bullshit? My religion, my beliefs are bullshit to you?"

"I just think you've bought into the same ancient myth everyone else has bought into."

"Myth?"

"God!"

"Jimmy, you can't be serious!"

"Hell yes, I'm serious!"

"Will you stop and listen to what you're saying!"

"Just yesterday these guys were knocking on my door. 'Hello sir, can we tell you about the glory of the coming of the Lord?' I mean, can you believe that? You want to know what I believe in? I believe in cause and effect. I believe in right and wrong. I believe in the haves and the have-nots, the rich and the poor. I believe in logic and reason and the genetic code. I believe in science and technology. I believe in medicine and evolution. I believe there's a lot of good in people, but there's also the potential for a lot of bad. I believe that genetics and socioeconomics have a lot to do with it, and God, very little."

Susan was glaring at Jimmy from the passenger seat. "Well, there you have it," she said, "the doctrine of the Church of Jimmy. It'll lead you right to the gates of Hell, just like him."

"Whatever. You know what I believe in above all else?"

"I can't even imagine."

"I believe in me! As messed up as I may be, I've gotten myself this far and I'll figure out the rest as I go along. Or maybe I won't, but it's up to me, not God! I don't have to pray about it."

"And what about me?" she asked. "Do you believe in me? Is it your choice to spend your life with me or without me?"

"How can I possibly answer that question right now?" he shouted.

Susan slumped over in the passenger seat in tears. She was crushed, and she'd heard enough of the Jimmy doctrine to last her a lifetime. She just wanted Jimmy to go away. She wanted him gone.

"Stop the car," she ordered.

"What? Why?"

"Stop the fucking car!" she screamed. Jimmy was jolted. He immediately pulled over on the shoulder, bringing the car to a screeching halt.

The sun was going down over the mountains to the east. It was a beautiful sight, the long, dark shadows spreading over the valleys like angels. Jimmy stared out of the car, and then finally looked over at Susan for an answer. He was tired and he wanted to get it over with. The drama queen was holding court.

"Get out," she said, "I want to drive."

Jimmy really didn't like the thought of her driving. She was tired and emotionally strung out, and she was really, really mad. He looked at her for a moment, searching her brown eyes. He'd never seen her so upset and he began to feel badly. He knew he'd just been pushing her buttons, it's not like he really believed any of that. Hell, he didn't know what he believed. He was saying everything he could to hurt her and he wasn't sure why.

Susan stepped out of the car and walked over to the driver's side, staring down at him. "Get out!" she ordered. "I'm driving."

He stepped out and tried to hold her and apologize. She could see it coming and pushed him away. She stepped into the car as Jimmy stood and stretched, looking at her miserably.

She rolled down the window. "Jimmy," she said, "I hope you find what you're looking for because it sure as hell isn't me."

The desert dust spit out from the wheels of the car as she took off down the highway. Jimmy stood there and watched as the Honda picked up speed and faded away into the mountains. He was in shock. He looked around – nothing but mountains and a deserted, lonely highway. Naturally, he only had on a T-shirt, shorts and sandals. The mountain air was growing chilly. Night was approaching and he found himself in the middle of nowhere. She'd left him there alone in the looming darkness. He couldn't believe it. He knew he'd messed up, but the punishment didn't fit the crime. He didn't deserve this. *What is her problem anyway? How could she leave me out here like this?*

Jimmy imagined that her crime must be a prosecutable offense. As he started walking, he saw himself in a courtroom making an oral argument in front of a jury of all men. He saw the foreman convinced, as he returned the verdict.

"Guilty your Honor," he'd say. "Guilty on all counts of abandoning Jimmy and leaving him alone in the desert to die. Without delay, your Honor, we recommend that the defendant, Susan Montera, be sentenced to a life of incarceration without any further contact with men, ever. It's the company of women that she deserves your honor. All men must be protected from her heinous ways. May God bless, Jimmy."

Afterward the foreman would stand in front of the cameras outside City Hall, telling them in no uncertain terms that they never bought into her "insanity by reason of hormones" defense and that Jimmy's immaturity was never a factor. A crime is a crime.

Jimmy kept walking, as the world around him became darker. With every step he took, the more angry he became, and the more tired and hungry. Blisters were beginning to form on his heels. His sandals were sliding all over the place and little rocks on the shoulder of the road kept slipping under his feet. He was exhausted. Even his thoughts of revenge dissipated. If Susan had driven up at that point, he would have said anything to be able to go with her. Jimmy was sorry and feeling very isolated. *What a fool. I'm such a fool!*

Susan was still mad; she sped through the mountains crying miserably. Then after nearly fifty miles, the guilt set in. *What had she done?* In her mind, she could see Jimmy cursing her as he walked for miles, wondering just how far he'd have to walk before she turned around to get him. Would he ever forgive her? At last, she turned around, heading back to pick him up. There was really no choice from the moment she'd driven off. She just needed to teach him a lesson. She knew she'd find him on the side of the road somewhere, mad as hell. The sooner she got there, the better off they'd both be. She was ready to apologize; it had been a long day and she was drained. It was time to find Jimmy and go get a room.

The late-model, dusty, red Ford pickup pulled up on the side of the road where Jimmy was sitting bent over on a large rock. Jimmy looked up as the passenger door opened.

"You know you really shouldn't be out here like this in the middle of nowhere," the driver said. "Lots of loony birds in these parts."

Jimmy stood up and knocked the dust off his shorts. He was tired and not much in the mood for small talk with a stranger, but he was also desperate. "Where ya headed?" Jimmy asked.

"Santa Fe," the driver said. "Hop in, I'll give you a ride."

Jimmy looked around behind him. What choice did he have? He got into the car, exhausted, just wanting to get a room and some sleep. "Thanks for stopping, man. You saved me."

"Interesting choice of words," the man said, smiling.

The driver extended his hand to Jimmy. "I'm Michael," he said. "Pleased to meet you."

"Nice to meet you; I'm Jimmy."

Michael looked over at Jimmy, barely able to contain his smile, his face glowing red. "Gabriel," he said.

"No, it's Jimmy." Jimmy looked up at him, not sure what to make of his new friend.

"Right, Jimmy. Jimmy. Sorry man, it's been a long day. I took some art and dropped it off in Taos. Helps with supplies."

"Supplies?"

"Yeah, you know food and stuff."

"Right — food. Man, I could sure use some coffee."

"Well, there's a little gas station up here a few miles down the road. It's on me."

"Thanks," Jimmy said.

"Say, what are you doing out here all by yourself, anyway?" Michael asked.

"My girlfriend kicked me out of the car."

"Is that right?" Michael said, chuckling. "The Lord does work in mysterious ways."

Michael just looked at Jimmy and laughed out loud like that was just the funniest thing he'd ever heard. He laughed so hard that even Jimmy began to smile, but not too much. He was a little weirded out by Michael. He figured he'd call Susan from a pay phone at the gas station and have her pick him up. *She had to have cooled off a little by now.*

Michael was around Jimmy's age, wearing jeans and a black T-shirt. Jimmy could tell the guy was cool, but there was also a strange quality about him that he couldn't put his finger on.

They pulled into the gas station, a little food mart with two pumps. Jimmy spotted a phone.

"How do you like your coffee?" Michael asked.

"Black."

"Okay, I'll be right back."

"Sure, I'm just gonna check out the restroom."

Michael laughed and stepped out of the truck into the light of the store. Jimmy could see him inside singing to himself. The guy was just a little too happy. Jimmy walked over to a pay phone and called Susan's cell phone.

"Hello," she answered.

"Susan," he said, "Where are you?"

"I'm 50 miles down the road just outside of Santa Fe."

"Santa Fe," he said.

Michael snuck up behind Jimmy. "Yeah, we're about 60 miles away from Santa Fe," Michael said. "Be there in no time."

"Jimmy, who's that?"

"Michael."

"Michael?" she said.

"Yeah, Susan," Jimmy said looking at Michael smiling. "Michael was cool enough to pick me up from the side of the road."

"I'm coming to get you!"

"How long will it take you?"

"Uh, uh," Michael said, interrupting. "Let me take you. There's no reason for her to backtrack this way. Just find out where she is and I'll drop you off. Really, it's no problem."

Susan could hear Michael and felt uneasy. "That's not a good idea," she said.

Jimmy looked at Michael and sized-up the situation. Finally, he said, "Just tell me where you are and I'll be there in an hour. It's cool."

"Yeah, no problem," Michael said. "I'll be in the truck."

"Look, it's okay. This guy's laid back, he's a hippie artist or something. He saved me from miles upon miles of walking and blistering feet. I kind of owe him the company to Santa Fe. You know what I mean?"

Susan didn't want to argue. "I'll be at the Holiday Inn on Cerr..."

"Cerrillos Road, right? The one I mentioned earlier before you kicked me out in the middle of nowhere."

"I'll get a room," she said. "Just give me a call on the cell if you want and I can pick you up when you get into town if he doesn't want to bring you all the way there. No big deal."

"No big deal, huh?"

She was trying to ignore him, but Jimmy wouldn't let her go without getting in a dig. "I'm sorry, Jimmy," she said, "but you were being such a jerk."

"Let's talk about it later."

"Okay. Just hurry up!"

Jimmy wasn't upset with her anymore, but he wasn't ready to let her off the hook yet, either. He figured if he played his cards right his new bargaining power might pay off down the road.

Michael handed Jimmy the coffee as Jimmy stepped into the truck. "I really appreciate this, Michael."

"No problem, man. I'm happy to do it. Sometimes people just cross each other's paths at exactly the right time, you know, it's fate. You were the broken down stranger on the side of the road. If I passed you up who knows what God would have had in store for me?"

Jimmy took a drink of his coffee and smiled politely. He couldn't wait to see Susan. The irony of Michael's biblical reference was not lost on him. Jimmy felt like maybe God was punishing him for his rant with Susan. *Karma is a bitch sometimes.*

It took about ten minutes before the drug started to kick in. "Man, I'm a little tired," Jimmy said, feeling a sudden wash of calm and an overwhelming desire for sleep. "You don't mind if I just..."

"Go ahead, Gabriel," Michael said. "Get some rest, my angel. We'll be home soon." Michael quickly took the coffee from Jimmy's hand that was hanging over the edge of the seat, spilling onto the floor. He pushed Jimmy's slouched body over to the door and leaned him against it.

The GHB, Gamma Hydroxybutrate, was a strong drug and he'd put a large enough dose in Jimmy's coffee to knock him out for several hours. Michael laid on the gas. He was excited and couldn't wait to get back to the ranch.

The revelation was being fulfilled. God was revealing his plans. The day of reckoning had just taken a giant leap closer to coming to fruition. This was a glorious day, a glorious day for God and his children. The angels would sing from the mountain-top about the glorious coming of the Lamb. And there would be a great celebration commemorating the appearance of Gabriel as foretold in Michael's great visions from God. The seeds of love would be planted into the fruit of Gabriel and then the flower would bloom, as it had with all the angels. The circle at the throne of God was nearing completion.

A grand day indeed!

CHAPTER 6

Jane Tierney was starting to feel the wine. She'd always loved vintage wine and jumped at the opportunity to drink the rare and pricey, highly sought-after 1996 Domaine de la Romanee Conti, when offered to her by Richard Novak, a man of means and fine taste. The wine was widely considered the finest from Burgundy, and arguably, the world. Since the Middle Ages, Burgundy had produced some of the finest wines ever to grace the lips of the most fortunate. And many connoisseurs believed Romanee Conti was the best of the best. That vineyard surrendered only 6,000 bottles to the world each year, and most wine xenophiles would never have the chance to drink even a small glass of the richly textured wine.

But, of course, Richard Novak had several bottles among his small collection of what he referred to as his "vintage traveling wines." Jane still couldn't believe they were on his private jet. As a rule, she never had drinks with her interview subjects, but Richard had proven to be a hard man to turn down. The fact that he owned GNN made it even more difficult.

They were sitting together talking in his private study on board the Gulfstream. Uriel was in the main cabin, dozing off in a chair. They were set to land in 45 minutes and then Jane would have to turn right back around to New York. She was due at GNN headquarters early Monday morning for the airing of her weekly segment. She simply had no choice. Such is the life of an ambitious newswoman; there were few choices, the schedule made itself.

Richard sat next to Jane in front of his dark mahogany desk and Jane noticed he'd been rather friendly. He was a married man, and also very powerful and charming. Jane tried hard to remain professional. She wasn't thrilled about the warmth she was feeling from the wine, but she couldn't pass on Romanee Conti no matter what the occasion. She hadn't stolen anything since childhood, but she playfully wondered how many bottles she could squeeze into her purse.

"So, do you really think you have a shot at being the next President?" she asked.

"Don't you?"

"Well, I'm not sure why you'd want to," Jane said. "The conservative right is going to jump all over you, given your stated religious beliefs. And obviously there's a risk people will misinterpret your message, and that you'll be viewed as a rich guy trying to buy a place in history."

"'The only good is knowledge, and the only evil is ignorance,'" said Richard.

"Pardon me?"

"Herodotus. The father of history."

"So you're not worried about these things – the risks involved?" Jane looked at him, trying to pierce his veil of invincibility, to find the cracks.

"'Great deeds are usually wrought at great risks.'"

"So you're not concerned?" she followed.

"Also Herodotus."

"Impressive. I'm sure Herodotus had an answer for everything, but I'm trying to get inside the man before me, not a ghost." Jane took a large gulp of her Romanee Conti.

Richard broke into a wide smile. He really loved that about Jane – her fire! "Sorry, Herodotus is just so much more interesting than I."

"Hardly."

"Look," he said, "at some point, if greatness doesn't choose you, then you have to choose greatness."

"Herodotus?" she asked.

"Richard Novak," he answered.

"Do you really think you can change the world? I mean that's what you said, right? In the interview, you indicated that we all have so much to give to the world, intimating that America should lead the way."

"Always the reporter?"

"Not always, but I think you should know what you're in for. You know the critics can't wait to rip into you. You just became the story. And as long as you keep talking like you did tonight, you'll be the story – for better or for worse."

"You think I don't know that? To hell with the critics, Jane. Do you think I can't hear them now? 'Look at the techno-billionaire, he's talking about a better world, but he doesn't pay homage to God.' 'How can we have a better world without God?' 'Must be nice to have everything and look down from the mountaintop.' But that's not what I said. All I said was, 'I do not rest my faith in God. I have faith in man.' And I won't apologize for that; I won't run from it."

"Well, you want honesty, Richard? America is not going to elect a man who doesn't believe in God. It just won't happen. And you cannot unite the world if you divide America. People won't be able to get past your religion, or lack of it."

"Would you rather I'd lied?"

"Maybe you should have held back a little, not for me, but for yourself," she said. "You know, *'Tell all the truth, but tell it slant, success in circuit lies, to bright for our infirm delight, the truth's superb surprise, like lightning to the children eased with explanation kind, the truth must dazzle gradually...'*"

"*'Or every man be blind,'*" he finished. "Emily Dickinson. She's a favorite of mine, as well. Her words are even more beautiful coming from you."

Jane blushed. "Thought I had you," she said.

"Oh, you have me, all right. You've got my undivided attention. But let's get something straight, just so you understand."

"What?"

"I am going to be the next President of the United States, Jane, and my goal is to unite the world. I want greater participation from the world's governing bodies in feeding the poor and promoting the highest quality of life for all, effectively moving the Third World into the future."

Jane took a deep breath and downed her last gulp of wine. Richard poured her another glass. "You see your future so clearly," she said. "Do you know something I don't know?"

"I know who I am," Richard replied. "I know what I believe and I know what I want. And most importantly, I know that when I want something I don't leave it up to others to make it happen."

"Maybe you forgot, but this is a democracy…"

"Of course, it is, Jane. I will win the support of the people. You'll vote for me won't you?" He gazed into her eyes.

She felt very awkward; he looked so intense, so serious. "I don't know," she answered. "Maybe."

"What would keep you from voting for me?"

"I don't know. I don't know enough about you."

"Well the devil's in the details. Get to know me. Help me allow the world to get to know me. Help me get my message out."

"I thought you said, 'unbiased and unabashed.'"

"I did, of course, and you will have complete access to me just like now. Am I holding back?"

"No, but the camera's not on, is it?"

"Then bring in the camera and start rolling. But, you like me Jane, and unconsciously you will show me favoritism. Naturally the world will follow. You simply won't be able to help yourself. You're under my spell."

She laughs. "Are you always so confident?"

"Why shouldn't I be? It's my destiny to lead this country, to help lead the world."

"Your destiny?"

"Have you no sense of destiny?" Richard asked. "It's everywhere, isn't it? We're surrounded by it. You think it's a fluke that I have all this wealth? It will enable me to make my place in history. Look at America, her place in history. Look at what the American spirit of freedom and democracy has brought to the world. Take the war in Iraq, for instance: Wasn't it our destiny to go there and conquer Babylon just like all the other great empires before us? The Sumerians, the Assyrians and the Babylonian king Hammurabi, the Chaldeans with their great king Nebuchadnezzar, Persia's Cyrus the Great, Alexander the Great. Then, after centuries lost and buried in rubble, along comes Saddam

Hussein, a dictator, too enamored with himself and wealth, to resurrect Iraq's place in the world. And now who is there, Jane? America! Think that's not destiny?"

"Okay, Richard, you know your history but…"

"I want to be a part of history and I refuse to be a small part! I want to be remembered among the greatest leaders to walk the Earth. Tonight was only the first step for me!"

"You've lost me, really," she said, "Maybe I've had too much wine. Maybe you have. Let's just call it a –"

"Jane, history and destiny are not irrelevant; they are part of the past and future merging into the present! We need to maximize our wealth, our power, our technology and our control in the world! We need to create a global bureaucracy with a centralized government and a centralized leader, with global taxation supporting the involuntary military necessary to hold the union together, as has always been necessary in all great empires!"

"That's not exactly the message you gave tonight in the interview! Do you see this evolving in the U.N. or some other mechanism?"

"Not now, Jane. We'll get there, you and me. We're telling it 'slant!'" He laughed. "The devil's in the details."

Jane felt a pain in her gut and she was sure it wasn't the wine. "Richard, Mr. Novak, Richard," she stumbled, "I'm sorry, I'm a little tired. Look, you're a very interesting man so don't take this the wrong way. I think you're fascinating, I do, but I care about my career, my integrity. I wouldn't subject myself to what you're asking, not for anyone or anything."

"I'm simply saying, '*Tell all the truth but tell it slant.*'"

"I know the poem, Richard!"

She was getting a headache and he wouldn't give up. "I know you do, Jane. And I get the impression you think I'm too over-the-top. People like you and identify with you. I want people to make that connection through you to me. It would be helpful to my campaign if you would cover me on the road as a network correspondent."

"Quit my current job to cover your campaign. You're crazy, you know that?"

"No, I'm as serious and as sane as I've ever been. I will be the next President and you're going to help me get there! So what's your price?"

"Why do you think I have a price? I'm not some fancy toy or some bottle of wine you have secret access to just because you own GNN and half the fricking world."

"Of course not! You've misunderstood me!" Richard said. "Let me be more clear. I desire *you*, Jane. What do *you* desire?"

She had no answer for him. She just shook her head and looked at the floor as she slipped her left foot in and out of her dress shoe.

Richard leaned over and took her petite hands into his. "You don't have to answer me just yet," he said. "Give it some time. Think about it. I'm confident you'll make the right decision, for you, for me, and for your career."

Jane peered into his seductive, dark eyes, which seemed cloaked in mystery. She made no attempt to pull away.

CHAPTER 7

The next day sometime in the late evening, the archangel Michael leaned over Jimmy at the altar rejoicing, the blood still dripping from Michael's naked body. The angels gathered, their shadows reflecting off the walls in the fiery light as they entered the room. The fire burned in the center of the tabernacle, crackling cinder and smoke flowing up into the rooftop and through the stone chimney.

The cry of the Lamb called out to Jimmy.

Soon it would be time for the *Ceremony of Angels* to begin. Jimmy was going to die, that was his sacrifice, the price of the glory of the Lamb. But God is so kind and glorious, the sinner would be reborn as Gabriel so he could fulfill his journey of sacrament, allowing him to take his long-awaited place in the circle of seven angels.

Jimmy began to wake.

Michael ordered the angels to take their seats on the rocks circling the altar. The GHB left Jimmy dazed and as he slowly lifted up from the cold slab, he thought he must be dreaming. He kept rubbing his eyes. The smoke was burning and he was naked, covered only by white linen that was soaked in blood. The angels watched in awe; the birth of an angel is an intoxicating, emotional rapture. Slowly, Jimmy began to rise and look around the glowing tabernacle. They all recognized the look in his eyes. He was so excited to be there, honored and anxious to glow in the light of the universe, the light of the one true being, the light of God.

Michael lifted his arms to the sky, and standing beside Jimmy, he began, "Lord, the circle of seven is nearly complete! You have offered us this man, who tonight will be born again in the first sacrament. And upon completion of his journey into the valley of darkness, he will rise again in the light, an angel, Gabriel, and it will have begun! The prophecy of the great wind of fire, hail and rain, sweeping down with your hand, will be swung into its final motion and like the sickle in the field of wheat, the harvest of souls shall cut through all the fields, and the Beast, the Anti-Christ, the Red Dragon of ten horns and seven heads, will be cast down into the fire forever and the new Babylon will crumble and perish into dust!"

Jimmy had heard enough, and he jumped down from the altar and ran for the front of the tabernacle toward the door. They cleared a path and let him run by. This was the glorious part; the dance of the Holy Spirit was filling Jimmy and his soul was singing. They were so happy for him that tears filled their eyes. He was so beautiful. The prophecy from the vision of Michael had made him seem so sweet, with the smell of a golden flower and honey colored eyes. But the reality was far better and they all felt so blessed and so endeared to God to have been chosen for this great service to the Lamb.

Jimmy slammed against the door. It was locked and he had nowhere to run.

Oh my God! Oh my God, what the hell *is going on!*

Jimmy turned to face the angels and he could see the whole picture. He couldn't breathe, he was suffocating in fear. They could see his pulse and they knew peace from the heavens was on the way. The great soldier, Gabriel, the great angel was there, the captain of God's army, the one who would lead them into the final battle. He was so brave and strong.

Michael walked toward Jimmy, and the angels split into two on each side of him for the *Walk of Rebirth*.

"Stay away!" Jimmy yelled. "I swear I'll kill all of you if you come any closer!"

They walked closer to Jimmy, smiling and filling their souls with his spirit. Jimmy took off, running through them, but they grabbed his arms and legs. He struggled to break free, kicking and throwing his arms for what seemed like an eternity. The GHB had made him weak, but he was still fighting as they dragged him to the altar, kicking and screaming and crying out for help. They laid him down as his screams filled the tabernacle. Two on each side, they attached his arms and legs to the altar with the white linens, using the iron rod loops as anchors.

"Let me go!" he yelled. "You motherfuckers, let me go! Please God, let me go!"

As if on cue, Michael, having heard Jimmy's prayers to God, began the ceremony. The animal sacrifice was led into the tabernacle and all the angels helped lift the beast onto the altar, placing it between Jimmy's legs. Jimmy looked into the eyes of the Lamb and they shared a moment of anguish. The animal was in pain and cried out; Jimmy screamed.

"Stop!" he shouted. "Stop, please! Stop! Don't do it, don't touch me! Please, stop!"

"Accept the moment, Gabriel," Michael said softly. "Go with the glorious Lamb into the heavens and return to us in his glory. It's your time to shine! This is your time, my angel! The stars have all aligned for you! With this sacrifice you are reborn!"

Michael raised the sickle high above Jimmy and the Lamb, as they both tried to break free of their captivity. The fear was exploding in their eyes.

"Behold the glory of the Lamb!" Michael shouted, as the angels all began to chant in unison, "Behold the glory of the Lamb! Behold the glory of the Lamb! Behold the glory of the Lamb ..."

The screams and cries filled the church as the blood washed down the altar to the stone floor. Gabriel was born.

CHAPTER 8

Susan couldn't stop crying. The young clerk at the front desk at the Holiday Inn on Cerrilos Road in Santa Fe was concerned for her and didn't want her to leave.

"M'am, you really shouldn't leave like this."

"No," she said, "I have to find him. Please call me if he comes here, will you?"

"Of course," he answered.

She packed her suitcase into her car and began driving down 68 North, toward Taos. Something was terribly wrong and she knew it. Jimmy would have shown up unless something had happened. He would have called her. Twelve hours had passed since she last spoke to him, and although it seemed like forever, the police still had absolutely no interest in helping find Jimmy. They advised her to give him a few days and see if he showed up, promising her that after their fight, he was probably out drinking and rough-housing – they saw it all the time.

They didn't know Jimmy. He was never big on drinking, and he certainly wouldn't have just gone out partying with some stranger while she was waiting for him. They had a fight, but she could tell when she talked to Jimmy that he was relieved to talk to her and things were going to be okay. She knew their fight wasn't over, Jimmy would still have some things to say. He's a prosecutor and he'd never run from a fight. Susan knew when she saw him he was for sure to go "lawyer" on her and she didn't care, she just had to find him.

When she pulled into the quaint food-mart with two pumps somewhere between Santa Fe and Taos, she spotted a pay phone and wondered if that was the same phone Jimmy had used to call her the night before. There was no one around outside. She parked and went inside the small store.

"Excuse me," she said, to the older lady behind the counter. "Were you working here last night around 8 o'clock?"

"Sorry, honey, just got on at 8 this morning. Ya need something?"

Susan glanced around the store. "Well, actually, I'm looking for someone. He's about 5'11" with dark, short hair. I thought someone might have seen him."

"From last night?"

"Yeah."

"He your boyfriend?"

"Yes," Susan answered.

"You guys in a fight?"

"Yes," Susan answered, looking blankly into the lady's eyes.

The lady shook her head. "Then he run off I bet," she said, her wrinkled face twitching as she spoke. "Men are always running off, the jerks. Honey, you'd have to talk to Marty, he was working last night. I have no idea if your friend was in here. We get lots of people passing by. He'll be in today at 4 o'clock if you want to come back later."

"Do you have his number? Could we call him or something?"

"Sorry, sweety, can't do that. Marty's the manager and he don't like to be bothered at home unless there's been a robbery or somethin' big. It's against his rules, might get fired – need the job – got kids to feed. Ya'll got kids?"

"No," she said. "We don't"

"Well, that's good at least! Consider it a blessing."

Susan nodded and walked out to her car. Behind the wheel she sat wondering how this had happened. She didn't know what to do or where to go for help. *Why did Jimmy have to be such a jerk! Why was I so stupid?* She hoped he was safe. This was the worst day of her life and it was all his fault. *Jerk!* She felt completely nauseous and sick to her stomach. *Please God, please let me find him. St. Jude, I pray to you for your guidance, please help me. Help me find Jimmy. Please let him be all right and let me find him soon.*

She broke down crying again over the steering wheel. She was so tired and strung out she just laid there against the wheel, helpless. If Jimmy only knew, he would be there for her, she was sure of it.

CHAPTER 9

The dodge-and-weave taxi ride through Manhattan on Monday morning following her interview with Richard Novak caused Jane to run late and stressed her out to no end. She was tired of having to race around the streets of New York chasing the news. She was ready for a change, ready for a good story to come along and captivate her. If Richard Novak had anything to do with it, he would be the story.

The interview with him was set to run in a 15-minute spot on that evening's news, during the 6 o'clock GNN News Hour. The interview was sure to set off some fireworks; the content had blown her away. She couldn't help but wonder how the public was going to react to the developing story. The executive producers at GNN had loved it, figuring the Richard's story was going to fill the news waves for several weeks and it was all starting with GNN, and he was their guy.

A few, however — Jane's direct boss, Max Weinberg among them — were privately concerned the association between GNN and the techno-billionaire, Richard Novak, with his grand view of the world, could cost the network credibility. Max, an old school newsy and one of Jane's biggest supporters inside GNN, was so concerned he personally supervised the editing of the interview to make sure the network maintained a professional, newsworthy approach. In the worst case scenario, they would wind up looking like the puppets of Richard Novak, especially because it was his network. In reality, he could do whatever he wanted, and it's that kind of power that makes news people especially nervous.

Jane walked into the corporate headquarters on West 66th Street in New York City and headed straight down the hallway to the make-up room to get ready for her spot. She was tired. The flight with Richard had cost her a lot of sleep, but what got to her more than the jet lag was the subject of their conversation and the look in his piercing eyes when he said he desired her. While Jane was intrigued by his proposition to cover his campaign, she wasn't sold on the idea of spending a lot of one-on-one time with Richard and wondered if the move would be right for her career. Richard was married, famous and powerful and Jane was no rookie when it came to complicated relationships. She didn't want to get caught up in another mess. She also didn't want to put her credibility at risk.

And then, of course, she knew GNN would have to replace her with another anchor while she was gone and she wanted to be able to come back anytime with no strings attached if she was not satisfied with the campaign assignment. She knew she was asking for more than the network would ever allow. Still, Richard had assured her it wouldn't be a problem and laughed at her when she said her boss wouldn't like it if she left to follow his campaign. Richard was accustomed to his power and enjoyed using it to get his way. He was well aware news correspondents were often assigned to follow top candidates and if Jane Tierney wasn't going to be the correspondent from GNN then someone was going to have to answer to him about it. Actually, he rather relished the idea of ripping into her boss and letting him know Jane Tierney was not to be messed with at GNN.

Richard wanted the best, and that was Jane Tierney, so she had a choice to make and she'd better make the right one. Jane wasn't smitten with the idea that one man she hardly knew was so easily able to make her feel so powerless. There was just something about him; he had all the charisma. Whatever the quality was that made people electric, Richard Novak had lots of it and Jane was drawn to him from the start. But, she had good reasons to be concerned. She had recently ended a relationship with a New York stock broker, and had walked away feeling betrayed. She just didn't trust rich and powerful men.

They were always hiding secrets, and although Jane had a few secrets of her own, she'd hated the secrets of the men she'd known.

Max stood nearby the set during the GNN News Hours, watching Jane closely. He was so proud of her; she had come to New York and taken the country by storm. She had a bigger fan club than a lot of celebrities. People were blown away by her wartime coverage in Iraq as she followed the Marines into Baghdad. She had a strong, captivating delivery and she had a special knack for being at the right place at the right time. His main worry with Jane was her affinity for taking too many risks. A news woman of her magnitude didn't need to, but Jane didn't see herself that way. Every good reporter just wants to be where the story is and that was Jane. She preferred being on assignment rather than sitting in the studio. "The real news happens outside in the streets with the people," she'd always say. "In here we may report it, but it's happening out there all the time." Max was really amazed by her. In his eyes, she'd always been special and he would have done anything to protect her.

When the story was set to wrap just after Richard's announcement that he was running for President, Jane followed with one last bit of news, and it was that piece of news that completely blew Max away and sent him walking swiftly to his office.

"And now one last thing to report," Jane said, "I will be leaving this broadcast for several weeks to report to you at home about the developments in the campaign of Mr. Novak. This is a special assignment that I am honored to accept on behalf of GNN, and when it's completed I hope to come back and continue to bring you the news. From all of us at GNN, I'm Jane Tierney. Thank you, and good night."

Jane took off down the corridor, chasing Max to his office. She ran across a garbage can Max had kicked over along the way. When he got to his office, she could hear the door slam from way down the hallway. Everyone was stunned and people stopped and stared at Jane as she stopped just outside of Max's door before entering.

"Holy shit!" Max yelled. "Holy goddam shit! Are you fucking nuts? Do you know what you just did?"

"Max-"

"Shut up! Goddam it, Jane, who in the hell do you think you are? Has your head gotten so damn big you think you can go on the air and make decisions about our broadcast future all on your own? Do you have any idea what you've just done? For god's sake, Jane, answer me?"

"This is for God's sake!" she said. "My God and your God!"

"What?" he asked.

She bore into him with her stare. "Max, he asked me to take the assignment-"

"Who?"

"He did."

"Who the fuck is he?"

"Richard Novak, the owner of GNN!"

"What have you done; lost your mind over another rich guy?"

"No, I don't care about him. He's just a story, Max! You saw the interview; you know that's going to be the biggest fricking story of the year! Come on, think of it, even if he fails and drops out in a few weeks, it's still going to be one hell of a ride and I want to be there for it. That's what I do! I'm a reporter and I want the best and the biggest story and this is going to be it!"

"Did you sleep with him?"

"Go to hell!"

"I am Jane — with you, remember," he said. "Well, did you?"

"I can't believe you can even ask me that! Who the hell do you think you are?"

"Well, Jane, I don't know anymore," Max said. "I thought that I was your friend. I thought that I was your protector."

"You are!"

"Well I also thought I was the boss around here, but apparently someone else has just usurped my authority on how to run this place." Max was weary from his rant and finally sat down behind his desk.

"Get over it!" Jane said. "This is the business we're in! People make news; we follow the people and report it! That's all I'm going to do. If you want to make it out to be something more, that's your fricking problem! We don't call the shots, Max, and we never have! The stories call the shots! And right now, Richard Novak just became the story! He will be on every news channel in the world and they will be playing our interview! That's how you make news!"

"Get out of here, Jane; go follow your goddam story! But you better make it great or else when you come back I will make your life fucking miserable like you've just made mine."

She laughed. "Max, you've always done exactly what I wanted you to do. You've always looked out for me. Always kept me safe, and you're going to keep doing that, so stop with the tough talk. I know where your loyalty lies in the end, and I think you know damn well what I'm talking about!"

"Do you know how many people I have to go explain what just happened to?"

"Max, you love me and you know it." Jane smiled.

"Right now, I hate you," he said. "Just make sure *you* don't become the story! Don't wind up his whore, or we'll all look like fucking idiots at a third rate news company!" Max winked at her with a nice, wide stick-that-up-your-ass smile.

"Screw you, Max! You tired, jealous, old man! It's been so long since you went out there and made news you don't even know what it's like out there anymore! You're out of touch!" Max smiled; she'd made him so goddamn mad he was hoping she'd just buckle over in tears.

She walked out of his office and slammed the door behind her. All eyes followed her as she made her way to the elevator. The truth of the matter was Jane hadn't really thought the whole thing through and was flying by the seat of her pants. *Damn Richard Novak, he better be worth all this!* She knew if he didn't turn out to be a sensational story, she would regret this move for the rest of her life. *Stupid men!*

CHAPTER 10

GNN.com

ASTRONOMY NEWS
The Universe, God and Us

Wednesday, August 22, 2007 Posted 9:30 AM EDT

NEW ALBANY, IN (GNN) – New Albany's own, Edwin Hubbell, the now legendary astrophysicist, who with his amazing telescope first proved our universe is constantly expanding. Yes, the universe as we know it today is said by scientists to expand across a distance of 93 billion light years. Understandably, most people have no idea how far that is, as average individuals have no real concept of how long 1 light year actually is, let alone 93 billion light years, because these are unfathomable numbers.

So let's put it this way, one light year is equal to

5,865,696,000,000 miles. Accordingly, to determine how wide the universe actually is you would need to multiply 5,865,696,000,000 miles x 93 billion. Oh, and good luck finding a calculator to do that math for you, and don't bother anyway because as we have already said, the universe is constantly expanding anyway. So, whatever number you come up with is sure to be wrong by the time you write it down.

Still the question lingers: Where do we fit in this ever expanding space known as the universe? We live on Earth, a relatively small planet that resides in the Milky Way galaxy. The Milky Way is a spiral galaxy, and among galaxies in the universe that we have identified, our galaxy is a fairly large galaxy. In our galaxy alone there are an estimated 200 billion stars. The closest star system is **Proxima Centauri and it is 4.33 light years away from Earth. Speaking a language that Americans can identify with, that's 5,865,696,000,000 miles x 4.33 light years.** And to further complicate things, scientists and computer models estimate that there are hundreds of billions of galaxies in the universe. In other words, space is huge, and we occupy a very small piece of matter in it.

Astronomers with improved technologies and telescopes have really only just begun to discover new planets revolving around other stars. Considering the number of stars in the Milky Way galaxy alone, and the fact that there are hundreds of billions of galaxies with hundreds of billions of stars, you can see quickly see that we are talking about potentially hundreds of billions of other planets.

Are any habitable? That's a question that we would love

to have the answer to, and we hope that someday we will. It's possible that all of the other planets are mainly just gas giants like Jupiter or planets with very unfriendly atmospheres and extreme temperatures like Venus and Mars. Yet, with the sheer volume of space and the numbers of the planets that exist in the universe it seems only logical that somewhere, perhaps, "In a galaxy far, far away," life exists, and not just plants or ameoba, but living, breathing beings with intelligence.

If we could only prove this think of the implications it would have on our existence. Obviously, there will always be new questions and mysteries for scientists to unlock about our universe, but if we learned life existed on another planet some of our long standing belief systems may also come into question.

What about God and religion? Would such an amazing discovery have implications on people's religious faith? Would doctrines just evolve and become more expansive, including the new world as part of God's creation? Today many religious foundations exist upon the belief that human beings are special and unique to only Earth. What if we find out that's not true? It's a fascinating discussion and one that will only continue to grow with the more we learn about the new frontier of space, where we have not even really begun to scratch the surface.

CHAPTER 11

The guarantee that brought so many great minds together in one place was, of course, money – lots of money. Richard Novak knew better than anyone its value to his campaign. And he knew that even this assemblage of intelligencia was not above setting their goals around the almighty dollar, yielding slavishly, in fact, to its offering. Richard hoped by bringing them together he could introduce them to his vision and win their commitment to his campaign.

Red Diadem's General Counsel began the late-evening, August conference requesting their signatures. It was hardly a surprise that every single one of the attendees signed the lengthy employment contracts. They were now Richard's people. He owned them. Once you signed on to work with him you accepted unquestionably that this was his show, his campaign, and it was based on his political ideas. They could help him shape those ideas and assist him in getting his message out, but they could never hope to change his view of the battlefield.

That's just the way Richard saw things. In his mind they were the foot soldiers and soldiers by themselves are nothing without a great commander. The commander plans their movements based on his extensive knowledge of the art of war. He's the one who masters all details of the battle design. Richard knew he did not get to where he was in life by chance; he was a great leader who had been ready for every opportunity that had come his way.

If life was a game of chess, Richard Novak made sure he was always the one to enjoy the pleasure of saying, "Checkmate!" From very early on he'd studied the great masters of war and leadership: Napoleon, Alexander the Great, Hannibal, Julius Caesar and Genghis Khan. These were the great ones, the conquerors and empire builders; these were his teachers. At night he dreamed of someday reaching out and grabbing his moment by the tail and swinging it high among the stars triumphantly. He imagined himself the great leader, the great conqueror, warrior of all warriors.

In his dreams Richard Novak was the shining prince emblazoned in the image of the Dog Star, Sirius, brightest star in the sky. Known as the One, it's located in the river of stars and is the gateway to lower and higher consciousness. While many have been misled by the North Star, it is the Dog Star that burns brightest in the northern sky. To the ancient Chinese, the Dog Star sat in the sky as the judge, the bridge between heaven and hell. Richard Novak saw himself as the living incarnation of the dog, a dog so fierce and fast that no one could escape its will.

Ancient lore has it that Zeus gave the dog to Europa, whose son Minos, King of Crete, then passed it along to the great Procris. The dog eventually ended up in Thebes, north of Athens, where he would have the glorious duty of hunting the fox that was terrorizing the community. No one had ever been able to even come close to catching the stealthy fox, but when the mighty dog unleashed his great wind, the fox could not escape its will. The dog was faster than the fox. Zeus turned both animals to stone, placing the dog into the heavens, making him the brightest star and closest to Earth. The will of the dog shined brighter than any he had ever seen.

Richard learned from the conquests and the mistakes of the great commanders before him and he applied the principles of war to all areas of his life. Anyone who didn't was simply naive and vulnerable. He had conquered his share of those weaklings along the way to building his technological empire. Every day presented a new conflict and every conquest was golden. Most importantly, everything was a battle that must be won, and every battle was won with planning and attention to detail.

The conference room was alive with anticipation. The walls were painted deep red and stately art of foxhounds on the hunt were displayed under low voltage picture lights. They were all there, perhaps the greatest minds of the 21st century seated around the oak conference table waiting for their new master.

Richard entered through the smoked glass doors in the rear of the room and made his charge to the head of the large conference table. All eyes were fixed upon him. Dressed in a dark blue suit with a red tie, he was indeed very regal and presidential. They were ready to meet The Man. From far and wide they had traveled across the country for this opportunity to chase greatness with America's newest presidential candidate.

He stopped behind the half-lectern and flipped off the lights. All eyes focused on the large plasma display screen behind him. "Good afternoon ladies and gentlemen," Richard said, in the half light of the room. "I am honored to be in your company. Thank you for joining me here today. Together, we are about to embark on the greatest campaign this country has ever seen. We are not only going to make history, we are going to make this country the greatest country in the world once again."

Richard turned to the plasma display behind him where a bald eagle appeared soaring above silver clouds. Then, with the sun peering up from below, the eagle boldly swooped to a perch on top of a mountain.

"This is where we want to be," Richard continued. "We are going to the top of the mountain, the apex of civilization, the heart of the modern world, the pulse, if you will, of the eagle soaring through the wind. We shall perch ourselves where only the mightiest have rested. This is our mission. This is no ordinary campaign. We seek not only to win the presidency; together we are going to win over the world. I kid you not! When we are finished we will seat ourselves in the White House and we will command the respect of all the world. And when we are done, there will be no doubt about the strength of our union, the strength of our country, the strength of our global, technological empire!"

A map appeared on the screen and starting with Hawaii a wash of red color began to sweep across the screen, turning the islands from white to red. Then Alaska and the western coast of the United States. It swept across the country coloring all land red until no state was left untouched. Then, like a flood, a river of red stretched out in all directions until the entire world was engulfed in red.

Then the screen appeared to blink and suddenly the red washed away leaving the land masses white once again. Richard pointed to the states. "This is not the goal!" he shouted. And with another blink, the flood of red again engulfed the world. "This is the goal!"

When the video presentation was finished, the screen went blank and the lights flickered back on in the conference room. Richard watched their faces as they all looked around at each other, bewildered.

"Are you surprised?" he asked. "Are you surprised by a man whose vision is so broad, so great that I would dream of America being the powerful centerpiece of a greater world dynasty? I bet you are shocked! I bet you are amazed!

"And why are you so amazed? Has it been so long since we've been allowed to dream?

"Has it been so long since we've been allowed to extend our dreams to the world, without boundaries and without separation?

"We will first make our country strong again, and then we shall make her rise above the clouds of poverty and man's inhumanity to man and perch in the place of honor on top of the mountain where the needs of all are met! We will bring food, drinkable water, sanitary living conditions, technology and all the strengths and opportunities democracy and capitalism have afforded us for so many years. And why? Because we know that the disadvantaged in the world continue to die for a drop of water, a breath of clean air and a simple offering of food. It is time to bring the world into the New Age of golden civilization! It is time to share ourselves and our riches with the world! Together, we shall achieve this goal!"

He paused and looked around the room. Many people looked like they wanted to run for one of the two exits, but instead remained in their seats, mesmerized, perhaps, by the grand lecture. This was no ordinary man. This man was not just seeking the presidency, he was planning America's evolution in the universe. Despite being unnerved, they were captivated by his message. He seemed so pure in his good will and so honest in his vision. They understood his use of allegory and metaphor with respect to his projections and hopes for the state of centuries ahead, and they marveled at his compassion and desire. He was not just reaching for the stars. He was a brilliant star in his own right and he wanted to serve as a beacon to lead the others stars in the room with him this night.

What they couldn't know at that time was that Richard saw himself as the living incarnation of the Dog Star, the star that burns brightest in the northern sky – the judge, the gatekeeper of higher and lower consciousness! He had great plans and he would use his new high-paid consultants to achieve his goals. And as always, he would tell it "slant." He couldn't reveal all of himself and all his plans and desires, not yet. They simply weren't ready for that revelation. The world wasn't ready, but the time was coming near.

His time.

He knew if he stayed the course, there were grand days ahead. After all, long ago in the desert dunes of ancient Babylonia, his glorious destiny was written in the stars.

In the back of the room a shaky hand went up into the air. "Excuse me," the man said, "but I'm not sure if I am hearing you correctly. Are you running for President or are you saying you ultimately want to turn the world into an empire ruled under U.S. power? 'Cause I have to be honest, if that's your goal, it's a little much for me and I think it will be a little much for the voters. If you go about your campaign with that as your message, you won't get elected, you'll get killed!"

Richard strode down on the left side of the conference room to where the man was standing. "Who are you?" he asked.

The man faced Richard. "John Burns, Rothchild Chair in Political Science at Harvard."

"Oh yes, of course," Richard said. "You wrote that treatise, *American Democracy in Foreign Policy.*"

"Yes, that's correct."

"Excellent work. That's why you're here. I read it twice."

The man smiled warmly at Richard, flattered by the praise.

"But don't you think it was a bit aggressive in its approach to the situation in the Middle East?" Richard followed. "If I understood you correctly, you felt war was the answer to bringing democracy to the civilizations in the Middle East.

"Don't you see that I'm not advocating any sort of bloody revolution, only a technological revolution and a charitable and social revolution? I don't advocate nonintervention, and let me be clear that if war becomes the only means to defend American ideals, then it will be done. But the key word is defending!

"Don't get me wrong, however. The world must and will eventually succumb to our ways as they are simply better. It will be essentially an American empire built on American ideals, but I was not suggesting that we exacerbate the tensions in the world by shoving our doctrines down their throats with the barrels of our guns! That would be your approach, Mr. Burns! The Bolsheviks tried it in the Russian Revolution and we tried it in Korea and in Viet Nam and now in Iraq. And has it ever worked? I am a revolutionary, yes, and I am a warrior, but I don't necessarily see how war can bring stability and democracy to any region."

"I see that we have differing opinions. Maybe I'm in the wrong place. I should go."

"No, please," Richard said, smiling, "please stay. You spoke your mind and I engaged you in debate. That's why you're here. We can benefit each other, you and I. I respect your opinion even if I do not agree with it. Just don't make me out to be an empire builder by war; I'm not Caesar and this is not Rome. This will be an empire, built over hundreds of years maybe, but an empire built nonetheless on principles of truth, justice and American ideals. And unlike Rome, we shall not fall!"

A female voice called out from the front of the conference room. "You want to change the world! So you're really saying the American way is better than everyone else's way, right?"

"I like freedom and prosperity and I want everybody to experience these things. Do you like your freedom to speak your mind, Ms. -"

"I'm Nancy Calloway."

"Ah, yes, Ms. Calloway!" Richard turned to address everyone, pointing back to her. "This is our resident expert on nuclear physics from Stanford; she's here to teach us about the virtues of nuclear power and all its sustainable uses. Let me just ask you something, Ms. Calloway. How many years can we make it on coal and natural gas? New technology is the answer. Is our technology better? Of course it is, and if you haven't yet admitted that to yourself then maybe you're not the right person to enlighten the world about the greatness of this new frontier and the environmental benefits of nuclear power. But I think you are. I believe in your work. I ask that you believe in me. I ask that you believe in the power that we have together to change the world."

She nodded politely and smiled, clasping her hands in front of her. Slowly, one by one, Richard was winning them over. He could buy their service, but he really wanted to win their minds and hearts.

The debate raged on late into the evening as Richard and his newly hired consultants exchanged ideas and argued on a wide range of topics affecting the United States and the world. Richard was having a great time. He had been preparing for this his whole life and he felt he was well up to the task. And he was winning over a very tough crowd.

A few in the room were still absolutely convinced he was an extremist revolutionary, but even they had to admit that he had some impressive ideas. However, if he was going to get elected, they were going to have to find a way to get him to focus on the U.S. and keep the lid on his foreign policy ideas for the time being. It's not that they weren't important, but he saw the world in terms of the American dream and many in attendance just didn't think the world was ready for his revolution. Funny thing about a billionaire: his money buys whatever he wants. Even those that disagreed still stayed put. They weren't about to turn over the $10 million that had been paid to each of them. Under the terms of the employment contract, it had to be refunded in full if they quit. That was the deal. It was confidential and it was lucrative.

And Richard knew that kind of money could buy loyalty, especially from the academics in the room. Their occasional books and treatises brought them mere pennies compared to what he was paying them for their service. Still, he wanted them to believe in him, but he knew it was going to take time. Richard knew they believed in his winning business ways, and he was certain that in time he would be able to transfer that confidence to his political ideas. He was a great man, a great leader, and yes, whether they understood their place in his grand scheme or not, he was an empire builder of the highest magnitude.

The discussion finally turned to the practical realities of getting him elected as an independent. That was the only real choice; he certainly didn't fit the mold as either a Democrat or a Republican. In fact, he vehemently opposed their monopoly on power and had been very clear in his plan to declare war on the two-party system.

Since the 1850's, only one third-party has ever had any success in establishing itself as a lasting factor in our democracy, and that was when Abraham Lincoln, a former Whig, brought prominence to the Republican Party with his election to the presidency in 1861. Despite public opinion polls that consistently show Americans prefer a third party in American elections, the result has largely been that third party candidates split the vote, thereby taking votes from the candidates of the two major parties, but rarely producing victory for their party or themselves. Never since Lincoln has a third party candidate taken the presidency.

Even Roosevelt, with his Progressive Party in 1912, couldn't do it; instead he split the vote enabling Woodrow Wilson to win the presidency without winning the popular vote. And where would Bill Clinton have been without Perot, who took 19% of the vote, including many votes that would have gone to George Bush. Perot didn't have a shot at getting the 270 Electoral College votes necessary to win the White House, and while he was a factor in the election, in the end he couldn't overcome the daunting problems that fly in the face of third party candidates.

Richard Novak, a student of history, knew well the obstacles facing his campaign, but he knew he had what it took to get the job done. He would do something the others had not done effectively. He would declare war not only against the individual candidates who were certain to steal from his ideas, but also against the two party system that in the past had been allowed to strangle the voice of third party candidates. He would do more than split the votes in the country's 3033 counties, he would win the popular vote and the Electoral College. This he would do by splitting the Democrat and the Republican voters and turning them into believers in the one man who could fix the problems facing the country – Richard Novak.

"If we are going to win this thing, we need to get several things accomplished," Richard stated. "First, we need to move a helluva lot faster than others who've failed before us. There is a lot to be done before the New Year. Perot and Nader showed us you can get on the ballots in all states, but you have to be incredibly organized. To that end, I appoint Ted Mitchell, who will be my right-hand man in this campaign, my campaign manager. He will be charged with the responsibility of getting the right network established to get us on all ballots for the 2008 election.

"As I am sure you all know, this will be a daunting task, but let me remind you that Perot's people, the Reform Party, accomplished it in seven months. We will cut that time in half! How? Well, needless to say, the war chest is up to the task and we are going to use the Internet effectively to circulate the nominating petitions and get the signatures we need. Ted, would you like to address this issue with respect to what we need to do to get this done?"

Ted Mitchell, a sharply creased, bald man, stood from the table and marched to the front of the room with the strong steps of a soldier. "Good afternoon, ladies and gentlemen," he began, with a gravelly textured voice. "I am delighted to be working with you on this campaign to get Richard Novak into the White House in 2008. It's a formidable task aside from the size of the war chest. These goddamn Democrats and Republicans have written the rules and requirements for third party candidates to get on the ballots! And people, they don't want us there! We'll have to file a declaration of candidacy and a certificate of a candidate's selection for vice president with the secretary of state before we can even begin to circulate the nominating petitions in the states. And if that weren't a big enough pain in my tired, old fat ass -"

The room erupted with laughter, and Richard stood off to the side against the wall with a wide toothy smile – loving his man.

"If that weren't a big enough pain in the ass," he began again, "we can't circulate the goddamn petitions until January 1, 2008. But that's okay," he said, smiling, "because that gives us five months to get our shit together! But let me tell you something, I've worked with Richard for nearly 20 years and if there is any one thing that helped get him to where he is today it is his ability to organize and absolutely out-fox the competition.

"Hell," Ted continued, "if Ventura can get elected governor in Minnesota with only an Internet site and one paid campaign employee, what do you think we can accomplish with this man's technological empire? The bottom line folks, is this: We'll get it done! You all already know why you're here and generally what the specifics of your jobs will be, as they're outlined in your contracts and we went over those things prior to today. So we can get down to business right away. Tomorrow I want to meet with each of you so we can get things going and get broken down into our committees and special task forces. Tomorrow you'll start to earn that money! Be here at 6 a.m. sharp. And here's a helpful hint: Don't ever be late!"

A hand rose in the rear of the boardroom. "I'm just curious," the man said. "Have we given any thought to who the running mate will be? I have some thoughts on -"

At that time the smoked glass doors in the back of the boardroom swung open and Jane Tierney and Uriel with his camera propped up on his shoulder charged into the room out of breath. Jane looked agitated to see the meeting was already underway. She looked at Richard who walked over to her with a huge grin on his face. Looking over at the man who rained the question, he said, "You let me worry about that. I've got someone in mind whom I think America will absolutely fall in love with as my running mate."

CHAPTER 12

The shining spotlights in front of Jimmy were blinding. In the back of the smoky tabernacle, he could see the back of a man with long, dark hair standing and talking to a small gathering. He couldn't make out their faces in the brightness of the lights and his mind was numb from the pain. Streamers floated from their bodies and they appeared through the smoke as if they were shining stars, illuminated in colors of a rainbow.

Jimmy had only been with the angels for a week and he had no idea how much time had passed. The sermon seemed to go on for days. The angels took turns and occasionally pitied him, bringing him bread and blood from the sacrificial lamb, smiling at him gently as they forced it down him. In the reflection of their eyes, he could see the reflection of the desecrated lamb and he crawled in his skin as if it were being peeled off of him by flesh devouring demons. At times he couldn't remember who he was anymore. He was so tired and the splinters from the wood were searing into his wrists. In the image of Christ, he was hung from a cross, which was tied to a rafter in the center of the tabernacle. He felt like he was dying, and truly, as he'd known himself, he was dying. That was their plan.

For the most part the angels showered him with affection as long as he answered to the name "Gabriel" and prayed with them. Whenever he screamed out in pain for his past life, however, he was beaten with a wet leather mallet and the rock below his feet was removed. When that happened, his body floundered against the cross as the blood soaked linens held him up in his place of light. They were reeducating him in the ways of the Lamb so he could accept his fate as a chosen angel in the circle of seven.

The reeducation process was intense. Angels in the circle of seven had to be equipped to endure the greatest suffering known to man for they knew the Beast was capable of inflicting greater torment than they could ever imagine. Gabriel just didn't understand. His rebirth and the rite of sacrament through the valley of darkness had only just begun. Soon Gabriel would learn as all before him had learned, to embrace the glory of the light, to embrace the glory of the Lamb, and to accept the sacrificial role with honor and enlightenment.

Still, Gabriel cried out for his past life, and they beat him mercilessly for it. Slowly, he began to lose the battle, his mind slipping further into their will with each passing hour. For each hour was more horrible than the last.

He cried in pain and soiled himself as the angels stood by and smiled compassionately. The walk of rebirth through the *Chamber of Light* was a wretched journey into one's soul. This was how it had always been done; every angel had to take the journey and confront their demons 40 days and 40 nights. Only then could they be purified and begin to understand their true place in God's Army. The angels implored Gabriel to let go. They explained that Jimmy was gone and would never return.

After all, he was chosen.

Gabriel's destiny was preordained. One day he would carry out his mission for God's Army, clearing the way for the coming of the Lamb. Then he would ascend with the Lamb into the light from atop the throne of Mt. Zion in the City of David. This they had learned from Michael, their blessed leader in the Great War.

Hour after hour, Jimmy hung there naked on the cross, becoming Gabriel. He was blinded by the light, praying for God's forgiveness. He no longer knew what he'd done to come to the archangel Michael and the angels, and to receive such unimaginable horrors in the *Chamber of Light*, but he was truly sorry.

He was sorry to be alive.

He prayed for salvation. He cried and kicked and occasionally he couldn't take it anymore and he would scream out in agony from the pit of his soul. And then Michael would dip the leather mallet into the Lamb's blood and begin again the purification of Gabriel. Then he would finally leave Gabriel to rest on the cross in the unconscious world where the few remaining bits of his old identity were disintegrating into dust.

All the while, the angels took turns praying for him. They were so passionate. The archangel Michael spoke with great force, but always with love. And his prophecy from the Lamb was grand.

"And it is written in *Revelations* that, 'I saw seven angels which stand before God; and there were given unto them seven trumpets ... And the seven angels which had the seven trumpets prepared themselves to sound ... When the fifth angel sounded, I saw a star from heaven fallen unto Earth: and there was given to him the key of the pit of the abyss ... And out of the smoke came forth locusts upon the Earth ... And the shape of the locusts were like unto horses prepared for war ... They have over them as king the angel of the abyss: his name in Hebrew is Abaddon, and in the Greek tongue he hath the name Appollyon.' We know him as Satan, the Antichrist, the Beast, the Red Dragon of ten horns and seven heads, as written in the great *Book of Revelations!*"

Michael's sermon reverberated against the walls of the smoky tabernacle. He shouted with his arms raised to heaven, the power of the spirit singing through him. "And the Beast will come preaching great blasphemies about the great modern equalizer, technology, and all of its grand power in his vision of the world. He will appear as the great peacemaker, the techno-prince of evil, who is a liar, hell bent on war! And the Beast will fornicate with the whore, Jezebel, who is surrounded on all sides by water, and with her seed he will make war! And who is Jezebel?"

"Babylon!" the angels responded.

"And who is Babylon?" the archangel Michael asked.

"America is Babylon," they chanted in unison. "She is the great whore who has fornicated with the Beast! She is the receiver and the deliverer of his blasphemies, the keeper of his commandments, the holder of his testimony! She will be stopped! For it is written that Babylon will fall and the Beast will burn in the lake of fire!"

Michael walked over to Gabriel, running his hand along the side of his blood drenched cheek. "And it is written," he said. "'I saw another sign in heaven, great and marvelous, seven angels having seven plagues, which are *the last*, for in them is finished the wrath of God! And I heard a voice out of the temple, saying to the seven angels, Go Ye, and pour out the seven bowls of the wrath of God into the Earth!'"

"And it is done!" the angels chanted in chorus. "Behold the glory of the coming of the Lamb!"

Michael nodded. "But fear not, my angels, for God's Army gathers. For although the Beast has risen, God has sent the great soldier into the desert where he appeared as foretold in the valley of the sun. He has come to us a virgin of faith! He is born anew, an angel — Gabriel! And wrath by wrath, bowl by bowl, plague by plague, the seven will be released unto the great whore — Babylon! We shall watch her cry out for war and revenge, as it is written in the prophecy! And the Beast will stand to lead Babylon. He will spit venom into the face of all that is good. For more than anything, he fears the coming of the Lamb! And with the last bowl of wrath, Gabriel will lead us into the final battle! A warrior, he will lead us into the abyss of Babylon. And alas, the clouds will open and the Lamb will return and God shall reign on Earth as in heaven!

"Are you with me, my angels?"

"We are with you, Michael," they responded. "Behold the glory of the Lamb! And, behold the glory of the coming of the Lamb! Behold the glory of the coming of the Lamb!" they chanted.

CHAPTER 13

LATE AUGUST, 2007

On a hot afternoon, Chase Davidson left Louisville in a rush. His trial had to be continued, set for a later date. A major personal injury case, he'd spent weeks in the war-room preparing for the showdown in the courtroom. The case was a multimillion-dollar lawsuit, the kind plaintiff's attorneys dream about. His client was messed up, and as Chase said behind closed doors, "The kid was tore up from the floor up!"

The kid, Bobby Rollins, had the misfortune of being in the wrong place at the wrong time. Young Bobby had spent his 18th birthday with his buddies drinking beers in the basement of a friend's house, not having a clue what destiny had dialed up for him in the hours and days that lay ahead.

Typical kids, the boys played drinking games and slammed more beers than they could really handle and left the house headed for the pool hall with their cues in hand, each one bragging about how they were going to clean the other's pockets. Bobby was quiet, he was the best player out of them all and really didn't feel that he had anything to prove. As they turned the corner for the hall none of them even noticed the semi that was barreling down the road, heading right towards them. Bobby stepped right in front of the truck and took the blow head-on. The collision was violent and it should have killed him, but he was lucky that the driver, anticipating a collision had managed to slow down and he was thrown into a grassy ditch.

The kid was busted up all over his body, just broken up into pieces. It was a miracle that he had lived and he had made great strides in his recovery, but he would never play pool again and he would never again walk to the corner pool hall with his buddies. Hell, he couldn't even talk to his buddies or remember their names. He was still in intensive therapy for his severe brain injury and it would be a long time, if ever, before Bobby Rollins could enjoy any normal quality of life.

Chase had poured nearly $50,000.00 in costs into the case and he was ready to take the insurance carrier and the trucking company to the cleaners. One thing was for sure, Bobby was going to be a very rich boy and he needed every penny, the cost of his future care was estimated to be at a minimum, $5,000,000.00. Although most attorneys would rake in 40% of the take on a case like this one, Chase had agreed up front to only take his costs out of the verdict.

That's the thing that few people knew about Chase, not even Jimmy – he played the big shot but he still had an equally big heart. He'd made a ton of money and it no longer motivated him. All he wanted was a sense of justice, he wanted to take a very bad situation and make it just a little bit better. He'd seen enough of these cases to know that there wasn't enough money in the world to make young Bobby Rollins whole again, but it made him feel better to give back on cases like this where the only word that could accurately describe the reality was, tragedy.

At first Chase was angry with Jimmy for causing this disruption in Bobby's case. Still, his last conversation with Susan was troubling, and he wondered where in the hell Jimmy had disappeared to and he knew that he couldn't ignore the fact that something was amiss with his failure to show up or at least call and explain where he'd gone. Jimmy was his own man, and did things his own unique way, but this was even a little aloof for him.

A week had passed since Susan's first call and there was still no sign of Jimmy. Susan had been everywhere. She went to all of the stores and art galleries in Taos; she'd contacted every hotel in both Taos and Santa Fe. She went to the police stations in both Taos and Santa Fe and had even contacted the FBI.

The authorities were gradually paying more attention to the case, but it just didn't grab their attention like a missing child and Susan had made it clear to Chase that they had to take this into their own hands if they were going to find Jimmy.

Time was wasting, and Susan had a terrible feeling. She was trying to stay calm and positive, but Chase could tell she was an absolute wreck. The flight to Santa Fe seemed to last forever, Chase closed his eyes and tried to think nothing but good thoughts. But even he had to admit something was wrong, Susan wasn't the only one with a bad feeling. He knew he wouldn't get any rest until he saw, Jimmy, smiling goofily and running his mouth at his "big-shot" older brother like always.

Chase began the drive to the hotel with a promise, once he found Jimmy, he was going to give his brother a big hug and then there was going to be hell to pay. This was just too much goddamn stress. How in the hell does a grown man, a strong man, a prosecutor for god-sakes just disappear and no one knows where the hell he is and no one has seen him. He just couldn't understand what could possibly explain this mess. He couldn't wait to get to the Holiday Inn on Cerrilos Road and sink his teeth into the search for Jimmy. He knew that he could find him, Susan had tried, but cooler heads would prevail just like in the courtroom. He was sure of it.

Chase knocked on the door and Susan peeked around the curtain and cracked a weak smile when she saw him. Quickly, she unlatched the locks and opened the door. Chase could tell she'd been crying again and she threw her arms around him and didn't want to let go.

Finally after a few moments, he was able to pull away and look into her eyes. He could see her pain and it just made him sick. "We're going to find him, Susan," he said. "We are going to find him! Do you hear me?"

"Yes," she said, "I do, but I'm just so scared, Chase. Where is he? This isn't like, Jimmy! I've been everywhere and nothing, no one has seen him. And this guy, this Michael or whoever the fuck he is, is a ghost, no one knows who he is and I don't know anything about him! Goddamn it! This is just an impossible situation!"

"We'll find him!" Chase said again. "I promise you we'll find him and we'll take him home. We have to think positive thoughts - do you understand? It's only been a week! It's going to be okay! Trust me, I've been through enough trials to know that every time you let a negative thought to creep in, it poisons the soul and takes you a step further a way from achieving your goal. Our goal, our only goal is to find Jimmy! And we have to get composed so that we can think logically, okay? Are you with me?"

She began crying again. "Yes, thank you so much for coming. I didn't know what else to do. My father is on a cruise in Alaska and I just figured-"

"Stop! It's okay; he's my brother! And although he's a pain in my ass sometimes, you know that I wouldn't ever let anyone mess with my brother! There's nothing more important to me than my family! We're going to find him and I'm going to beat the living shit out of him for driving us nuts like this, that's what's going to happen!"

Susan smiled. "I used to think that Jimmy was so strong that he could handle anyone, but I'm not so sure anymore."

"Hey, what did I just tell you? He's going to be okay! He's going to be okay!"

"That's what the police keep telling me!"

Chase turned away from her and looked around the hotel room that had more charts and maps on the walls than his war-room at the law office. This was serious and he knew Susan was right to be concerned and freaked out. He knew that Jimmy wasn't the type to put people through something like this unless something was wrong. He wondered where Jimmy was and he prayed that he was okay.

"Well, let's get started," Chase said. "I want to know everything that you've done, I want to know every place you've been and everyone that you've talked to — law enforcement, store clerks, the whole list. Have you've been keeping the journal of names and activities like I asked you to on the phone?"

"Yes."

"Good, well fill me in on everything. I've got some ideas, but first I want to know that I'm not missing anything. We're going to do this right! We're going to find him and I am going to kick his ass! I'll beat the living shit out of him just like the old days!"

Chase rolled up his sleeves to his white oxford and sat at a small table and began looking over the map that was spread open across the table.

He was preparing for an all out assault on the area. He knew enough about missing person's cases to know that time was of the essence, and he feared that too much time had already passed. He was sorry that he hadn't come sooner. He just didn't know how to tell a family that had been waiting for their day in court for over a year that he had to go out of town and look for his brother, a grown man that had disappeared after a fight with his girlfriend. Although he'd rationalized his delay at the time, he knew that if they didn't find Jimmy that mistake would haunt him forever.

They simply had to find him! There was no choice!

CHAPTER 14

Seattle has always been known for its dreary skies. Even in late summer, the clouds hover above the city. What's hidden under its reputation for rain and sullen skies, however, is the paradise it offers for those who love the water. The city is situated amidst the deep-water Puget Sound, about 75 miles inland from the Pacific Ocean, with Lake Washington just a few miles to the east and Lake Union in the north, it's a city virtually surrounded by water. With the vast, dark blue waters of the Sound, the shimmering lakes, the shadowy Olympic Mountains and the snowcapped volcanic peak of Mount Rainer, the natural horizon of Seattle is simply stunning from all directions.

Richard helped Jane step up into the cabin of the shiny, red Bell 407 helicopter atop the landing deck of RDI Tower. The rotors were whipping violently on the rooftop with the force of a gail wind. Jane's hair was tousled in every direction and she was burning with anger.

She was furious about the fact that she'd just flown all day trying to get to the conference when Richard must have known all along that she'd show up just in time to see it end. She sent Uriel back to Alexis Hotel with none of the promised footage to return to GNN. She was trying to contain her emotions but she was mad as hell.

Already Richard wasn't holding up his end of the deal.

He was playing games with her and she knew it, but she hadn't gone that far to go home without a story. She thought that she might as well try to figure him out, to get the fricking story, that's after all what any good reporter would do in her shoes. So with reluctance she accepted his invitation to take a little hop to dine by the water. In her mind the questions were percolating like Seattle coffee and she couldn't wait to throw the brew into his face. She was just waiting for the right time to pounce on her prey. *Richard Novak – big deal – this man is no match for me.*

The pilot banked left around the infamous Space Needle and flew just below the low hanging clouds, buzzing through the air toward the Sound. Richard handed Jane a headset and turned a knob on the side. Jane peered through her side window admiring the view of Seattle below.

"You're awfully quiet today," Richard said.

"You think?" She kept her eyes to the window.

"Is something wrong?"

"No, not at all. Why would anything be wrong?"

"You seem a little distant."

"Do I?"

Richard, an ardent student of human nature, knew enough about women to recognize the warning signs of subtle hostility brewing beneath the surface. He knew she was upset with him. That was all part of the plan. He just couldn't help himself. He enjoyed toying with her, her fire was a delight to see and he looked at her admiringly, taking strength from her spirit. He knew he had a winner with Jane. People loved her. She just had charisma; she was a star in the making. She was a bright, beautiful star, shimmering in the sky with the Dog Star. Together they were going to conquer the world. She just didn't know it yet.

In fact, she knew very little about Richard Novak and the extent of his plans, or to what lengths he would go to get what he wanted and to stake his claim to what he viewed as rightfully his, to not only make history but to be the master of the greatest story ever told.

This was his show and he loved every minute of it.

The money he could do without, but the power, the power was the greatest drug in the world. And he wanted to have so much power that he could bathe in it and let it soak into his veins and fill every drop of his blood and his every breath so that every time he spoke the Earth moved and the wind swirled with his burning energy. He was an empire builder, it's all he had ever known how to do and now he could take his design to the world, one small piece at a time.

He wanted a revolution. He wanted absolute chaos.

And in those troubled waters the world below would look to the sky praying for a savior, and he would be there for them. He would rise to lead them into the annals of history, into the new world order, the greatest empire the universe has ever seen, the one that the prophets always knew was coming. That time had arrived.

As they flew out over the dark waters of the Sound, Jane was surprised to see they were flying away from the city as the lights fell behind in the distance. "Where are we going?" she finally asked.

"To eat by the water," he answered.

"Where?"

"Aboard Red Trinity."

"You didn't tell me we were going to a boat."

"Would it have made a difference?"

"Maybe I don't like boats."

Richard smiled. "When's the last time you were on a boat?"

"I don't know," she said. "What's the difference? If I don't like boats, then I don't like boats!"

"Well if you don't like it then we'll leave, but this is a pretty nice boat. I assure you dinner will be absolutely mind blowing."

"You know, I really don't care too much for your macho, call-all-of-the-shots bullshit! If I'm going to cover your campaign, we're going to have to get some things straight."

Richard tried to fight back his smile. "You're very beautiful when you're mad, full of fire!"

"You just don't get it, do you? And why is that? Are you so fricking smug that you don't even realize when someone is not turned on by your rich boy games. I'm a reporter. You're a story. That's all this is."

He turned to her, a very crystalline look in his dark eyes. "In the end, Jane, isn't that all every thing is, just a story? How do you want your story to be told? That she was an excellent reporter who always got the big story. Don't you think that's a little low on expectations? Aren't you just an instrument for the real newsmakers? Is that all you want?"

"Go to hell! Who are you to judge me?" she said. "Look at how you live! This is not the real world! People don't fly around on private jets, make billions, live in mansions and talk about ridding the world of its plagues! This is a modern day freak show! The average American can't relate to a man like you! You're not their guy! You'll never be their guy! I don't know if any of your lackeys back there had the guts to tell you, but don't you realize how hypocritical it's going to sound when you start preaching to Americans about making the world a better place with your technology and their tax dollars?

"What have you done for the average American, that their ready to support you on Project-Save-The-World? You don't even know the first thing about equality! You live like a fricking king, and the rest of us are just serfs in your kingdom! Wake-up!"

Richard reflected for a long moment and then turned to Jane. "'The nations of our day," he said, "cannot prevent conditions of equality from spreading in their midst. But it depends upon them whether equality is to lead to servitude or freedom, knowledge or barbarism, prosperity or wretchedness.'"

"Herodotus?" she said.

"No, Tocqueville."

"That's great! Just terrific!"

"Just trying to lighten the moment."

She forced a smile. "But this isn't a joke!" she began. "Try to sell those lines to the voters, the people who pay taxes and work their asses off to pay their monthly bills! Just how do you plan to win people over? Why would they warm to your politics and your MIT education?"

"Seriously?"

"Yes, seriously!"

Richard looked up through the cockpit out the front window. He could see the lights of Red Trinity as they approached. "Well, I have a secret weapon," he said, turning back to Jane.

"What? Money? Fancy marketing?"

"No."

The red Bell 407 helicopter touched down on the landing deck on board Red Trinity. The yacht, over 200 feet in length, was more than a boat, it was a mega-yacht. Jane was not surprised, she'd figured as much. Every rich guy she'd ever met had loved showing off his toys, and Richard had been no different from all of the rest in that regard.

She figured the toys were used as distractions to keep the women off their mark. The men seemed to know that if the toys didn't get them to bed, then their lack of depth was certainly going to be a major problem. These types rarely surprised her. But Richard was far from ordinary and even further from predictable.

As a steward ran to the helicopter and opened the door, she turned back to Richard before stepping out. "What's you're secret weapon?" she asked.

"You are!"

"Me!"

"You!"

Jane threw up her hands in surrender. "I haven't got a clue what you're talking about! It must be nice to live in your little world, but it's a million miles away from the real one!"

She stepped down onto the hard-deck and Richard followed. The rotors of the helicopter bellowed in the wind at their backs as they raced to the door and into the labyrinths of Red Trinity. Just inside the door, Jane turned to Richard and pushed her hand against his chest. "What are you up to?" she asked.

"Let's eat dinner first," he said. "Then I'll let you peer into my little world and we'll see if it sounds any more real to you."

She laughed. "Oh, I just can't wait," she said. "I'm sure it'll be a real hoot!"

In Jane's humble opinion, Richard deserved credit for being right at least about one thing, dinner was delicious. They dined on buttery lobster in the formal dining room on the main deck which was open to the high-windowed saloon. He was spoiling Jane. She savored several glasses of vintage Bordeaux, 1868 Lafite-Rothschild Pauillac, as the moon glowed in the night sky over the San Juan Islands.

The yacht was a marvel of modern craftsmanship and technology. The red mahogany interior was open and spacious, filled with traditional antique furnishings sitting elegantly atop the black marble floor. After dinner, Richard led Jane into the 50-seat theater room on the 3rd deck. She took a seat in a soft leather recliner while he fiddled with a remote. The large plasma movie screen lit up and he sat down hurriedly next to her.

"Allow yourself to open your mind," he said. "You might find the subject matter of this a little strange but there's a point I'm trying to make here. Think of this as a presentation. This is my presentation to you."

"What is this? Why don't you just tell me?"

"First I want you to watch this video and then we can talk about it. I'm going somewhere with this so just sit tight, okay?"

"Okay."

The soft theater lights went out and the show began. The documentary was titled, *Great Women in Power,* and the commentator was no less a woman with a deep, exotic voice.

"What's this?" Jane whispered. "A home movie?"

"Not quite," he said. "This is your potential."

"My potential?"

"Greatness!"

The video began with Nefertiti, the great queen of Egypt in the 14th century B.C. She was described as beautiful and powerful, the wife of Akhenaton, who worshipped in Egypt what was a very unique religion at that time, the belief in only one God, Aten. The next subject was Cleopatra, the queen of Egypt from 69-30 B.C. Her reign was marked by her struggle to hold onto Egypt's independence, but she needed the protection of Rome. For that she bore a child with Caesar and fell in love with Marc Anthony. In the end her romance with Rome came back to haunt her and her beloved Egypt, bringing war and Egypt's defeat at the hands of Octavian in 31 B.C. Not only was she was a dynamic, calculating leader, but her rule of ancient Egypt has forever made her a star in the realm where not enough stars of her kind have been allowed to shine so bright – history!

"But she succumbed to defeat at the hand's of Rome," Jane whispered.

"Yes, and so did everyone else," Richard said. "But what made her special was her ability to hold off Rome longer than most. By seducing the Romans, she kept them at bay."

Upon the screen the video turned to Joan of Arc. The sultry moderator noted that for centuries the role of women in combat has been debated. Joan of Arc, however, was a great military leader before a modern gun ever fired any shots.

She was fearless and powerful. She led the French army of Charles VII into battle against the English. Her price for her bravery was steep and she was eventually captured and burned at the stake. Her place in history? Immortality!

The video continued. One by one it went through a long list of great female rulers and heroines: Catherine the Great, the Russian Empress from 1729-1796; Victoria, Queen of England from 1819-1901, the longest reign in English history, usher of the Victorian age who orchestrated Britain's rise as a great colonial power; Eleanor Roosevelt, the First Lady from 1933-1945, social revolutionary of woman's suffrage for most of her political life; Margaret Thatcher, Britain's first female Prime Minister.

The moderator next talked about the inequities of the Equal Pay Act of 1963, the national impact of the Civil Rights Act of 1964, and the landmark case of *Roe v. Wade* in 1973, which declared a woman's constitutional right to abortion. She spoke elegantly about the unratified Equal Rights Amendment of 1972, designed to abrogate state and federal laws that discriminated against women. She also discussed many of the landmark decisions and the lasting impact of Sandra Day O'Connor and Ruth Bader Ginsburg, respectively the first and second female U.S. Supreme Court justices on the high Court. The list went on and on, and Jane was very intrigued and fascinated with the presentation. She was impressed but she was also very wary. Although she had no idea where Richard was going with any of this, she understood that somehow it was meant to come back to her and she wasn't yet making any connection between any of these women and herself.

Sure, she admired and marveled at all of them, having a great respect for their accomplishments in a world that was not always willing to accept their leadership with open arms. These women earned their way into the lore of history, and their importance was not lost on her. Jane couldn't figure out the point of the history lesson. Then when the presentation ended with, Geraldine Ferraro, the running mate of Democratic Party presidential candidate, Walter Mondale, in 1984, the wheels in Jane's mind began to spin rapidly and as the theater lights clicked on in the room, she was standing and looking down at Richard.

Typical Richard, he just beamed with a bright smirk. "What?" he asked, breaking the silence.

"You're crazy!" she said.

"You tell me that a lot, you know."

"Are you serious?"

"About what?"

"Don't be coy with me!" she said, peering into his eyes. "You know what I'm talking about!"

He stood up, towering over her but gazing down into her eyes with purpose. "Jane," he said, "with you as my running-"

"Oh my god, you're fricking nuts! You are! You're absolutely nuts! Hell no, I won't do something like that!"

"Yes, you will," he said calmly. "You'll run with me and we'll win the White House! You and me! You'll have a place right alongside the most powerful women in history! How about that for a legacy!"

"But that's not what I want, I'm a journalist!"

"Don't you want to make a difference? Think about the things that you could achieve! We'll set the world's agenda! You'd be the most powerful woman in the world!"

"Yeah and what if we lose? Have you thought about that?"

"No! We won't lose -"

"What if?"

"Are we negotiating now?" he asked.

"No, we're not negotiating! I'm pointing out the fact that I would be ruined as a journalist!"

"Ruined as a journalist! For one thing, I don't know what world you're living in but you'll be the most famous female face in the world, that's far from ruined! Plus, if you do this with me, if we were to lose, which we're not, but if we did, then GNN would be your empire. I would make you the president or whatever you wanted! Either way, Ms. Tierney, you stand to lose nothing and you have everything to gain."

"I don't have a political background!"

"You graduated from Georgetown Cum Laude in Political Science before moving on to Journalism. You've covered politicians from every angle. You are a woman of intelligence and opinions, and guess what?"

"What?"

"You're very popular with the American people!"

"As a journalist!"

"As a character, a personality, an intellectual! You're beautiful and energetic and they connect with you! And when I bring you on my ticket, you'll bring them with you in hoards! It's bold and it's brilliant! We're unorthodox and we're novices and they'll admire us and they'll be intrigued with everything we do and say! Once we have their ears, then we can capture their minds! They won't even see us coming! We'll knock the socks off of the establishment and the American public and there won't be anything the other candidates can do about it! Don't get me wrong, this election will be won by ideas, but charisma and fame, intelligence and beauty will also win it! You may not realize it, Jane, but I'm a fucking genius! I love this idea, it's out there, but it will work! Trust me!"

"'A genius! Trust me!'" she said, laughing. "You're nuts beyond anything I could have imagined! Really, you need help!"

"Of course I do! I need your help! What do you think?"

"What do I think?" she said. "I think all men are evil and are in love with power! That's what I think!"

Richard smiled. "Well," he reflected, "not all men."

"I still don't understand why you're doing all of this," she said. "You have everything already."

Richard moved within a breath of her and looked deeply into her eyes. "Ever since I was a young boy," he began, "I've known that one day I would leave my mark upon the world!"

"Your mark?"

"There's no escaping destiny, Jane. You can't hide from who you are; the universe will always find you. The light will always pull you from the shadows. Just like I discovered you."

"What make you so sure it was you who discovered me?"

He smiled. "When I first saw you I could see it in your eyes all that you were capable of being. I knew at that moment that you were destined for greatness. I knew that your name would some day be a part of the great names in history, that you would rise to the occasion. It is all written – written in the stars – burned into the genetic codes of our being. We are simply encrypted with our destiny, always marching to the moment as the trumpets sound and the drums of nature roll. It's who we are.

"I'm simply asking you to be who you have always had it in you to be, nothing more; nothing less. Many have said that, 'everything happens for a reason.' Well it's also true that some stars are meant to burn brighter than all of the others in the night sky. We aren't created as equals. According to our internal settings, we burn like the fire of the stars, shining our light onto our external world. We are the lightning strike of nature! It was always meant to strike at exactly that moment, in exactly that spot with precision and power! So too must we strike now, and with all of our might! For it is who we are; it's our destiny!"

Jane sat silent and still. She was completely mesmerized by him. His words were spinning in her mind like a willowy web, and she felt drawn to his power.

"Perhaps, you think I'm simply mad, a hopeless demagogue preaching a hapless message, and you'll turn your back on destiny and walk away. Just rest-assured that the universe is sure to find you hiding, and when you become a stranger to your destiny you become lost and lonely and your fire inside burns to ash.

"Shine like the star that you are, that's all I'm asking! That's all that anyone can ever ask of another, and that's all that I'll ask of you. You were born for greatness! That's just who you are! It's not a choice! Accept it, that's all you have to do! Just accept it!

"And know that achieving greatness requires you to walk down a path where only a few have ever had the fire to tread! Walk that path with me and we'll set it on fire! Our time is here! Our time is now! And you can't deny it, Jane! You can't deny your destiny! And I care too much about you to let you just walk away from me, this was meant to be and it shall be done! Our time has come!"

CHAPTER 15

The church bells in downtown Taos rang out at the noon hour. The town with the panoramic view of the mountains was already buzzing with tourists, shopping in the roadside stores and galleries and dining in the cafes. The town is a Mecca for artists, many came to the town in the 60s in droves and never left. With over 80 galleries in Taos, art is a major attraction drawing artists and consumers from all over the world. The span of eclectic genres, from Native American, Spanish and modern contemporary art, makes for a splendid array for the tourists who are drawn there to see primarily Native American and Southwestern art and find a much broader theme. To be sure, Native American art is plentiful, as Taos is located in close proximity to the Taos Pueblo, the homeland of a proud people who first inhabited the valley over 1000 years ago.

Only a week after his arrival, Chase and Susan had been walking the streets all morning, talking to store clerks and hanging up 'Missing' posters with Jimmy's picture, description and other pertinent personal information. Neither had slept in days.

Yet, they weren't about to give up. They had people helping them now and the search had broadened. Several of Jimmy and Susan's friends had flown in to assist in the search and they were spread out all over New Mexico at the direction of Chase, who was orchestrating a carefully designed mission to find Jimmy. Many felt that they weren't likely to find him alive but they wouldn't dare say that to Susan or

Chase, and Chase wary of such negativity sheltered Susan as much as possible.

The authorities were helping but their investigation hadn't turned up anything. The search was primarily focused on Taos and Santa Fe and all areas in between. Jimmy was just outside of Taos when Susan last spoke to him and he was headed in the direction of Santa Fe, or so she thought he was anyway. They had very little to go on except for the statement that Jimmy had made about Michael being a, "hippie artist." It was that information that had brought them to Taos. They were hoping to talk to someone that might know Michael, but with no other information about him, they knew that they were working on hope and a prayer.

Chase kept telling Susan, "It's just a matter of time. We'll find him."

However, even he began to wonder if they were looking in the right place. Had someone taken off with Jimmy and taken him out of the state? Was he alive? Was he hurt on the side of the road somewhere? There were so many questions and no answers. They'd spent the week before in Santa Fe doing all of the same things, hoping and praying that somehow all of their effort would pay off. The more they searched, the more it just seemed like Jimmy had just vanished into thin air and that they were never going to find him, and worse than that, they weren't going to find him alive.

Just that morning there had been a short article buried on page 3 in the Taos newspaper about the mysterious disappearance of Jimmy. The most significant effect of the article was the toll that it was taking on Susan. She was distraught and physically sick. She was a ghost of her former self; she hadn't been eating and she looked bad and she'd been waking up in the mornings vomiting. Chase had noticed that Susan looked bad, he also felt like a shell of his former self so who was he to judge. But he wasn't about to let that stop him. How could he? Jimmy was still out there somewhere? *God-damn it we're not giving up! I don't give a rat's ass how we feel! That's my little brother out there somewhere and if I have to crawl all over these god-damn mountains then so be it!*

And so they pushed on, store by store, gallery by gallery into late afternoon. The sun was beginning to fade behind a mountain as they entered the small little Christian art gallery called, *God's Work.* There were a few customers and Chase and Susan made their way to the clerk, a young Native American man, standing behind a canvass upon which he was in the process of painting a small, old Spanish style church.

As always Chase carried the charge and interrupted the young man. "Excuse me," he said. "We're looking for my brother. I wonder if we could just have a minute of your time."

"Sure," he said, taking a leaflet from Susan. He politely stared at the picture of Jimmy and read the description. "I'm sorry, but he hasn't been in here. I'm pretty good with faces."

"What about the name, Michael?" Susan asked. "Do you know anyone by that name?"

"That's a pretty common name. Know a couple of Michaels."

"Any of those hippie artist types?" she asked.

"Sorry," he said, fighting back a smile. "Look around here almost everyone is a hippie artist or an Indian, and sometimes there's not a lot of difference to outsiders."

Susan was no longer in the mood for politeness. This was a desperate search and no one seemed to understand. "Please," she said. "I think the last person he was with was named Michael, he picked him up on the highway to Santa Fe. If you think of anyone at anytime that it could have possibly been, or maybe several Michaels come to mind, doesn't really matter. Would you please call me on that number?"

Chase and Susan turned and began walking toward the door.

"Wait a minute," the man said. "There is a guy, this Michael freak. The guy's a real quack; I met him when my brother brought him to the pueblo a few springs ago. He was interested in our religious rituals. He had all sorts of questions. He really upset some of the elders. Our ceremonies are sacred and everyone felt there was nothing sacred about his intentions. The guy came off like a real fruit cake. The only time I see him now is when he's trying to pawn off the art. Usually comes in every couple of weeks. Always on a Monday. K'un, that's what my grandfather called him. I always think of it when I see him. Cracks me up. My grandfather's a spiritual man. He thinks he can see things in people; read their auras. He made my brother promise to never bring this guy back to our pueblo, he's superstitious like that. K'un."

"Kon?" Chase said.

"No, K'un."

"What's it mean?" Susan asked.

"It means to be dark. My grandfather used it as a reference to the color of his spirit, dark."

Susan looked at Chase. They both knew that this was the first real break that they had received since they began this forlorn search. They didn't know what to make of it, but they knew they had to find out more about this Michael character and they weren't about to dismiss anything. "Do you have any idea where this man lives?" Susan asked.

"No," he said, "I have no idea. You might talk to my brother though. He's the one that first met him. I doubt he knows, but you never know. He might be useful to you anyway, he's a tracker."

"A what?" Chase asked.

"A private investigator," the man said, smiling. "He refers to himself as a tracker though, like the ancient ones. Cracks me up! The best he's done so far is track down a few of the pueblo drunks and the occasional man that's late on child support."

"Turns them in?" Susan asked.

The man smiled. "Well, you'd have to ask him. Sometimes, maybe, but he might deal with them the Indian way."

"The Indian way? What's -"

"My brother's older than me, and he's a little out there – intense. The elders call him 'Old Redwood.' I call him whacked! He takes himself and his way very seriously."

"Could we talk to him?" Chase asked.

"Sure, I'm getting ready to close up here. You'll have to come with me back to the pueblo. I'm Dan, by the way. Dan Aranjo."

"Nice to meet you," Chase said. "We really appreciate your help. We're looking into any connection we can make. This is all new to us, you know. We just want to find Jimmy."

"I understand," Dan said. "You have to keep the faith. Think good thoughts."

Chase looked at Susan and smiled. He liked the optimist in young Dan, just his kind of man. He hoped that Susan was catching the spirit, she needed a boost. They both did. Maybe this was it, maybe his brother could locate this Michael character and that would somehow lead them to Jimmy. Neither of them knew, but they were going to find out; they weren't about to give up their search.

CHAPTER 16

The Taos Pueblo sat nestled in a valley at the base of the Sangre de Cristo Mountains. The ancient adobe complexes had been home to the Tiwa speaking Native Americans since around 1350, several centuries after they first inhabited the area that had come to be known as Taos. They are a proud and distinguished tribe whose pueblo stands as testament to their perseverance, and the fact that they still occupy it, after hundreds of years of modernization of the white man's society provides the most compelling evidence of their commitment to maintain their way of life and pass it on to their young.

The multi-storied, stacked room pueblo sits on two sides, north pueblo and south pueblo, divided by a river which flows down from high in the mountains from sacred Blue Lake. The Indians know the river as Red River Creek. More than an ordinary stream of water, the Indians depend on the small brook for drinking water, not only for themselves but for their livestock as well.

These Indians, out of their great wisdom, have made a simple choice to depend on each other as a community, a tribe, and to lend their patience and virtues to the fortuitous songs of Mother Earth. The residents of the pueblo have all chosen to forego modern amenities such as sewers, electricity and all of the normal luxuries of the white man's world. Inside the walls of the pueblo, it is their world, their land, and their sanctuary where the ways of the past are still remembered and practiced in every day life.

However, there had been a few adjustments in their Native ways to further their social independence. Originally established as an agrarian society, the Taos Pueblo Indians integrated their traditional indigenous religious practices with a blend of Catholicism brought to them by the Spanish, and they have woven their lifestyle much like an Indian wool rug, seamlessly blending the old world with the new. These are intelligent, spiritual people, maintaining their rich history and fostering their native footprints far into the future with their economy that is fortified by tourism, and the sale of their specialty craft items, such as rugs, drums, pottery and jewelry, and of course, a modern, state of the art casino.

Dan Aranjo led Chase and Susan around north pueblo, and they walked along the front of the enormous 5-story, mud-brick structure. The old pueblo was a marvel of ancient architecture. They walked behind Dan in awe of the complexity of the structure, until they reached a doorway to an apartment.

Once there they followed Dan into a small shadowy room where there was a small couch and several Indian drums of various sizes stacked alongside a wall. The room was tidy and a thin layer of dust filled the air. A wooden crucifix hung on the wall above a doorway going to a side-room. In the corner of the room, leather and materials for drum making sat neatly stacked on a table. Dan asked them to wait there in the room as he left to go find his brother.

Susan sat down on the couch and laid her head back and closed her eyes. "I'm so tired," she said.

"Are you going to make it?" Chase asked.

"I'm fine. Do you think this is a waste of our time?"

"Probably."

"Then what are we doing here?"

He looked at her, eyeing her closely. "We're desperate, remember?"

"Oh yeah," she said. "How could I forget?"

"You look bad, Susan. When we get out of this place, we're taking you to see a doctor."

"No, I'm fine."

"Yeah right!"

"No! I'll be fine! I just haven't slept or eaten-"

"I know. I know. It's hard to rest, isn't it? When he's still out there somewhere and we don't have a clue what's happened to him. All of the fliers and nothing, not a goddamn thing! That's why we're here!"

"How could we ignore the first lead we've had, no matter how strange?"

"Well," Chase said, contemplating the question wearily, "we couldn't."

At that moment they heard steps and looked up and there was an old Indian man standing in the doorway. When he saw Chase and Susan, he stopped in the doorway and stared. He was tall and dark with a ponytail, casting a long shadow into the room. Chase nodded at the man, but the old Indian failed to notice. He was staring at them but it was clear that his mind was somewhere else. He was distant. At the sight of them, it seemed as if he had slipped into another state of consciousness.

Dan finally came up from behind the old Indian and touched his shoulder. He looked at Dan and spoke to him in their native tongue; his pitch was deep and gravelly, aged no less by the hard silt of the mountains. They both took turns speaking and looking back over at Susan and Chase, who were watching closely but not understanding a single word that was being said. Then without warning, the elder Indian pushed young Dan aside and walked over to the couch. Chase jumped up and extended his hand, but the man just looked at him briefly and then focused his glistening eyes on Susan.

"You part Indian?" he asked.

"Yes," she said.

"What tribe?"

"Hopi. My mother was full-blooded Hopi. My father is Mexican born of Spanish descent."

The old Indian smiled, his wrinkles engulfing his tan face, he turned and looked back at young Dan with a cold stare. "I told you so," he said. "This is the one. They are finally here!"

"Excuse me?" Chase asked.

The Indian looked at Chase. "She's pregnant," he said, pointing to Susan.

"What?" Chase said.

Susan buried her head in her hands. Chase quickly sat down beside her. "Susan, is it true? Are you pregnant?"

"I don't know. I think I might be."

Chase looked back at the old Indian, stunned and short of breath. "Let's get out of here," he finally said to her. "We've got to get you to a doctor."

Young Dan, feeling the stare of his grandfather, hurriedly brought him a wooden chair so the elder could take a seat close to Susan and Chase.

"When I was a much younger man," the old Indian began, "I was meditating one moonless night in the Kiva and I had a vision of this day when you would come to hear the story of my vision. I saw a great fire in the black sky and behind that fire there was an eagle circling over a burning lake and many spirits were walking toward the lake. They were led by the dark one. They bore the mark of his hate, and one by one, they were led into the flames where they were burned alive. I could smell their burning flesh; I could hear their screams. I remember the cold stare of this man. He was a white man, but his spirit was dark, his aura black like coal.

"And the screams reached out into the heavens. And then the wind began to swirl and lightning filled the sky as thunder and rain hit the lake with a mighty storm of blood rain, chasing away the flames with the energy of the buffalo running from the spear in the final moment. And then there was a bright light and I remember the vision was too powerful and I was overcome with emotion. I asked the Great Spirit how we could avoid this vision of the people and the lake of fire and the white man with no soul. And I laid down in the Kiva and went to sleep and in my dreams I heard the voice of my father from the other side, telling me that Mother Earth was calling on me to deliver a message to the great warrior! The one who could make the rain and the wind howl like a mighty winter storm over the lake of fire."

Chase looked over at Susan, and extended his hand. The room was growing darker as night was approaching fast. "C'mon," Chase said, "let's get the hell out of here."

The old Indian moved closer to Chase, right up in his face. "You are a warrior!" he said.

"No buddy, I'm just a lawyer."

"No, you're a warrior! You're the warrior in my vision!"

Chase looked at Dan for help. Dan shook his head, offering none. "I don't understand," Chase finally said.

The old Indian smiled. "In the vision," he began, "the warrior, the circling eagle that showed no fear in the face of the fire bore your face and he came to me in the dream with a young woman, a woman who was pregnant with child. The woman was 1/2 Indian in blood, full Indian in spirit. For many years I've waited and now you've finally come. So now I can rest in peace. But you, you're journey has just begun. Take with you my oldest grandson, Billy. He'll guide you on your journey."

"Thanks, but I-"

"There's no arguing with him," Dan interrupted.

Susan stood up and peered deeply into the elder Indian's eyes. "What's your name?" she asked.

He smiled proudly. "I am Walter," he said, "Walter 'Red Hawk' Aranjo!"

At that time they were interrupted by another Indian, a middle aged man with a deeply furrowed brow, who'd entered the room in a rush as if he'd been summoned. Red Hawk turned to him and they spoke in the tribal tongue – Tiwa. The man stood there for a long moment, his hand stroking his chin, he looked at Chase and Susan closely and then left the room.

Red Hawk turned back to Susan. "With you," he said, "a child grows and will come to Mother Earth, brave and golden like the warm rays of the sun in the dawn. You must go home! Go to your family!"

"I can't," she said, "I have to find him!"

"No! You must go home now! The white warrior will find him!"

Chase just shook his head, too damn tired to argue with old Red Hawk. Susan began to cry, knowing that she couldn't go on in her condition and that the old Indian was right.

Red Hawk turned to Chase, grabbing onto his shoulder, looking him eye to eye. "You must look deep inside your soul and gather all of your strength, for your journey is the most dangerous journey of all and it is only beginning. You must find the dark one and stand like an oak in his way so that the wind and rain can fall on the lake of fire and it shall burn the spirits no more! You must be brave! You must be strong! Mother Earth rests in your hands!"

Chase let out an exhausted smile. "You're an interesting man," he said, "but I'm going to find my brother and then we're going home!"

"Yes, you will find him, for he is the key to the dark one! Follow his tracks and he will lead you to the lake and the great battle will roll like the thunder. Only then will you know what you must do!"

Chase was off of his game.

He just stared back at the old Indian. He was stunned and when he looked into the old man's eyes he saw something that he had seen only a few times before in his life – truth! He remembered young Bobby Rollins had that look in his eyes when he asked Chase to end his misery at the hospital. Chase was simply beat down. He decided that he would go with the tracker and see if he could help find Jimmy. And from there, he really had no clear idea where in the hell he was going.

CHAPTER 17

For hours Jane watched the shadows dancing on the ceiling. To her the shadows created by the burning candles looked like trees in a burning forest. The more she stared at them the more naked she felt. She could almost see faces of demons glowing on the ceiling as if she were being watched.

The dream had really shaken her.

The eagle's glowing eyes awakened all of her fears and he was chasing her and she was running for her life, screaming with her arms flailing helplessly as she ran. The wind was searing and cold and it soaked through her skin and hail the size of golf balls poured down from the black skies and she could barely see in front of her. She was scared and she just kept running toward the light.

And the closer she got to the light the warmer she felt and the more people that she'd run into along the way, all heading for the warmth of the light. And she'd look behind her and the eagle was still there in the sky, flying after her and she'd keep running, feeling so lost and tired and hopeless.

Then she'd reach the light, and to her despair, it was the abyss, a raging lake of fire where people were jumping into the flames to avoid the grasp of the man chasing them.

Jane could hear their screams and smell their burning flesh as they melted in the flames of the Beast. The horror of the screams and the smell of their flesh made Jane cry out for salvation. And then the eagle's eyes bore deeply into her, piercing her soul, ripping at her heart.

Then she would always wake.

She'd been having the same dream, on and off, since childhood. Her father was a minister and he had two passions, the War of Northern Aggression, or what northerners refer to as the Civil War, and the other passion, preaching fire and brimstone. His preaching about the *Book of Revelations* and the coming of the end had left their mark on Jane. In fact, the older she became the more intense the dreams were becoming. Her father always told her that the dream meant her time was coming. He believed that she was special beyond what people ordinarily deem as gifted. She'd come to this world with a true purpose, a calling, a path ordained for her since her birth.

A preacher's daughter, Jane was profoundly driven to succeed and also very driven to explore every inch of the universe, ignoring for some time every little thing her father had ever taught her about her role in the universe.

Richard was sleeping as she walked away from the bed. She slipped on his red silk robe, careful not to wake him. She had no idea what time it was and it didn't really matter, after the nightmare she could never go back to sleep. All she knew was that she needed to clear her mind and gather herself, there were a lot of things that she needed to think about. Things with Richard were moving at the speed of light and she was breaking all of her own rules: never sleep with a married man; never sleep with the subject of the story; and, never at any time become part of the story. *God-damn this man!*

Still she couldn't deny that she was intrigued by his offer. Jane had always admired politicians, even the ones who were in it just for the power. *These are the movers and shakers of the world! Politics is always a consuming story, and politicians, the best and the worst, all find their chapters written into the most encompassing story of all time – history!*

Jane worked very hard to get her career going and being a woman with great ambition, she knew that Richard was offering her a rare opportunity into the game. She'd always admired Karen Hughes, a member of George Bush, Jr's White House cabinet and she couldn't deny the pedigree. Hughes had been a reporter for 8 years prior to getting into politics. Jane knew, win or lose, her stock in the world was going to rise. Running for the White House with a campaign backed by Richard's war chest was sure to be an endeavor not taken lightly.

As a woman she almost felt a sense of duty to jump on the opportunity that was being presented to her. But it was crazy! Jane was well aware that as politicians, neither one of them had any credibility at all. Richard, however, had argued vehemently that she was wrong. He assured her that what voters wanted was someone new, off the radar with integrity and leadership. He assured her that America wanted them! She thought about her father and what he would want her to do at this moment. She knew the answer, as it had been given to her many years ago.

Still cloudy from the wine, Jane sat down at the computer that sat on top of the mahogany desk in front of the floor to ceiling window that peered out into the dark waters of the Sound. She watched the clouds as they engulfed the moon, turning the night pitch black. She intended to do what she'd always done since she was a young girl growing up in Georgia.

She began typing her list of pros and cons. One by one, she added up the reasons to accept his offer and all of the reasons why she should run like hell and never look back. The ritual was a family rite passed on to her from her father. When she finished she always took out a coin, assigning a side of the coin to a side of the list, pro or con. Whatever the coin landed on, she'd follow it with the question of whether or not that felt like the right choice. Whenever her first reaction was to flip the coin again, she knew her answer. She'd made all of her major decisions this way and she never looked back.

Jane had been at the list for over an hour when Richard snuck up behind her, placing his hands on her shoulders. "Wow!" he said. "You see, this is another reason why I need you."

"What's that?" she said.

"Attention to detail. You've got 345 cons and 321 pros. That's amazing!"

"It's a big decision."

"Indeed it is. But maybe you should forget about all of those reasons, good and bad, and just make a decision based on your own sense of destiny. Ask yourself what's written in the stars and then go with it."

She laughed. "Well I was just getting ready to flip a coin." She raised her hand, holding a shiny silver dollar.

"You're kidding, right?"

"Oh no," she said, "I'm as serious as the dickens. This is always the way it's been done for me. For guys like you, maybe it's written in the stars. Bur for a girl like myself, I leave it to gravity. It's always certain to give you an answer. And if you feel like flipping twice, then you still have your answer."

"So flip and get it over with," he said. "I'm dying to know whether I've got a running mate or just a mate."

She smiled. "Well if I wind up your running mate, there won't be any more of these nights. I believe in separation of sex and power. Hell, I might even propose a Constitutional Amendment for that one."

Richard smiled. "Maybe your power is derived from your sex, and that's not such a bad thing. Think of Cleopatra."

"Well then maybe I'll just become more powerful by holding it back."

"I'll take my chances," he said. "Flip the damn coin!"

With that Jane called, "Heads for pro and tails for con," and then she stood and tossed the coin high into the candlelit ceiling. They both watched intently as it flipped several times before landing on top of the desk and falling to the floor.

"Does that count?" he asked.

"Oh it counts," she said.

She walked over to the coin and when she saw it she looked back over at Richard, her eyes exploding wildly with excitement like firecrackers on an otherwise quiet night.

CHAPTER 18

Two weeks had passed since Susan had flown home to be with her father in Arizona. Chase was still no closer to finding Jimmy. His new best friend, a gangly Native American named Billy, was the quiet type and it was driving Chase nuts. Billy had been little help. He kept telling Chase to "Relax and just be patient," but that just wasn't his style. He needed action, sitting and waiting didn't feel like searching, it felt like dying. All of the other searchers had packed up and gone home and the authorities still had no leads. Jimmy had completely vanished, and Chase wondered if he'd ever see him again.

Jimmy was his blood, his brother, his only real family and he couldn't believe he was gone. Their mother had passed seven years earlier and he rarely saw his father anymore. He'd never been married and he didn't have kids. In fact, his only serious commitment was his law practice and if he stayed away from it much longer he figured he wouldn't have any clients left when he returned. But he was determined to stick it out. There wasn't really an option, he knew that.

Chase and Billy were sitting outside *God's Work*, hoping Michael would show. He hadn't been there since they started looking for him. They had been everywhere and although some people knew who Michael was, they didn't know anything else about him other than he was an artist. The few that knew him had no idea where he lived. Finally they decided their best chance was to sit outside *God's Work*. So for almost two weeks, they'd been sitting there waiting.

Chase and Billy didn't talk much to each other and the days were long and tiring. Chase spent his hours trying to think of anything other than Jimmy, it just hurt too much to think about where he might be so the only answer was to wash those thoughts away as quickly as they came. Chase wondered if Billy liked the silence or if it was just him that Billy didn't like. Whatever the reason, he felt like Billy was just there because the old Indian had given him the order and that was the only reason. Chase had told him several times that if he wanted to go it was okay. But, Billy stayed.

The air in the Chevy Malibu was stale with the sweat of two grown men and it was always worse in the afternoon sun. They sat there with the windows down, parked behind a Jeep Cherokee three cars down from *God's Work* on the curb of the street. They had a clear view to the front door and it was nearing closing time. The red chili was turning over in Chase's stomach and he was thinking about a run to the restroom. Then it happened.

"There," Billy said, pointing at a man walking down the sidewalk. The man had long flowing brown hair and wore jeans and sandals.

"Him?" Chase asked. "That's Michael?"

"That's Michael!"

"Looks pretty normal to me, are you sure he's -"

"Well I was sure until I started hanging out with you. You white men seem to always judge a book by its cover."

Chase laughed; old Billy thought he was pretty funny. "Okay, Tonto," Chase said, "when he comes out let's hope he's headed home."

Billy turned to Chase and cracked his first smile in several days. "Tonto?" he said.

"I'm only kidding. Don't you have an Indian name or something?"

"My name is Billy and because I'm an Indian that makes it an Indian name," he said.

"Sorry, didn't mean to offend you," Chase said, grinning from ear to ear.

"No, it's okay Beaver."

"Beaver?"

"Yeah, you call me Tonto, I'll call you Beaver."

"As in builds a dam?" Chase asked.

"No, as in, *Leave it to Beaver.*"

The two broke into laughter and they were laughing so hard that it brought tears to Chase's eyes. He was worn out and he felt guilty for laughing but he couldn't stop himself. The stress of the waiting had taken its toll and now that they'd actually seen Michael go into the store they were just losing it. Neither had been sleeping well. Chase was having nightmares about Red Hawk's vision and he just wanted to find his brother and take him home.

The whole thing with Michael was a long shot. Just because he was a hippie artist and maybe a little odd didn't make him responsible for Jimmy's disappearance. But that's how desperate Chase's search for Jimmy had become. He needed to rule out this guy or after everything that he'd heard from Red Hawk, he wouldn't be able to live with himself. More and more, he started to think that Jimmy was dead somewhere on the side of a road. He wanted to keep hope alive, but the more time that passed the more difficult it became to keep the faith.

Susan wasn't much help; she just seemed so down. She was carrying Jimmy's baby and she didn't know if he was ever even going to know about it. Her father told Chase that she stayed up all night praying for his return. Chase understood her anguish; he'd been doing a lot of praying himself. And now here was some guy, Michael, who looked rather ordinary, his only mistake being that he'd convinced a few Indians that he was a creepy white man, a white man with a dark soul.

Michael walked out of the gallery with his art in hand. Dan rarely bought any, and few galleries ever found his work appealing. His work was too graphic. The bloody religious scenes were disturbing and beyond the taste of most galleries and art buyers. They watched as he walked across the street, threw his art into the back of a red pick-up truck and sped off down the street.

They took off after him. Chase was thrilled to be moving at last.

Michael weaved in and out of traffic through several narrow streets. The sun was fading back into the mountains when his truck finally headed south on highway 68 in the direction of Santa Fe. Billy was driving and he was keeping a safe distance. As they followed Michael, reality seemed to set in with Chase and he became more and more quiet. Billy could sense he was becoming despondent. But Chase just knew that if this turned out to be a dead-end, he wouldn't know where to turn next.

The pressure was definitely closing in on Chase. He didn't want to give up, but he was in danger of letting his practice slip from his grasp. Judge Reinhold had begrudgingly moved the Rollins case 6 months down the docket and he was clear that he wouldn't do it again. The bottom-line was simple, Chase was a man that had gotten used to throwing his weight around and getting his way and now he was riding shotgun with an Indian through the shadowy mountains of New Mexico, following a starving artist named Michael. He was quiet because he was lost deep in the caverns of his mind, desperately trying to figure out how things had become so hopeless. And then he thought about Jimmy, and he knew he had to keep going.

Jimmy had kept his distance from Chase after their mother had died of cancer. That was a tough time for both of them. Chase wanted to talk about things and share the grief. Not Jimmy, that just wasn't him, his way of grieving was to crawl into a shell. Jimmy took the loss really hard and Chase figured that he was just a reminder to Jimmy of all that he'd lost. He could tell that Jimmy didn't want to spend much time with him and he wasn't sure why. Whatever he'd done, Chase just wanted another chance. He couldn't stand the thought of losing someone else. Not his brother, he needed Jimmy, whether Jimmy really understood that or not.

As they followed several cars behind, Billy broke the silence. "So if this turns out to be nothing," he said. "What's next for you?"

"I don't know," Chase answered. "I've been thinking a lot about that. I'm not sure. What if he's just gone?"

"You mean dead?"

"Gone. Dead. I don't know, is there much difference if I never see him again? "

"Well if he's dead, he's not gone. He's just in another realm, on the other side."

Chase smiled. "The other side?"

"Yeah," Billy said. "I take it you're not a spiritual person?"

"I believe in God. I just don't know what happens when we die. When my mother died, I spent a lot of time thinking about it and I never got to that peaceful place, you know that I had any answers."

"Answers? No one has the answers. Listen," Billy said, "the Spanish brought my tribe Christianity, they forced it on us, but they didn't bring any new answers. No religion really does. We integrated Christianity with our own sacred beliefs and Christ gained a place in our spiritual world, with our own religious messiah, Pohe - Yomo. Sure, the Spanish missionaries were saving our souls. In their minds, we were the savages.

"But, over the years, my people have come to realize that we knew more than our conquerors. You can bring technology and all of your answers. The white man can cure disease, he can build empires and conquer new worlds and savage peoples, but unless there is harmony in the universe and peoples of all worlds are respected for their own identities, with good energy sweeping in the wind, there will always be new conflicts and new diseases. No matter how tall the buildings rise or how fast the cars go.

"And what's on the other side, who can tell you that but someone on the other side. My people believe that all things are connected, and that even death is connected to life. We seek harmony with the universe. It's the seekers who often become the discontents. They want to stamp their identity onto the world, and that goes against the spirit of Mother Earth, against the force of life. I don't believe people die and everything ends, life just moves to another stage of life. But I don't claim to have the answers, just a way of life that brings me happiness."

Chase was quiet for a while. Finally, he said, "Why are you helping me?"

"Because my grandfather told me to," Billy said.

Chase laughed. "No seriously, why?"

"You think I'm joking? Our elders get respect in my society. Red Hawk would have me skinned. Still, there are other reasons," he said. "I knew Michael, and I saw into his spirit and if I didn't think he was capable of something, I wouldn't be here right now. The guy has issues."

"Issues?"

"Hard to explain. Some people find their identity in religion, but they don't find the Great Spirit. Michael's one of those. His stream flows east, and the Great Spirit's flows west. But Michael would have you believe, and he probably himself believes that he is somehow doing the Great Spirit's work. He's dangerous. He's a charismatic person and he's smart, but he's lost."

"How'd you meet him?"

"I met him at Ranchos de Taos. I was working there at San Francisco de Asis Church. The church, an early 19th century Spanish church is a tourist attraction and I was the curator for a couple of years. It's an interesting place. You've probably seen pictures of it before in magazines. Ansel Adams has photographed it and Georgia O'Keeffe has painted the old place several times. It's famous for its enduring adobe, Spanish architecture and as a refuge for white men to hide out from Indian savages."

Billy smiled at Chase, always enjoying trying to make him feel uncomfortable. Chase was unmoved. "You said that," Chase said, "not me. Ansel Adams, huh, I've always loved his work."

"He's not bad. He photographed our pueblo many years ago, like back around 1940 or something. Red Hawk was a young spirit then; he actually tried to get the guy drunk and he says he took his roll in poker. Who knows, Red Hawk has a lot of stories about the old days. He was wild back then.

"There's a painting there at the old church of San Francisco de Asis," Billy continued, "and every evening the shadow of a cross appears behind Christ's shoulder."

"Okay," Chase said, "you got me!"

"No, it's true," Billy argued. "Hell, scientists have studied that painting and no one can explain it."

"I'll bet that brings in the freaks."

"Well that's where I met Michael. He came in one day and started asking questions about the painting. He came back several times and spent a great deal of time studying the painting. I kind of got to know him a little and the guy was interesting. He said he was an artist, a huge fan of religious art. His mother was an artist that came to Taos in the 60s. He showed interest in our heritage and asked if he could come over to the pueblo. He said he was doing research on religious ceremonies. But it was a mistake on my part. I'd misread him.

"I took him back to the pueblo for dinner one night and he starts telling this crazy story about how his mother and father had met at a party in Taos and married and that he was actually born in the San

Francisco de Asis. He believed that his mother gave birth to him under the painting of Christ at the same time the cross was mysteriously making its appearance over Christ's shoulder. Supposedly they'd been caught in a storm and took shelter in the church. The elders were very disturbed by his story and they blamed me for bringing him there. I'd known he was strange. He said his father was some rich guy and that his mother was dead. He was 'looking for his people,' his place in the world."

"He sounds like a lost soul – a real freak."

"Just another creepy white man," Billy said, smiling.

Chase laughed. "Well look Billy, I appreciate your help, it can't be easy hanging out with a white guy like me," he said. "Seriously, I can pay you if -"

"I'm not here for the money. My grandfather had a vision and you were a part of it. You saw it in his eyes. He has talked about the white man with the pregnant girl coming for many years. This is real, you know, this is not Indian hocus pocus."

Chase stared at Billy closely. "Do you really believe -"

Billy slammed on the brakes and Chase went flying into the windshield, catching himself with his arm. "Of course I do," Billy said, "I wouldn't be here if I didn't!"

"Sorry!" Chase yelled. "Damn! This is just all very strange! Why'd we stop?"

"Michael just turned down that road. There you see the dust?" Billy said, pointing to a dirt road. "We'll wait here until dark."

"Great," Chase said. "I can't wait."

CHAPTER 19

GNN.com

U.S. NEWS - EDITORIAL
American Extremism Meets Islamic Extremism

Thursday, August 31, 2007 Posted 8:45 AM EDT

NEW YORK (GNN) – And now we are tunneling down the road to Hell, only creating new enemies and wars that we'll be fighting long after anyone remembers what we're fighting for.

We fight for the red, white and blue and the stars and stripes. We fight for the West. We fight for what we say because we know best. We fight for oil. We fight because we must. We fight to end terrorism. We fight because we're right.

We fight for freedom, ours and all others, men, women, children, sisters and brothers.

The enemy, Islamic extremists, they fight for the eradication of all other faiths. They fight for Allah. They fight for the destruction of the infidels and all who are not Muslim. They fight because their neighborhoods are poor and burning. They fight because America, the great Beast has come, as they knew we would. They fight because they believe they can win. They fight because they must. They fight because without their faith, they have no hope.

What if both sides are equally arrogant and ignorant, and equally at fault and equally wrong, in fighting to bring each other to its knees?

What if Allah is no more on the side of the Islamic extremists than she is the common honey bee? And just what if the Western culture of America is no more advanced or deserving of superiority and power than all of the other empires that have long since come and gone? What if we're both just the Roman and the Germanic barbarians fighting in the hills of Bastogne all over again, destined only to fight, never having anything to do with what is right.

If there be a God – Allah, why would she play favorites? If God is wisdom and the light of the universe, then why would God, creator of all matter, take sides in the battle of a red ant against a black ant?

Are they any different from us? Are we any different from them? In God's eyes, if there be a wise God, probably not. So why are we fighting? So why do we hate? Perhaps that's just what we do, we focus on each other's differences and turn our distrust into hate. In the end, with our increasingly, sophisticated modern weapons of destruction, all that's really at stake is the existence of humankind. With the universe as vast and bright, if we beings are truly that stupid, then perhaps it wouldn't matter much if we were gone. We are living in an illusion of superiority in a fake empire. So, ironically, are the enemies we fight. We have more in common with them than each of us would like to believe. Think to yourself how a visitor to this planet would view our spectacle of warfare waged against one another, tearing up our lands, wasting our natural resources. They would rightfully think we were all idiots.

Arrogance and ignorance, yes, we all have a lot in common after all.

CHAPTER 20

The helicopter landed on top of RDI Tower around 6 o'clock, just in time for the news conference. Richard charged ahead underneath the wind of the rudders, determined to execute the plan according to his grand design. Security was in full force under Richard's command, who knew that as the storm gathered momentum it would take on a life of its own and he wasn't about to take any chances.

As he entered the boardroom everyone was waiting. The bright lights of the cameras hit him and followed him to the podium at the top of the table. The press from all over the world was gathered there for his show, and he was primetime. GNN, of course, paid particular homage to him by detailing every campaign move that he made. And this grand spectacle was no exception. The privilege of ownership was that he could control his image at all times. The officers at GNN would never admit it, but behind the scenes Richard was not just making news, his people were now controlling every aspect of how they presented him to the American people.

Even Max had flown in for this one, a long time friend of Jane's and her boss, he wanted to see her big secret unveiled. He had no idea what she was planning, but he was pretty sure it was going to be a mistake. He still wasn't sold on her recent career decision to follow Richard's campaign. Still, he loved Jane and admired her brashness in a man's world.

Richard, as always, commanded attention. He was wearing a regal, black suit with a red tie. He was the center of the universe and he absolutely loved it. The Dog Star, shining brightly with the world at his beck and call, he was seeking his place in the heavens. He was sure they were going to be smitten as ever with his next chess move in the game of life, a game he wasn't only winning, but artistically dominating like the great warriors of old, only better. When he was through, in the end, they would all know that the man who would be king, was the greatest warrior of all and that forever he would be revered and served, his named etched on the stone of the highest mountains, his glory filling the universe with the blood of his enemies, his conquest leaving no stone unturned.

The man was more than an ordinary man, he was the Dog Star, the brightest star in the sky and his glory wouldn't be fulfilled until he'd set the whole world on fire with his vision. And one piece at a time, he was doing just that, stoking the flames and watching them grow and breathe, rising to become a glorious beast, sweeping from ceiling to ceiling and house to house, capturing the world by storm.

"Good evening ladies and gentlemen," he said. And from his first words he had them, his voice spilling his energy into the room, filling every space of air with his intoxicating fire. "I'm so glad you could make it on such short notice. As I am sure you are aware the timing of this meeting just so happens to coincide with the opening of the Republican National Convention. It is my hope and my desire to send the message to the Republicans and the Democrats that we shall not run from the fight.

"This campaign shall honor the spirit of our democracy and the freedoms bestowed upon us in our great Constitution, but we want the world to know and you are all invited here as witnesses that we are taking on the establishment. Make no mistake our timing is not intended to offend, it is intended as an attack on the two party system that has crippled the progress of this country, stifled our foreign policy, exported our technology and made us weak in the eyes of the world.

"Yes, while the plagues rage on in the lower economies of the world and people continue to starve and thirst for a clean glass of water, and they continue to grow weak and to capitulate under the attack of germs and diseases for which we have yet to really turn to them and offer our modern medicine with the same fervor that we send our soldiers off to war against terrorism.

"And yes, terrorism is a problem for us that is not to be ignored, but yet the modern day plagues that continue to ravage the world, we have not gone to war against them and every day they grow stronger, they kill more people, they make more young sick while we ignore their plight and fight the wars that we see as more important. Somehow we have grown so fond of ourselves and our democracy that we have decided that everyone should have it, even before they have health and technology to support it and anchor its freedoms that mean nothing to the sick of mind, heart and soul. And the wars rage on as we bring our gift to the world.

"Are we any different than those empires who have failed before us? Where the world once envied us as being on the mountain high, they now see us way down in the valley below, as they perch themselves on the rock with the virtue of greater wisdom than our own. How did this happen? How did we become so weak?

"I believe that we can thank our friends in the Republican and Democratic parties for placing a stranglehold on our government and making it virtually impossible for a new voice to rise amidst their islands. Well, I am a new voice to the political world, but I am not a novice to leadership. I urge all Americans to click onto my website, RichardNovak2008.com and find out more about me and my vision and how to get on board and rise with the sweeping tide that will wash away the worn out agendas of these two parties that have long since lost their way and their touch with the American people and the world at large. Join me in this greatest of all endeavors and you shall perch with me again on the mountain high!

"I can't tell you who is speaking right now to the Republican constituents gathered for their convention, but I will bet you that when the ratings come out tomorrow it will prove that the American people weren't interested. I'll bet you that our numbers here will compete, and when we are finished with this campaign, they won't even know what hit them.

"America loves the underdog. Well here I am, America, I am your dog! And I will be your star because I will not forget that you, all of you, from coast to coast are my constituents. I don't need the PAC money, won't take it! I don't need the campaign contributions, don't want any! And I know a little bit about what you don't want! You don't want our deficit to continue to rise! You don't want higher taxes, but if you do pay taxes you want your money to be well spent! Can you trust your government to spend your money wisely? You all know the answer to that question, don't you?

"Commit with me to take back America from the career politicians who see your taxes become their earnings, their kickbacks, and their reward for being voted into office! Commit with me and together we shall make this country, without question, the greatest country the world has ever seen!

"How do we make this country great? Great leadership – do I know great leadership when I see it? Well, let me just say that my companies have made me a billionaire for a reason, and the number one reason is my leadership and the key leaders that I've surrounded myself with. Some people just have it, they have that magic to inspire and they make you want to follow them, in their eyes you see their conscience and their wisdom. So without further ado, please allow me to introduce someone that you all already know, someone that has spent many nights in your homes from the highest rated news hour in the world, Jane Tierney, my running mate, my choice to be the next Vice President of the United States of America."

The enthusiasm for Richard and his maddening storm had spread like wildfire and everyone in the room felt empowered. The bulbs in the conference room began flashing and the cameras were rolling and clicking nonstop as Jane barged through the glass doors with authority. Her red power suit with the white blouse made her look beautiful and elegant for her grand entrance into the political spotlight. Jane strode to the lectern and shook Richard's hand, standing side to side with him and facing the flashes. The room was filled with electricity and Richard and Jane let the energy soak deep into their veins.

Finally, as order settled in, Jane stepped up to the podium. "Good evening," she said. "You know, I've been a reporter for 12 years now and I'm sure you all are wondering why I am qualified to be a vice president of this great country. Well maybe you're right, maybe I'm not. Maybe I'm just another woman stuck in a man's world. Or, maybe not! Maybe, just maybe, I am just another American citizen that thinks they can make a difference, and maybe our little melting pot needs a little shakin' up! What if people never tried anything because they didn't think they were qualified, didn't think they could make a difference? Would we have electricity, would we have running water? Heck, would we have democracy?

"I want you to tell me who told the Founding Fathers that they were qualified to set up the principles for the greatest nation that was ever born! I want you to tell me who told the Wright brothers that it was their place to revolutionize travel, taking us from land to air! I want you to tell me who told the black slaves they had the right to be free! I want you to tell me who told women they had the right to vote! And then let me tell you something, America, if you wait around for somebody to tell you to do something, then it might not ever happen!

"The time is now for a woman to be Vice President of the United States! And I am that woman! Together, Richard Novak and I will take back this country from the two party system that has lost its voice! It's time for women to have a greater voice in the course of America's journey! We will not so much as bring a new voice as we will allow the voice of the people to speak!

"Too often we see politicians get elected and they fall in love with their own legacy, and forget about the people! Well, I may be just a small town girl from Georgia, but I can tell you this, we are going to bring the fight to these two parties like never before! There's a lot of fight in this little girl! The old boys in Washington ain't never seen a woman like me before and they'll be wishin' they hadn't lost your trust – but it's too late for that, America – it's time for change. And I assure you, change is on its way!

"Thank you."

The conference room broke out into cheers. Several reporters were hurdling through the crowd trying to get to Jane and Richard as they exited quickly out the side door of the conference room. Richard wanted this to be a hit-and-run introduction for Jane. He loved to stoke the media's fire and was an expert at playing to the masses. For a political novice, he was already proving to be a genius. The timing of the press conference was shrewd and he was just getting started. Jane was by his side now – America's darling, he couldn't lose. He would give the world something they'd never seen before. It was time to set the world on fire!

CHAPTER 21

Billy led the way, ushering Chase along in the night with hand signals. The moon was full, a glowing disc of white light, ducking in and out of clouds and occasionally breaking free and providing a respite of light upon the path that led up to the ranch. And they could see in the distant valley three small buildings at the base of the Sangre de Cristo Mountains. There was a hint of moisture in the air as the threat of a rain shower loomed behind the dark clouds. The dry terrain was carpeted with brush, and Chase kept running into Cacti, cursing Jimmy every step of the way for putting him through this madness.

In just a few weeks time he'd gone from his law practice to a trespasser onto somebody's ranch with an Indian in New Mexico, even Chase had to laugh, if only his clients could see their lawyer now. They inched alongside the dirt trail for at least two miles. They were far off from the highway when they first saw the headlights coming from the compound from what appeared to be a large, U-haul type of truck. They hid off to the side of a creek bed and waited for it to pass.

When the truck was gone they started again towards the buildings. The road led them all the way up to the first building of the triangle, and it appeared to be a small tabernacle. A small cross rose from the center of its octagonal roof. The wooden church was rustic and appeared to be a remnant of the early 19th century. Not far off to the side of the church, about 20 feet back, sat a log cabin with dark logs and mud filled joints that resembled an old settlers' farm house.

Chase and Billy snuck up to the side of the cabin and peered through an open window. Inside the cabin they saw several single beds lined up like a barracks, and there was a kitchen with large silver pots and pans stacked on top of an old wooden island.

Suddenly they heard a strange noise coming from behind the cabin and they both swallowed their breath. Billy looked at Chase and motioned for him to walk slowly toward the noise. The moved deftly and hovered close to the side-wall of the cabin. Then they heard it again. This time it sounded like a can was being kicked around, but they still weren't sure. Chase could feel the hair on his neck standing straight up. He felt sure they were going to get shot, and although he believed in the mission that brought them there, he didn't relish the thought of having to explain it to a New Mexico trooper. Billy dropped to his knees as he reached the back of the cabin and slowly peaked around the corner.

At that moment he saw the white lamb kicking its metal dinner bowl around the small pen. Chase inched up beside them and they both stood there, watching the lamb play and letting the air soak back into their lungs.

Then Billy saw a trail a few feet behind the lamb's pen and noticed that it led up to the third building. Chase followed closely as they crept down the path. They stopped in a brush clearing 20 feet from the screen door that was swinging open in the breeze, the flimsy frame sending an eerie noise into the night. With a nod, they both agreed to check it out and they slowly walked toward the lighted entrance. Billy got there first and crept up the wooden steps. A loose step creaked and they both stopped, waiting for a moment and making sure that no one had been alarmed by their presence. They peered through the screen door and were stunned by the complexity of the contents of the large room which looked more like a government command center that belonged on Los Alamos than some old, worn down ranch.

On the walls there were two large plasma TVs that tied into computers, displaying detailed maps of cities and charts and graphs with detailed demographics and logistics. And there were several computers and hardware in front a horseshoe shaped bay area, where a workstation with tall bookshelves housed a library of books and treatises on various sundry subjects: aerosol technology, plastics, molecular biology, radiation, cell division, high tech munitions, computer viruses, the black plague, tuberculosis and various diseases.

The oddest site in the small building, however, was the steel wall separating the front room from another with a steel door as the only entrance. Quietly, they walked to the door and Chase turned the pressure locked handle, which released and opened into a hermetically sealed room. Inside the room was a laboratory with soft lights and three rectangle, stainless steel tables shimmering under the lighting in the center of the room. On top of the tables were several high-tech microscopes with wires interfacing with computers and expensive looking medical equipment. In the back of the room there were two large sliding, glass-door freezers and Chase walked over to survey the contents while Billy guarded the door.

The air conditioning system kicked on in the room and Chase didn't even notice the small infra-red light when he walked past the lab tables. He slid open a freezer door and pulled out a sealed culture dish that sat in the freezer among hundreds of culture dishes and vials and several plastic bags, the bags sealed tightly and containing a clear fluid. When he read the label on the dish, his breath sucked deep into the cavity of his chest and he looked at Billy, his eyes screaming wildly, "Holy shit!" Billy looked back at the screen door and didn't see anything and motioned for Chase to get out of there. Chase carefully put the culture dish back into the freezer and left the room in a hurry. They made their way for the door, and then Billy stopped and grabbed a large vanilla envelope off a desk and glanced down at it, showing it to Chase who studied the name of the addressee and the postmark.

The creaking door slammed hard against its frame and they both turned into the blows, which felt like the horns of a herd of charging bulls slamming into their heads. They were both rendered unconscious before they even hit the floor. The angels formed a small circle around their bodies, their eyes glowing at their uninvited guests.

CHAPTER 22

Jane was running late for dinner with Max, her strategy meeting with Richard after the announcement had lasted longer than she anticipated. The glass elevator ride up to *Sky City*, the restaurant at 500 feet near the top of the Space Needle, was simply breathtaking. The day had been truly wonderful. Jane felt as if she were Charlie in *Willy Wonka's Chocolate Factory*, as if the elevator was suddenly going to explode out of the needle into the sky. There was simply magic in the air and Jane felt alive.

The panoramic view of Seattle was amazing and she could see all of the natural surroundings without obstruction. The Cascade Mountains were enormous and green and snow capped Mount Rainer stood out as a 14,000-foot giant in the western horizon. She could also see Puget Sound in the distance and all of the tiny little boats and ferries in Elliot Bay.

A new accessory to her rising status on the political landscape, Jane was being escorted by a trio of highly trained security guards. The presence of the guards provided a stark reminder of how much had changed. They shadowed her every move, with one even accompanying her up to the revolving restaurant and the other two taking positions at the base of the needle.

Richard insisted on the security and she knew that she'd better get used to it as long as she were running for vice president with a man who could afford to cover the details. But it didn't matter to Jane; she loved the attention and basking in the limelight that was befitting to only the brightest stars. A modern day Charlie of the female gender, she'd just broken through the "glass ceiling" and she was going to be one of the highest profile women in America. Still Jane was wary of eating at the biggest tourist attraction in Seattle, but Max had insisted on *Sky City*. He'd been there before and assured her that tourists aside, the sunset from the restaurant was something that she'd never forget.

Jane saw Max sitting at a table as she exited the elevator. His big red cheeks glowing, she was sure that the beer on the table was not his first. She strode over to the table and on her way it happened.

"Ms. Tierney," the little old lady said. "You're my hero! Would you sign this for me? Please, it would absolutely make my day."

Jane's eyes sparkled and she smiled and obliged the request and before she knew it she was completely surrounded by a mob. Men, women and children of all ages were lobbying for her signature or just a kind word with her. She was a magnet for attention. And the thing about Jane was, she'd always been very magnetic, but now people had an even grander reason to approach her. She was officially a politician setting out on a journey to make history and she was going to need their support.

They, on the other hand, the buying public wanted to get to know her and they also wanted to be a part of history and glow in her greatness. They wanted to be able to tell their friends, their kids, their grandchildren, that they shook hands with Jane Tierney on the night of her famous announcement back in 2007. They'd brag about getting her autograph and speaking to her. They felt honored to be in her presence. They were asking her all sorts of questions, some of them promising her their votes in the general election, and they didn't even know much about the platform.

"I just love the fact that you and Mr. Novak are going to be taking on the establishment! It's time to send the Republicans and the Democrats a message that time has run out on the two party system! We need a new party with muscle! We need a change!"

Jane agreed with the man and slowly made her way to Max, the crowd finally dispersing when she took her seat at the small table not far from the maitre d's station near the center of the restaurant. Richard was right about Jane; her popularity was going to win votes.

The showing of support impressed even Jane; she'd figured that most people had missed the press conference, instead watching the start of the Republican National Convention. Apparently she was wrong. Richard and Jane were the night's big story. They were the new stars in the universe, and Jane was adjusting rapidly. Always a girl sharp on her feet, she knew how to work a crowd and she was very good with people.

"My, look at you, Madam Jane Tierney, candidate for Vice President of the United States, I am duly impressed and honored to be in your company," Max said, standing and then bowing dramatically in front of her.

"Stop it," Jane said, laughing. "That's embarrassing. Has everyone lost their minds'?"

"And you haven't?" he said. "I always knew you were an ambitious woman, but I had no idea."

"Well the opportunity presented itself and I jumped on it. What can I say?"

"Does Mrs. Novak know that you jumped on it?"

"Max, are you going to start that crap again? Give me a frickin' break here! Mrs. Novak has everything she wants and from what I've heard, she enjoys shopping and decorating her mansions more than anything else. And granted that's a full-time job but I'm building a career here. I'm breaking through the glass ceiling. Hell I'm planning on shattering it in one of its last great strongholds – the White House. C'mon Max, everyone wants to know when we're going to have a female President. Well I think this is as good as a place to start as any. Don't you? Besides, I think I make a pretty hot politician and the old boys' network needs a little shakin' up."

"I think we both know that this is about more than that, Jane."

"Max, when I make the call to you, you understand that-"

"You know I'll do whatever you ask," he said.

She just grinned.

Max had always worshipped Jane. "Jane," he said, "I'm so proud of you. I don't know much about Richard Novak, but if he's got you by his side, his chances of actually making this crazy campaign work and getting him to Washington have just risen dramatically. You're contagious! People love you! Novak, he's no fool, he's chosen you because he thinks you can help him get elected. He doesn't want you running the show or changing his ideas though, you know that, don't you?"

"I've thought a lot about that. He's a brilliant man, but he's not going to be the boss, Max."

Max smiled, knowingly. "He's not, huh?"

She grinned defiantly. "Well, of course not!" she said. "This is about me! This is my time. Richard's a supremely intelligent man and he knows things that ordinary men will never know. But his politics aren't as far from my beliefs as you might think. I do think it's time that someone made a credible attack on the two party system. I think it's appalling to think that everyone's views are being fairly represented by the Republicans and the Democrats. Mine aren't! Are yours?"

"My views are your views!"

"Well, see, even you'll vote for us."

Max smiled and turned his gaze to the view for a moment and then back to Jane. "You've always had my vote, Jane," he said, still grinning. "Maybe," he said, speaking quietly, "something happens to Richard if he gets elected, so you can get a shot at the big seat in the Oval Office sooner rather than later."

"That's not very nice!" Jane said, grinning mischievously. "But I'd make you a cabinet member."

"Are you crazy? I don't want any part of politics. Leave me out of it, I'm too old to change my ways."

Jane looked down at her red heels and then rolled her eyes up to meet Max's. "What about this old girl," she said, "think I can learn some new tricks? I was class president in college but it's been awhile? And that was just a popularity contest!"

"Jane, in many ways this is also a popularity contest. You know the world of politics as good as anyone. You've covered it for years. And you're a born leader. Hell, you've never done anything I've ever asked you to do. You'll be fine."

Jane smiled. The waiter came and took their order and Jane ordered some Chardonnay. Dinner was fabulous, Jane had the salmon and Max engulfed a steak and three more beers. The best of friends, they sat and dined and enjoyed the pink and gold sunset over Mt. Rainer. The sunset glowed like a halo over the Cascade Mountains and lit up the sky, casting a golden light into *Sky City*. Max began telling stories about the old days and they caught up on everything that was going on at GNN. Max was complaining a lot about the stress of being in management and indicated several times that he was thinking about getting out of the business altogether and opening a small hardware store. The thought of Max running a hardware store was cracking Jane up to no end.

Jane, smiling, finally interrupted Max. "I've got a secret to share with you, Max. Promise me that you won't ever tell anyone."

"I promise, Jane, what?"

"If we lose in this election, I'll be promoted to the head of GNN."

Max choked down a gulp of beer, his eyes turning red like his cheeks. "What?" he said. "He can't possibly do that?"

"He owns the company. He can do whatever he wants!"

"You're dealing with the Devil, Jane."

"Hey, I am the frickin' Devil!"

Max smiled. "Well, get that in writing? That's all I'm saying."

"Relax, okay, I'm running for vice president on his ticket! He's not going to outfox me! No one can control me! You know that! He's a smart man, but he's still just a man! When I want something from him, believe me I'll get it! He wants to leave his mark on the world, well so do I! No one's going to stop me! Not even Richard Novak!"

"Take whatever you want! I surrender!"

Jane shook her head excitedly. "You surrender my ass!" she said. "You're my inspiration! You're my protector!"

"You mean servant?"

"No, protector!" she said. "You've pushed me harder than anyone I know besides my father. What is it you used to say? That quote, 'If I advance, follow me. If I stop, push me. If I fall, inspire me.' I need you Max; I need you to be there for me."

"I'll always be here for you. Don't ever worry about that? Just be careful with this man. Always make sure you get something in return for everything you give. And I don't have to tell you this, but the media will be looking to find any skeleton they can find."

"Jeez, you're paranoid! I'm a big girl now and I was born and raised for this. We've had this talk a million times. I don't ever do anything I don't want to do, and nothing has changed. You can count on that!

I'm a tough girl and I'm going to take that damn glass ceiling and obliterate it! They might be seeing a female, but they'll get a leader! I'm not going to be anybody's pushover! You'll see! And skeletons, so what! Let them look!"

"That's my girl," Max said, smiling. "I'm so proud of you! You knock em' dead, Jane!"

Her eyes were dancing wildly as she reveled in the excitement she was feeling. "Oh, you can count on that! Hell you can bank on it!" she said. "I'll find a way to get you into this mix – you just wait!"

"No way!" he said.

"What? Are you underestimating me, Maxie boy?"

"Never. I'm begging you though. Please leave me out of it. I'm happy where I am."

"Oh horseshit! You are not! And besides when I call you, you won't be able to say no. No matter what I ask of you, you'll do it."

"Anything but that! Even servitude has to have limits. You've seen me at GNN; I don't have the diplomacy skills. I just don't like kissing asses and all of the bullshit that goes with it."

"Nice try!" she said.

"You're killing me here!"

"Don't worry, I'll leave you alone as long as I can," she said, "But if I ever need you, you'll have to come to my side. You know that!"

"At your service, my lady," he said. "Just be kind, don't lose yourself in all of this madness! There are crazy days ahead, it's bound to happen. You're having fun now, but the responsibilities you're taking on are tremendous. But, just look at you, you're a superstar; you'll rise to the occasion no matter what happens! That's just how you are."

Jane beamed. Max always made her feel good. It wasn't the flattery that warmed her but the look of devotion in his eyes. She could trust Max. He was an ally, a confidant, a protector and she needed his loyalty and protection now more than ever.

CHAPTER 23

Chase opened his eyes and at first he thought he was dreaming. His head was pounding and he felt weak and he was unable to move his hands, which were bound behind his back. The heat from the fire coming from the center of the room was intense and through the smoke he could see a familiar face.

"Jimmy!" he said. "You're alive! You're okay!"

Jimmy just stared back, a glazed look in his eyes shadowing his thoughts. His beard was scraggly, and he'd lost a lot of weight. Chase was groggy and his thoughts were registering slowly. He looked down at himself and discovered that he was completely naked and he tried to stand but his hands were tied around a steel ring at the bottom of the altar. Instantly he was engulfed by fear. He couldn't make sense of his surroundings. The stone floor was cold and he began to realize that something was not right about Jimmy. He was just kneeling there in front of Chase, praying, completely unmoved by his awakening.

"Jimmy, are you okay? What is this place?" he asked. "Jimmy, please look at me! What happened to, Billy? Did you see the man I was with?"

"I'm over here," Billy called out from the other side of the altar. "I'm tied up to this thing. I've been awake for a little while; long enough to know this isn't a good place to be. The darkness in here is real. This place harbors evil."

"Jimmy's here," Chase said. "How's your head?"

"I'm seeing double but besides that I'm okay," Billy answered. "Jimmy's not going to help us, Chase. Look into his eyes. He's gone. Can you move your hands?"

"Jimmy, look at me," Chase said. "Please, Jimmy, please just look at me."

Jimmy never looked at Chase. He never moved. He was chanting something over and over softly, and Chase couldn't hear his words over the crackling fire.

"Jimmy!" Chase cried frantically. "What have they done to you? Please snap out of it, it's Chase. It's Chase, your brother, please -"

"Look, Chase, we've got to get out of here," Billy said. "We'll take him with us, but you've got to try to get your hands free. Mine are coming slowly. It's taken a while. Get started. Rub the knot against the altar."

Suddenly, Jimmy, cloaked in a white linen garment, stood and stepped closer to Chase. Chase knew he'd finally broken through to him. *Thank God!*

"You're my brother, Jimmy! We can deal with this," he said. "Untie me! Help us out of here."

"Your brother has passed," Jimmy said, staring down at the stone floor, "his soul has been enveloped by the spirit and the blood of the glorious Lamb. I am Gabriel, a soldier in God's Army. Soon the wrath of God will be known to the world! Soon the Lamb will come! Behold the coming of the Lamb!"

"Jimmy!" Chase cried. "You're Jimmy Davidson. It's Chase, please-"

"I am the seventh angel of the circle and I will deliver unto Babylon the last bowl of wrath!" Jimmy Shouted. "I know what you want! Michael has told me! I say to you now, repent! Repent and you shall have nothing to fear! For behold the coming of the Lamb is at hand!"

"What the fuck, Jimmy? What's wrong with you?" Chase screamed, trying to free his hands and get to his brother.

"Don't listen to him!" Billy yelled. "Chase, focus on your hands!"

"God does not request your service here!" Jimmy said. "You shouldn't have come! You've brought danger to us and now we must protect the circle! The wrath of God will be done!"

"God-Damn it, Jimmy! You listen to me before you get us killed! This is bullshit! This is not real, this fucked up place, this shit they've fed you is not real! You're not some fucking servant of God, you're just fucked up! This guy's crawled into your skull and fucked you all up! Listen to me, just untie me and I can help you! I'm here because of you! Don't do this, Jimmy!"

"Gabriel, step outside and wait for us," a voice called out from the front of the tabernacle.

With that Gabriel finally looked up at Chase. "I have to go now," he said, and he walked away.

"Jimmy, damn it Jimmy, don't go!" Chase screamed.

"He is a soldier of God! He is Gabriel!" Michael yelled, his voice filling the tabernacle with his anger. "Your arrival is unfortunate! But please know that the glorious Lord hath brought you here for a reason! You are to be cleansed of all of your sin! You will not bear witness to the battle that draws near! You represent the ignorant and unknowing! God has chosen this moment for your awakening, the awakening of all mankind follows! You are so blessed, so loved! The blood of the Lamb shall cleanse your spirits and shall give you new life! Go to him now, my children, the angels here have so much work to do and there is so little time. The revelation is at hand! The great Beast, the Red Dragon of ten horns and seven heads has risen and we must pave the way for the coming of the Lamb!"

Chase just stared back. He didn't have any words. Michael walked over to the wooden tabernacle door where the angels were waiting with the Lamb. They led the Lamb to the altar. The chant began in unison, "Behold the glory of the coming of the Lamb! Behold the glory of the coming of the Lamb! ...."

"Take hold of the Lamb," Michael commanded, directing Chase and Billy to grab hold of the Lamb. He waited until they had followed his order. Then without warning he pulled the sickle from behind his back.

"Behold the glory of the Lamb!" Michael shouted, lifting the sickle high above his head, as the angels all began to chant in unison, "Behold, the glory of the Lamb! Behold, the glory of the Lamb! Behold the glory of the Lamb ..."

And then the screaming began. A river of blood made its way to the tabernacle door and down the front stoop where Gabriel was sitting quietly. Over and over he chanted, "Behold the glory of the coming of the Lamb! I am Gabriel! I am the seventh angel of the circle of seven! I carry the last bowl of wrath – the wrath of God! I am a soldier in God's Army! I am Gabriel!"

CHAPTER 24

Richard had ordered the strategy session and he was running late. Jane was standing in the cloud cloaked boardroom at RDI, clicking her heels in front of the floor to ceiling windows, gazing down at the tops of the tall mirrored buildings in downtown Seattle. Ted Mitchell, their tough-as-nails campaign manager, was reading through his notes, already full of venomous ideas to help shape the campaign's message. No stranger to nasty political campaigns, he was anxious to forge ahead and get started writing the policy and formulating the slate that would clearly rebut and rebuff the attacks that were just getting started on Richard's candidacy.

The article in *The Washington Post*, written by the infamous preacher and one of the many Republican leaders of the Religious Right, Paul Larson, who had recently slammed Richard for his humanist ideology in a speech on his religious network, claiming in no uncertain terms that his faith in man, over God, and lack of recognition of God, was a moral travesty of a billionaire that could not lead the multitudes, let alone, get elected with his lack of spirituality and belief in the Almighty.

Richard knew damn well that the war had begun, and his enemies were powerful. President Barton, the Republican incumbent, was not only allied with the Religious Right, but he was their spiritual leader, his every move and decisions were inspired by God, who he believed was the only true source of law.

Richard knew his enemies all too well.

They were the Christian fanatics that inspired him to get into the mix sooner rather than later. The Democrats had proven ineffective at stopping them, scared of inciting the backlash of Christian voters and fearing the personal attacks on their reputations. The Religious Right had sought Richard's support back in 1992, only to discover that Richard Novak was not in their camp.

At the invitation of Paul Larson, Richard attended a series of clandestine meetings of a secret Christian society of right-wing conservatives, whose aim is to make America a Theocracy, instituting Biblical law into the Constitution, and destroying the secular wall between the separation of church and state. They were fools to invite Richard, having known so little about him at the time. They'd regretted it ever since, and the svelte talking spokesmen of this most secretive movement, Paul Larson himself, had personally taken the blame for what was now deemed the Richard Novak fiasco. They'd just assumed with his contributions to charity that he was a religious man, a believer of Christ, their savior. They wanted Richard's financial support to further the movement.

Their sole purpose was to bring Theocratic government to the U.S., and then to the world. And so explains the link between the war in Iraq and terrorism. There wasn't a link. The designs of war in the Middle East were laid out in secret meetings of the Religious Right long before any planes ever hit the World Trade Center or the Pentagon. Richard was deeply concerned because he understood the power of these men better than anyone else. They had successfully taken control of the Republican Party and they had gained majorities in both Houses of the U.S. Congress. And next on the agenda was the Judiciary, which would give them control over all three branches of the government.

But, to accomplish that task, they desperately needed to retain control of the presidency. These are the same people who spent millions of dollars discrediting Bill Clinton in a barrage of attacks that eventually turned his lying about an elicit sexual affair, a sin against God, a violation of the *Ten Commandments*, into an impeachable high crime under the U.S. Constitution. Richard knew that they would stop at nothing to incorporate Biblical law and the *Ten Commandments* of the Old Testament into the Constitution, making it the cornerstone to a new Theocracy. Already he had seen them embed themselves into the government, taking advantage of the blind eyes of voters, quietly and stealthily transforming America into a Christian nation.

But they wouldn't stop at gaining power of the U.S.; they wanted the world to get their most important message, that "Christ's Kingdom is not a Democracy!" These men were empire builders, already deeply entrenched into the American government, and they were having great success fighting the new crusade against what they believed to be a decaying society, which they believe is in large part due to the freedoms bestowed upon the U.S. citizens in the Constitution. Richard also wanted an empire, only his vision excluded religion as the binding force. He wanted an empire built on technology, economics and Democracy.

Yet to the Religious Right, he now boldly stood as a giant foe to the Biblical law and to their battle for dominion and control of the United States. Larson had spared no punches in his speech, calling, "Richard Novak a nonbeliever that would seek to further tarnish the soul of America."

The article didn't tell Richard anything he didn't already know, he was dealing with fanatics, religious fundamentalists, that truly believed that they knew the way to glory and that there is no other way.

Only Richard didn't believe in their path. In his eyes, it was time to wake up the apathetic voters of America and turn their eyes to exactly what was going on behind the scenes. It was time America learned what the Religious Right wanted to keep a secret until it was too late to do anything about it. Their goal was to limit freedom. Their goal was the imposition of Christian ideology and practice onto the entire world. Their goal was to achieve this by any means necessary, believing in all sincerity that the end would justify the means.

Richard had seen this coming. He had lived long enough to see the Islamic extremists rise from a small group to a large army of terrorists bent on making the world suffer for not following Allah. And he'd studied enough history to understand that the Nazi party was born in similar fashion in small, backrooms where the discussions and the minutes were held secret until the time to seize dominion was right. The liberty of the United States and the world at large was at risk, and Richard had long dreamed of being the savior, the Dog Star, the brightest star in the midnight sky, the empire builder, the greatest empire builder who ever lived, uniting the world with his technology, enlightenment and Democracy.

And if Richard knew anything for certain, it was that the Religious Right could not stop him. Richard believed, as Machiavelli once said, "It is double pleasure, to deceive the deceiver!"

The conference glass doors swung open as Richard charged in to start the meeting, wired from several cups of coffee, his fiery eyes were racing wildly at Jane and Ted. He sat down at the head of the long mahogany table, completely infuriated, throwing the newspaper down in front of Ted as Jane took her seat at the table.

"They want a holy war! We'll give them a holy war! They don't have a clue what they've just begun!" Richard said.

"A holy war," Jane said, stunned.

"It was just an article, Richard," Ted said. "You knew religion was going to be a major card for these guys. What is it that Pat Robertson, the leader of the Christian Coalition once said? I think it was something like 'There is no such thing as separation of church and state in the Constitution. It's a lie of the left, and we're not going to take it anymore.'"

Richard loosened his silver tie. "Yeah, Ted, I recognize that, but this guy Larson came out swinging pretty hard. He practically called me the Antichrist!"

"Well he didn't go that far, but who really cares what he said. These people are all fanatics!" Ted said. "You know that better than anyone, you've been to their secret meetings – the damn Religious Right isn't underground anymore, they're entrenched and they're not going to let you just walk in and take over without a fight!"

"Yeah, speaking of Robertson, wasn't it him that was quoted in the Denver Post, back in 1992, talking about taking over the Republican Party?"

"Exactly," Ted said, "if I remember correctly, he said something like, "We want ... as soon as possible to see a majority of the Republican Party in the hands of pro-family Christians by 1996.'"

"What are you all talking about? How do you equate these things, and make this giant leap to a holy war?" Jane asked.

"Jane," Ted said, "I mean no offense by this, but there's a lot you don't know about what's been going on in this country. Let me read you something I printed off the Internet for this meeting, this is the mission statement of the National Reform Association and I think you should listen carefully. 'The mission of the National Reform Association is to maintain and promote in our national life the Christian principles of civil government, which include, but are not limited to, the following: 1. Jesus Christ is Lord in all aspects of life, including civil government. Jesus Christ is, therefore, the Ruler of Nations, and should be explicitly confessed as such in any constitutional documents. 2. The civil ruler is to be a servant of God, he derives his authority from God and he is duty-bound to govern according to the expressed will of God. 3. The civil governments of our nation, its laws, institutions, and practices must therefore be conformed to the principles of Biblical law as revealed in the Old and New Testaments.' Then it even adds, 'We believe that the Bible requires any nation, including these United States, to confess the King of kings as its Lord.'"

"Okay, that's pretty scary," Jane said, with a look of disbelief.

"Yes it's scary, Jane!" Ted said. "These people don't just want a holy war, they're already waging a holy war and if this country doesn't wake up and smell the coffee pretty damn soon, then these guys will be trying to change our name to the Holy American Empire!"

Jane looked at Richard, smiling and shaking her head. "He's good! The Holy American Empire – now there's a conspiracy theory for you."

"Jane, you've covered politics," Ted said, "then you tell me what the Hostettler bill was all about?"

"Never heard of it," she answered.

Ted laughed. "Well, I'm not surprised. Do you remember back in 2004 when all of that attention was paid to the monument of the Ten Commandments in the lobby of the Alabama Supreme Court?"

"Yes," she answered.

"Well while that was going on, the U.S. House of Representatives passed the Hostettler bill. They tacked it on as an amendment to an appropriations bill. The amendment prevents the federal government from spending any federal funds to enforce the 11th Circuit U.S. Court of Appeals order to have the monument removed. Now, is that power or what? And it passed by a landslide, 260-161."

"That's interesting, I'd never heard of that -"

"Well, I'm sure you've heard about the Houses of Worship Political Speech Protection Act, then haven't you?"

"Yes, I'm familiar with that one," Jane answered, smiling confidently.

Ted smiled. "Then you probably recall that that's the one that would allow campaign donations at church to be anonymous. You wouldn't have to pay taxes on them. Hell, you could just throw your big checks into the collection plate."

Jane was tired of this rant on the Religious Right and Ted was getting on her nerves with his tirade. "Ted, let me just ask you one question," she said.

"You're the reporter!" Ted said.

"Who killed John F. Kennedy?" she asked. "Castro? The Mafia? Oswald? What do you think?"

Ted laughed and smiled at Richard. "Okay, I can take a hint. Once I get going on that subject I can't stop," he said. "She's a keeper. I like her. We'll get along just fine."

Richard just shook his head, not amused. "Great, I'm glad you two are clicking but we've got to respond to this attack. Any suggestions?"

"Look, why don't you just let it slide and see if it gets any bigger. If we need to we can respond later," Jane said. "There's nothing to gain from responding."

"I disagree," Ted said, avoiding Jane's stare. "You have to let them know where you stand and that we are not afraid of this issue. How long have you and I been saying that it is the fanaticism in this country that is driving it to destruction. American people have been asleep. Their apathy let the Religious Right come to power, but stand up and be proud of who you are and they will love you for your honesty!"

Richard smiled. "Maybe I should just change my slogan to, 'I am the Antichrist! Vote for me and we'll set the night on fire!'"

The room broke into laughter. Then Jane became quiet. "Well who knows who anyone really is anymore," she said, smiling. "So are you the Antichrist?"

Richard looked at Jane, as Ted buried himself in his notes. This is what Richard loved about Jane. The relentless questions, she wasn't scared of anything. While he assumed she was only joking, he didn't mind stoking the flames. "What if I am, Jane, would you really want to know?" he asked.

"I asked the question, didn't I? I want to know who you think you are."

Richard smiled. "Yes, but can you handle the answer?"

"What answer," she said, "what are you talking about?"

"You asked me if I am the Antichrist. I presume you are taking that reference from the Bible, is that right?"

"Yes," she said, smiling. "But I know you're not. I was only kidding you, Richard."

"Well as a reporter," Richard said, "you should know that there are always two sides to everything. Where there is light, there exists darkness. Where there is truth, there is deceit. Where there is a rainbow, there was first a foreboding storm. There are always two sides, and the Bible is just one side, from a Christian perspective it is the truth. From my perspective, it leaves out nearly all of the best parts of the story."

"Great, this sermon again, can we talk about the campaign," Ted said, abruptly.

"No, this is important; I want her to hear this!" Richard shot back.

"Jane," Richard continued, "there are always two sides to every story, and the truth lies in the middle, the center, the apex. Have you ever heard of the Delphi Oracle?"

Jane shook her head. "Isn't that some place in ancient Greece where a prophet gave oracles, revelations of some sort?" she answered.

Richard smiled. "The Delphi Oracle found truth in the middle, the center of the world. Legend has it that Zeus sent two eagles flying in opposite directions, each in search of the center of the world and that they eventually landed after years of flight, at Delphi. This is also the site where Apollo, Zeus' son, killed the great serpent python and then later in honor of the battle erected the temple in that same spot, the center of the world, the apex of the universe, Mt. Parnassus, in the ancient town of Phocis. Herodotus wrote that the Delphi Oracle made predictions and revelations at the Temple of Apollo. It is said now by modern historians and archaeologists that she, the priestess, Pythia, entered a trance while sitting in a tripod position, hallucinating from the toxic fumes which came up from the Earth at exactly that spot."

"What does this have to do with anything?" she asked.

"I'm trying to tell you the other side of the story, Jane. Please listen carefully. The Christians at that time, stirred by the preaching of St. Paul that had swept through the entire region, denounced the Oracle at Delphi as evil and called the oracles and revelations from Pythia, demonized rantings, the preaching of darkness, but that was not the case."

"Well what were they then, if not ramblings from a freak on a good chemical buzz?" Jane said.

Richard smiled. "She wasn't a freak; she was fulfilling her place in the order of the universe at the center of the world. The fumes were real, and they were her opiate that enabled her to reach her trance state. But, her ramblings were more than that, it was in fact, prophecy.

"She was the seeker of truth who spoke to the high one through the omphalos stone, the stone sat in the center of the temple, the center of the world, the center of the universe, the stone that bore the arch similar to a rainbow.

"On one day, Pythia told a prophecy similar to that found in *The Book of Revelations*. There were many similarities in her prophecy, but also blaring distinctions. For instance, the Oracle predicted that there would be a great battle fought by the two sides of good and evil, and that in the center of the battle a great fire would emerge where gray smoke would flow into the heavens covering the Earth in darkness that would cloak the world like a cloth for several days. The sun, the moon and all of the constellations and stars were lost in the darkness. And the people wandered around the land, blind and unable to continue their everyday lives. They became paralyzed by the darkness.

"In the end, however, the Bible's version tells us that Satan, the Antichrist, the Beast, is cast down into the fire and the Lord, the glorious Lamb comes again and all of his believers go with him to heaven. Well that is vastly different from the oracle that was given by the Oracle at Delphi, who said that finally when the gray smoke began to clear there was one light that shone out above all others, a bright star, Sirius, the brightest star in the sky and it casts its light over the Oracle at Delphi and what emerged from that point on was not a clear winner in the battle of good and evil, but a grayer world where good and evil will always be intertwined.

"The Christians for centuries would rise and fall and rise and fall, but through it all the star would always shine in the midst of the gray. That star has had many names: the Dog Star, the Star of Islis, and the Nile Star. In ancient Egypt its appearance marked the summer solstice, giving rise to the oft heard expression 'the dog days of summer.'

"Always remember, my dear that not everything is as clear as some would have you believe. Who can tell you the Bible is the whole truth? Truth always lies somewhere in the middle, in the gray areas where only the strongest lights can shine. The Oracle at Delphi saw my coming in the light of the Dog Star. The prophecy she foretold has come true, I know because I am here now. She knew because she saw it when she looked into the eyes of the fire and my face was shown to her on a winter's night."

"Are you serious, Richard?" she asked. "Because I was only kidding when I called you the Antichrist? Do you really think you're a prophet or some kind of a -"

"Jane," Richard said, searing her soul with his piercing stare. "I am the light that breathes fire into universe! I am the only light in the valley of darkness, the flame of eternal life and the energy of all that some would call evil! I am the Dog Star, the burning fire, the brightest light in the northern sky that is never beholden to God! I am the light of the universe and I fear no man or woman or god! And my time has come!

"Am I the Antichrist? The prince of darkness? The Beast? Does it matter what they call me? The *Book of Revelations* uses the name, Apollyon, which in Greek means the destroyer! The Greeks relate Apollo, as a derivative of apollyo, which also means to destroy. Apollo just so happens to be known as the Greek god of the sun, the god of light! Did you know that the symbols often associated with Apollo are wolves, ravens, crows, snakes, gold, and the silver bow and arrow.

"Just as Orion was a hunter, I am also a hunter. Do not be afraid of me because I bring you no harm. But who am I? In Hebrew, they use the term Abaddon! So many names, so little time! This is a holy war! They want to create the second great Christian empire since the fall of Byzantium, the empire which was established by the Roman Emperor Constantine and engulfed at the height of its power almost all of Asia Minor, becoming the longest enduring Christian empire the world has ever known. They will say, of course, that I am the beating heart of

Babylon, the emperor of the unholy city, the Antichrist. But, I don't know that it would serve my glory to answer such a question when it is so boldly asked.

"I am who I am! The only thing I need to know from you is that you accept me for who I am, and you must only know that I will always accept you for who you are."

Jane was stunned. She'd figured he was just joking, trying to scare her, but he was so intense and so pure in his steely delivery that she was left without words. Her father used to tell her that a false prophet would appear and lead the way for the true one to take over the world. She wondered what her father would think of Richard and his shtick. The whole thing left her more amused than anything else; she'd always loved arrogant men who were in love with themselves.

"Jane, look out on the ledge outside the window, do you see my friend?"

She turned her eyes to the window and could not believe her eyes. A beautiful, sleek bird landed on the ledge, its feathers jet black with deep purple tones. Jane felt chills tingle through her spine. She felt as if the raven were looking into her eyes, penetrating deep into her soul. She locked eyes with the dark creature with the fiery eyes, and then as suddenly as it had appeared it flew away.

Jane was amused, and shook her head in distrust. "Okay," she finally mumbled. "Was that a -"

"A raven," Richard said. "Yes, I believe it was."

"Damn, you're good! Lands there all the time I bet! Indigenous to these parts maybe, the mountains and all! Wow, you're too intelligent for your own good, very quick on your feet! That's a great skill. It will be very useful in this campaign. I guess I need to be careful what I ask you from now on. That was intense, you are the mad genius, but please don't include that prophecy in any of your speeches on the campaign trail! Damn!" she said. "I never know what you're going to come up with! You are quite the piece of work!"

Richard sank back into his chair, reveling in her words. He loved the sweetness of her voice. She was such a prize, a worthy jewel for his kingdom.

"Jane," Ted said, a crooked smile raising his cheeks. "If he is the Beast, you and I are in it together! I won't let him pull any of that

Revelations shit on us, so don't worry! We'll be fine! It's our world for the taking!"

"Okay, enough," Richard said. "Let's get back to the subject of the meeting – why we're here tonight!"

"Oh yeah, the holy war," Jane said, smiling and rolling her eyes at Ted.

"This isn't a joke!" Ted said. "Richard, she has listened, but she still has not heard! This is a holy war! They have majorities in both Houses of Congress and they have an incumbent in the White House! The Religious Right wants every civil government to be Christian to prepare the way for the second coming! Call me a nut or a conspiracy theorist if you want, but I think you should open your eyes! You're not seeing what's in front of you, Jane! You're in the middle of something that you don't understand!"

"Suggestions?" Richard repeated calmly.

"Richard, she needs to know! She needs to understand!"

Richard focused on Ted with a cold stare. "In time," Richard said, "all will understand."

"Don't dance around it, Richard! You know what I'm talking about here. Isn't that what Iraq was really all about? We've talked about this, you and I on several occasions. It's no coincidence that we walked right into the heart of ancient Babylon. It's practically a fucking crusade that's going on right now and these guys are leading the way! Paul Larson, the guy they're quoting in that paper helped put these people in power. He sets the agenda behind the scenes. This war is about religion! They don't want the globalization of Democracy; they want the globalization of Christianity! And the first place to start is right here at home. Hell, a few more years in power and I wouldn't be surprised to see the *Ten Commandments* become a part of the Constitution! Their goal is Theocracy!"

"I can't believe we're still having this conversation," Jane said.

Ted pointed at Richard, ignoring Jane. "You're going to have to let people know who you are! You have to try and ease their fears!" Ted said, his breath rasping with every word. "'A charge to keep,' remember that?"

"I remember," Richard said. "You're referring to the title of George W. Bush's autobiography."

"Oh it's more than that, my friend. He kept a painting in his governor's office in Texas. The painting depicts a horseman charging up a high mountain. It was a reminder to him that he served God!"

"So he's a Christian," Jane responded, "don't make a mountain out of a mole hill!"

Richard laughed at Jane's remark, while Ted shook his head. "Laugh if you want," Ted said, "but my point is that you're not going to win over the fanatics. You have to attack them with everything you've got or you don't stand a chance. And forget about the Democrats, they're not going to take you head on about your religion, they'll expect the right to do it for them, and they will."

"All right then, let's set up another interview!" Richard said, standing. "I want primetime on GNN! Set it up for next Thursday night! Ted, I also want to see the reports you've been working on for the campaign with the others, and a full progress report on our status in every state for getting on the ballots. No messing around on that, I want a record set! Get these reports to me no later than Tuesday afternoon."

"Well you know me," Ted said, "I'm divorced because that's all I do is work. That's why you like me so damn much. Don't worry Richard, we'll get it done. We're going to shock the world! Then what you do with it from that point on is your business and your problem! I'm retiring after this!"

Richard laughed. "You're never going to retire, Ted. I won't allow it!"

"Listen to him, Ted, he's the Antichrist," Jane said, laughing.

"Jane, a word to the wise," Ted said. "Have you ever heard of Friederich Nietzsche?"

"Yes, of course," she said. "His idea was the superman, wasn't it?"

"Well, yes, but he had lots of ideas," Ted said. "The one that comes to mind for me when I look at you though, is a quote of his where he said, 'Whoever battles with monsters had better see that it does not turn him into a monster. And if you gaze too long into an abyss, the abyss will gaze back into you.'"

Jane shook her head. "Wow, pretty scary. You're almost as good as Richard at that. But I've never been afraid of the dark fellas so don't worry about me, I'll be just fine."

CHAPTER 25

The smell of pine blew in the breeze and the bald eagle with its sweeping wings flew over the tops of the trees high towards the mountain's peak. The slow and steady beat of a drum echoed in the distance. Chase steadied the chestnut Mustang, holding gently onto the reins and cinching his boots into the stirrups as they made their way up the steep grade.

The rugged trail was well traveled and the mountainside dotted with pine, spruce firs and the occasional cottonwood. Chase could see the small silver stream flowing down into the valley. His journey was only beginning, and he had no idea where he was going. The majestic eagle seemed to be leading him to an unknown destination up on the hillside. Small game was everywhere. Chase saw several big-eared rabbits bouncing along in the sagebrush. The sky was clear, a beautiful day, and as he ascended up the mountain the cool breeze ruffled the golden wildflowers near the edge of the creek.

After a few hours and several miles on horseback, an opening appeared at a place where the sun seemed to fall into the mountain, soaking the area with streaming rays of light. Chase looked into the ravine and he saw the eagle land on a large boulder. His horse made its way, charging up the hill to reach the ridge. As they reached the rim of the tree line to the ravine, the eagle took flight again, this time its powerful wings lifting it gracefully over Chase and his old horse. Chase watched in awe as the eagle flew into the sun and vanished. When he finally looked down into the opening before him, he saw a splendid blue lake nestled into a valley on the mountainside. The surface of the lake was glistening like a giant ruby stone as the sun showered the valley with a glowing red sunset.

The energy of the lake was magnetic and it drew Chase in as his breaths became relaxed and his mind became still. He dismounted his horse and walked over to the edge of the lake. When he looked across the lake into the red sun he saw the strangest sight. There was an old Indian, wearing a feathered war bonnet, standing near a small canyon and waving Chase over with his eyes.

Chase walked around the lake and began to follow the Indian, who led him to a small canyon and at last into a small cave. Inside the cave it was dark and Chase could barely see as the Indian performed his ceremony around a small fire, chanting and meditating in a strong and forceful prayer in his native tongue. Chase sat by the small fire and closed his eyes. The drumbeats from the distance grew closer and their rhythm put him to sleep.

When he finally opened his eyes, it was as if the world had completely stopped. The Indian was gone. The fire was out. The drumbeats were beating no more. The cave was engulfed by fog and he stood and made his way to the opening. When he saw the lake from the distance, he could see that something was happening on its surface and he instinctively walked to the water's edge.

It was there that he saw them in the reflection of the lake. The inferno was raging wildly. The sky filled with black smoke. People, people of all sizes and shapes and skin colors were on fire and screaming for help. One by one, they looked to Chase, and then into his eyes, and they penetrated his soul with their screams and their frightened, melting stares. Chase sank to the ground, filled with their pain and their hunger for salvation. The faces in the fire had seen the abyss, and he could see the horror in their eyes and he felt it bore into his soul. When he could bear no more, he screamed out, "Why? Why me?" he screamed. "What do you want from me?"

And then the voice spoke to him. "If they aren't stopped, the faces you see will melt away in the flames. Your brother is the last of the seven, and with him he will bring the inferno of hell to Earth. Prepare yourself now for the day that will come soon when God shall call upon you to choose between your brother and the people of the lake. Deep inside you, your true self knows all answers and will lead you to the place where it shall be done. You must not ignore who you are. Go now! Be swift and bold like the eagle! For in this battle, you are the chosen warrior of God and it is your will that shall be done! Discover now who you are and in doing so your will is revealed."

Chase fell back onto the ground exhausted and he closed his eyes. His head was throbbing, and when he finally opened his eyes he was in a dark room, only the light of the moon filtered in through an open door. He saw a man hovering over him chanting in a foreign tongue, and he remembered Jimmy raising the mallet as he begged for mercy. The cry of the Lamb rang out loudly in his mind and all at once he couldn't take it anymore and he jumped up and knocked over the man, pushing him against a wall and running outside into the night. The horrors of the angels ran through his mind like an explosion and he just kept running. He was running at full speed when he was tackled from behind, forcing him to roll hard onto the ground and land on his back. A man jumped on top of him.

"Chase," he said, "We made it! It's okay! That was Red Hawk you nearly killed back there!"

"What?"

"Chase, it's me, Billy! Remember?"

Chase looked past Billy and he could see the adobe pueblo in the background. "I thought we were still there. I was trying to get away and-"

"I think he's feeling better," Red Hawk interrupted, holding his hand to the back of his head. "He knocked me over like I'd been holding him under water."

"I'm sorry," Chase mumbled. "I didn't know."

Red Hawk eye's were deep and intense like an old owl's, but he looked down at Chase and smiled. "You were dreaming, yes?" he asked.

"Yes, I must've been."

Billy sat beside Chase on the ground, out of breath. Chase could see that Billy's head was bandaged; his eyes were swollen and bruised badly.

"Chase, what you're remembering wasn't a dream," Billy said.

"Jimmy came back inside and they left him there with us to finish it. You tried to reason with him, but he wouldn't listen. You bought me time to work on my hands, and if you hadn't done that we wouldn't be here right now."

"What happened to, Jimmy?" Chase asked.

"I don't know. I just remember him picking up the wood block and he came at me swinging. He knocked me pretty good, and you, too. We lost two days there. I finally got free and went for help. Luckily I ran into an Indian brother on the road. We were lucky. They'd deserted the camp. They took everything and left us there to die."

"Have you called the police?"

"He's your brother. I didn't know what to do. I had my friend make an anonymous call to the FBI and he gave them the location of the ranch. I'm sorry, but I had to do something. He told them that they were some sort of fringe religious group that was extremely violent and up to no good. That's it."

"You did the right thing," Chase said.

"We didn't say anything about, Jimmy or Michael," Billy said. "I'm not so sure it was the right thing but it was the only thing I could do to help my brother."

Chase looked up at Billy and smiled. "Your brother?" he said.

"After what we went through," Billy said, "we're brothers. We were bonded by a nightmare, and now it is up to us to prevent those bastards from bringing their nightmare to someone else."

"I have to get Jimmy. He's still my brother."

"Of course he is," Billy said. "Let me help you find him. If we don't, he'll be gone forever. They've fucked him up real bad."

Chase nodded. "Yes they have," he said softly. "But I'm going to find Michael and I'll kill him when I do."

"Killing isn't the answer," Red Hawk said. "The answer is in your dreams."

"How'd you know about that?" Chase asked.

"You had a vision, didn't you?" Red Hawk asked.

"I guess you could call it that. It was strange. I was climbing a mountain on a horse, and a bald eagle flew high above me in the sky, always ahead of me as if directing my way. Way up on the mountain, there was an opening and there I came upon a blue lake with water that shimmered like a crystal in the red sunset. Then I saw an Indian in a headdress. He was old, and his eyes were full of direction. He led me to a cave and I fell asleep to his chanting over a fire. It was really bizarre. I remember when I woke up, he was gone and everything seemed pasty and there was a lot of fog. And that's when I walked over the to edge of the lake and I saw it."

"What did you see?" Billy asked.

Chase looked at Billy and then back at Red Hawk. "People," he answered. "Thousands of people burning and bleeding and surrounded by fire and smoke. It was like a lake of fire."

Billy looked at Red Hawk, stunned. Red Hawk nodded, as if to say, "I told you so."

"Then I heard a voice speak to me," Chase said.

"And what did the voice say?" Billy asked.

Chase just looked at Billy and shook his head with eyes that said, "You don't really want to know that."

"The lake in your dream was Blue Lake, up there in the mountains," Red Hawk said, turning to the mountain behind him. "A sacred place to my people, the source of our energy and life, we return there when we die. The red sunset you saw has been called the blood of Christ, hence the name Sangre de Christo. You're vision has meaning. Let it guide you on your mission."

"My mission?"

Red Hawk smiled. "Chase, you know what I'm talking about."

Chase looked down at the ground, ignoring Red Hawk's piercing stare. "My mission is to find my brother, that's my only mission."

"We'll find him," Billy said.

"I'll have to make some arrangements with my practice. I won't be going back until this is done. This is war now. They've declared war on my family."

"Let your vision guide you," Red Hawk said. "This is more than a war on your family. This is a war against humanity."

Chase ignored Red Hawk. He was trying to block the dream from his mind and just focus on Jimmy. "I'll call Susan and tell her that we're still looking," he said. "I'm not going to tell her what happened. She doesn't need to know. We'll find Jimmy, I can feel it."

"You will find much more than, Jimmy, I'm afraid," Red Hawk

said, as he turned and began walking back to his apartment in the adobe complex.

Billy looked at Chase with a worried look engulfing his tanned face. "Do you remember that letter?" he asked.

"Yep. How could I forget it?"

"We'll start there then."

Chase sighed deeply. "I'm not sure what is worse, where the letter will lead us to or the contents of the dish from refrigerator in their lab."

"I forgot about that," Billy said. "What was in that thing?"

"That thing was a culture dish," he said, "and what was in it was something that could get Jimmy in a lot of trouble if we don't find him first."

CHAPTER 26

MID-SEPTEMBER, 2007

Robby Gonzalez was just another rabid, young baseball fan. His favorite team was the Los Angeles Dodgers, whose hometown is LA, a city of 15.8 million people, the 6th largest city in the world. Numbers aside, Robby knew he had to be the biggest fan the team had ever had. He absolutely lived and breathed baseball, and the Dodgers were more than just a team, they were family. His father had introduced him to all of the players. At 9 years of age, he was already dreaming of a career in the majors. And it wasn't exactly a far-fetched dream. He could already hurl a fastball 60 miles an hour, a feat that had made him a local prodigy. In the draft at the four star league in LA, he was the first player chosen the last three years. Blessed with athleticism, size and speed, he was already belting homers at age 6.

His father, Roberto Gonzalez, Sr., the Mayor of LA, was a first generation immigrant from Mexico City, Mexico. He was a standout player in his own right in the early 80's as a late-teenage prospect. He played ball with Fernando Valenzuela in the Mexican League in 78', a few years before Fernando's breakout season in LA with the Dodgers in 81', when he dominated the league like no other rookie ever has before, winning the Cy Young award easily. Roberto was never a Fernando type of prospect, but he could bring the heat. Unfortunately, a lot of great athletes never make it to the majors, and Roberto threw out his arm in a tryout with the Oakland A's and he was never able to make it back to top form. After that injury, his fastball became average, and he knew he'd missed his shot.

The thing that wasn't lost, however, was his ambition. Never mind baseball, he married and became a U.S. citizen and went to college, majoring in Political Science at UCLA. After college he worked his way up the food chain at city hall and became a name in LA politics. He was elected as the Mayor of Los Angeles in 2004 in a landslide. He was very popular with the people in LA, they respected his roots and appreciated his ability to connect with all individuals, not falling into the trap of championing only the wealthy elite, but remembering the average citizen's struggles as well.

Still, all of his own personal accomplishments aside, nothing made him more proud than to watch his son fan kids at the park with his fastball. Little Robby was doing things at the ballpark that he'd never dreamed of being able to do at that age, and most times, it was against kids much older than him. Roberto understood that fruit sometimes falls close to the tree, he also understood that sometimes, if you're very lucky, the fruit is naturally engineered perfectly in such a way that only comes along on rare occasions.

This was a big day for little Robby. Since his mom had passed 6 months ago, he'd been down in the dumps and Roberto was trying everything that he could to snap him out of it, which wasn't easy since he was also heartbroken. Her two favorite men sorely missed, Maria Gonzalez. Her death from pancreatic cancer had been tough to watch and even more difficult to survive.

Sometimes the clouds of depression after such a loss can prevent one from seeing that the sun still shines and that the world is still spinning on its axis. It's like looking through a kaleidoscope, you see what's inside of it so clearly, but everything outside of it is muddled because your focus becomes limited to what's inside. Roberto knew that if there was one way to bring a smile to Robby's face it was to take him to a Dodger's game. Afterward they were coming home to celebrate his 10th birthday with family and friends. This was going to be his first birthday without his mom there so Roberto had made sure it was going to be a blowout, the plan was to keep Robby too busy to think.

Robby couldn't wait to get to Dodger Stadium. He was so excited that he talked the whole way to the game. "Who's going to be on the mound for the Dodgers? Did you check?" he asked.

"Sorry, Robby, I didn't get a chance to look at the -"

"I'm going to eat hot dogs until I'm sick!" Robby blurted. "The dogs at the park are the best I've ever had."

Roberto just laughed as Robby continued.

"I can't believe we've got seats behind home plate. I can feel the heat coming off those pitches already. I wish I could get out there and shag a few. I bet I could do pretty good."

"I can only imagine," Roberto said.

"I can see it," Robby said. "Just like you always tell me, you have to see it in your mind first before it can happen. I'm gonna make it to the bigs one day. You're going to be so proud."

"You don't have to make it to the big leagues to make me proud, Robby. I'm already proud of you. Whatever you do, I just want you to be happy. What good is life if you're not living it to the fullest and giving it your best? Just keep going for it like you have been, and you'll be just fine."

"I'll try my best! Mom's watching!"

"You better believe it! You've got an angel on your side, kid!"

The game started at 12:10 PM. Ariel was working the concession stand closest to home-plate, just inside the stadium corridors. He couldn't stop himself from looking up at the air shaft directly above the people standing in line at the concession stand. He was so proud of his invention. He was an electronics genius, and his new aerosol release device was second to none. Love was in the air, and he could feel it. The love of the Lamb! What a pleasure it was to serve God, and to be chosen and beholden to such a great assignment made him so proud. It was truly a glorious day. *I'm coming Lord. I'll be there soon. And with me, I will bring you a flock.*

To the people in line at the hot dog stand he was just a friendly, skinny fella with a long beard and starry eyes, a man that was just a little too happy to be serving hot dogs on such a beautiful day at the ballpark. What they didn't know was the electronic aerosol device attached to the air vent was releasing the virus into the air directly over their heads. Robby loved his hot dog so much that Roberto had to make two more trips to the concession stand, each time tipping the friendly gentlemen at the stand generously. Robby was in heaven. Hot dogs at the ballpark brought tears to his eyes. They always tasted better than anywhere else, and these dogs were no exception. He literally ate until he was so stuffed that he was belching hot dogs burps the whole game.

The stadium wasn't filled to its capacity of 56,000, but there were easily 36,000 in attendance to watch the Dodgers play the St Louis Cardinals in the early afternoon game. Dodger Stadium opened in 1962 and covers 300 acres of land. The stadium is known as a "classic pitcher's park," and none have done more to boost that reputation than Fernando Valenzuela. Robby knew everything about him. His dad was a friend of Fernando's and he even had an autographed ball from Fernando that was actually used in a game – Robby's most prized possession. Although Robby had never seen him play, Roberto had all of his televised games on tape and Robby grew up watching them. There was nothing bigger and more exciting in LA than when Fernando Mania swept the city. To the Mexican-Americans, he was a legend, a man who came to the U.S. barely able to speak any English, and with his fastball became an ambassador of what a Mexican immigrant could achieve in the land of opportunity.

The pitches whipped from the mound with the hiss of a snake and snapped into the catcher's mitt, as Robby and the mayor soaked in every moment. After all, this was Robby's birthday and what a day it was going to be. The Dodgers, not having a great year, had come to play and even managed to pull out a 4-3 win over the Cardinals. Robby dreamed one day that it would be him out there, just like the great Fernando, kicking the dust off the plate on the mound, loading up and bringing the heat. He figured if he just kept working hard, it was only a matter of time.

On the ride home, Roberto could tell that the game had worked – mission accomplished. He figured it was due in no small way to the angel that was watching over them. Little did he know?

"Thanks for taking me to the game, Dad! Baseball is the greatest game in the world!"

"Yes, I agree," Roberto said. "And you're the greatest son in the whole world!"

Robby just looked over at his Dad, his eyes were swelling. Roberto had been keeping to himself a lot since his mother died, and he needed him now more than ever. They needed each other.

"Just remember," Roberto said, "what am I always telling you about this country. We've been blessed! Baseball is a great game, and if you make it as an athlete that's fine, and if you don't, there are plenty of other ways that you can accomplish your dreams. The most challenging game in life is politics. Someday if you become a leader, that's where you can make a great difference in the world. And you've got it in you. I've seen you in action!"

"Do you mean for Mexican-Americans?" Robby asked.

"No, come on, you know better than that! All Americans!" Roberto answered. "Freedom and opportunity, these are the great gifts that all Americans should be able to enjoy."

"I'll do my best," Robby said.

"I know you will, son. You always have."

The party by the pool was awesome and Roberto enjoyed seeing Robby kick back with his cousins and his friends. The kids swam in the pool, playing Marco Polo, until their skin was blue and wrinkled. The Gonzalez house was a large stucco, red tile roofed, California mansion and the pool area was paradise for kids in the summertime, but this was the first time that Roberto had seen Robby enjoy it this year. High up in the mountains of the Hollywood Hills, the view from the edge of the pool in the evening was like a window to the city of lights. And the city was a great portal to the world at large. And the world at large would soon discover that something was happening that would change the city of lights into the city of darkness without mercy. The time for mercy was over! The wrath of God had begun!

CHAPTER 27

At first the symptoms were mild. Robby and Roberto, Sr. had been complaining about having headaches for about a week. Then Robby developed a fever, and the rash followed. In time the rash became lesions, and then scarring scabs. Still, when the symptoms began Roberto, Sr., with all of his training on bioterrorism did not suspect that these symptoms were anything other than an ordinary virus. This was a mistake beyond proportion. In the first days of symptoms, he simply ordered his son to bed-rest until he felt better and planned to call his brother to get some medication for him and Robby to take, fearing that they might have had the chicken pox. Being the Mayor of Los Angeles, Roberto felt a great duty to keep working, and he tried to work through his symptoms with positive reinforcement to himself, but it just wasn't working. When his secretary, Rosalie, noticed the small lesions appearing on his skin, she'd seen enough.

"Roberto," she said, squinting her eyes under her wire-rimmed glasses at the sight of him. "Those bumps aren't normal, and you're walking around here like a zombie and you've taken a fever. Go to a doctor! That's an order! I don't want to scare you, but you look like you have the chicken pox!"

"That's what I was thinking. Robby's at home in bed. I think I'll go call my brother. This started about a week ago."

"Well, whatever it is, please keep it away from me! I'd just die if I brought that home to my granddaughter. The poor little thing has enough trouble with her asthma. You know, I hate to tell you this but ever since Maria died, neither of you have been taking very good care of each other. You don't eat well! And with the heart problems that you've had, that's no good, Roberto! And that boy can't just live on meat! You should hire someone to help you all out at home!"

Roberto slumped over; he was ready to pass out in his agony. "I promised Maria that I would take care of Robby," he said. "I'm doing the best I can. It just wouldn't be right to hire someone to come into her home. I can't do that."

Rosalie frowned and started walking back to her desk. "Well, you're the mayor, who am I to tell you what to do?" she said.

"I promise I'll have my brother come by our house tonight. We probably just need some antibiotics."

"Now there's an answer," she said, turning back to look at him. "Doctors these days give them out like candy. That's part of the problem."

Roberto shook his head, and headed back to his desk to call his brother. As every minute passed, he began to feel worse. Whatever it was that was plaguing him and Robby, he knew they needed some good medication and fast. Sometimes there's nothing like a little dose of antibiotics and some rest, the combination had become the chicken soup of modern medicine, and Roberto yearned for a remedy to his plague.

CHAPTER 28

GNN.com

WORLD NEWS

Major Smallpox Outbreak in Los Angeles

Wednesday, September 24, 2007 Posted 1:30 PM EDT

LOS ANGELES (GNN) – The headlines tell the story: *Terrorism Suspected in LA Smallpox Outbreak*, The New York Times; *Mayor Roberto Gonzalez First Victim of Smallpox Attack*, The Washington Post; *Los Angeles City Hall Subject of Investigation in Smallpox Attack*; The Los Angeles Times; *Thousands May Die from Smallpox Outbreak*, U.S.A Today; *Biological*

Attack in U.S., The London Times; *World Horrified by U.S. Smallpox Epidemic*, The Japan Times, *52 Deaths, 1252 Reported Cases of Smallpox in U.S. Outbreak*, The Times of India; *U.S. Seeking Muslim Suspects After Smallpox Attack*, Arab News.

In the most horrific smallpox attack in North America since the British handed out blankets infected with the virus during the French and Indian Wars (1754-1767), the U.S. has now been attacked in the city of Los Angeles. The attack is believed to have occurred by an aerosol release somewhere within the city, and city hall is considered a possible target. The entire city is under curfew and quarantine. The Mayor of Los Angeles was the first victim to die in the attack, which is believed to have taken place at least five weeks ago, location still unknown. Mayor Roberto Gonzalez, Sr., elected to office in 2004, was 43 years old. He is survived by his 10 year old son, Roberto Gonzalez, Jr., who is also suffering from smallpox and currently being treated in the Los Angeles quarantine facility at LA County Hospital.

While officials continue to investigate the outbreak, the numbers of victims suspected of being contaminated with the virus are mounting. Already 1,252 people have been diagnosed with smallpox and of those victims, there are 52 reported deaths. The Los Angeles International Airport and all businesses in Los Angeles have been ordered closed until the city can come to grips with how to handle the investigation and at the same time impede the growing outbreak from reaching outside the city limits. People are being asked not to panic and not to travel unless absolutely necessary.

Given the epidemic numbers this has become an international crisis. Most countries around the world have discontinued flights and all other forms of travel to and from the U.S. until this outbreak can be contained. Officials in the U.S., while well trained and prepared for an attack, were caught off guard by the nature of this attack due to the delay in the onset of symptoms and the number of those infected. By the time the first victims reported their symptoms to health officials the outbreak was already a major epidemic.

Fittingly, there has been a massive response by authorities locally, nationally and worldwide. In the U.S., the U.S. Centers for Disease Control and Prevention and the U.S. Department of Homeland Security are working together with state and local officials to contain and investigate the attack.

"The intelligence we're receiving indicates that this was an attack carried out by Islamic extremists, possibly Al Qaeda," U.S. Attorney General Blakely said in a news conference. "Although we must report that several groups have come forward taking responsibility, it will take authorities some time to sort through all of the leads. However, as sure footed as I stand here today, we will find whoever committed this cowardly crime against humanity, and they will pay for their sins! So help me God!"

While officials have urged people not to panic, fear is

widespread and people have clogged the expressways trying to flee Los Angeles, which is exactly what officials are trying to prevent.

"If we give in to fear, then they've won. The disease will spread, and thousands will die. The only way to stop this outbreak is to contain it and implement the inoculation plans that are already in place," Michelle Abrahmson, with the U.S. Center for Disease Control said in a statement issued on Tuesday in response to the public's reaction to the outbreak.

Smallpox is a highly contagious viral infection. The disease is preventable by vaccination, however, once infected the death rate is 30-40% in healthy persons and higher for those with weakened immune systems. The incubation period prior to the onset of symptoms is typically 12-14 days from the time of exposure. Symptoms include many characteristics of other illnesses, particularly the chicken pox, and include a high fever, headache, body aches, and a quickly spreading rash. Those infected with the disease who survive are usually scarred for life from the lesions.

Public health officials are requesting all people with symptoms to report to one of the nearest quarantine facilities that have been set up all over LA and the U.S. to treat and contain the disease. Anyone who believes that they may have come into contact with a victim is also being asked to report to the designated health agencies as set forth in the hourly public announcement by county and state officials nationwide. All states have already put their emergency response plans into action and are prepared for victims. Smallpox vaccinations are now being administered in accordance with the federal guidelines for an outbreak.

While the possibilities are endless, authorities from the FBI to the president insist that the nation must remain calm while they continue to investigate this matter thoroughly. The entire city of Los Angeles has in effect, become a crime scene. The roads now lead to nowhere, as police continue to block all perimeters to keep people from leaving the city. As a result, many people have abandoned their vehicles in their places on the expressway, creating miles upon miles of log-jam, which remains at this hour, unresolved. So far over 200 suspects have been detained by federal authorities and the FBI have made raids all across the U.S., seeking several other potential suspects. Many communities are outraged, as most suspects have been foreign, Muslim immigrants.

These issues and the outbreak will be addressed from the Oval Office by the president tonight in his prime-time address to the nation following the evening news.

CHAPTER 29

Jackie Cole always preached that God's gift is creation, and Satan's, the Beast's, is destruction. And the medium of each, God's and Satan's, is man. It is through man that each will accomplish its giving and the taking away. Man was so perfect an instrument, always torn by its love and hate for one another; there's a little bit of heaven and hell in every human being. There is, however, a price for man's imperfection. In the Lord's book it is referred to as Armageddon. The ultimate weapon of Armageddon, of course, was created by man: the atomic bomb.

The Germans, during World War II, started the race for the great weapon. They knew, as the Americans knew, that the first country with the bomb held the cards to the future of the world. They would be the master of the universe. Or so they thought, anyway.

Albert Einstein, the German-born physicist, was contacted by two Hungarian, Jewish scientists who convinced him to write a letter to President Franklin D. Roosevelt about the Germans and their nuclear program. He wrote that the Germans with their discovery of fission were getting close to developing an atomic bomb. He made a case to the president that the U.S. should use its brightest scientists to develop the weapon first with the aid of the government.

Jackie grew up around these great minds; her father was friends with them all. They often ate barbecue and drank beer at her house, talking about their great "gadget," as it was called. Her father was the great protector of the great destroyers. She knew about it all. She'd heard all of the arguments, studied the treatises, and asked all of the questions. And over time she'd learned, as she lost her family, one by one, to cancer, that science was not the great equalizer of man, but its greatest destroyer.

She had personally witnessed the light. It was so bright and powerful, she felt as if it was imbedded into her brain. And the light brought her darkness, and she made darkness her friend. The flash of the light was awesome, and what followed was silence and darkness and despair. She had seen the power of man explode into the bomb, many bombs, created by men who were grasping at straws to stake their claim in the battle of man versus nature.

Fission meant nothing to her, but death, and fusion, just meant more death in a different manner.

Atomic or Hydrogen, what difference did it really make, the result was the same, a smiling Beast in a shattering storm of heat and blazing wind, scorching the sand and melting it into glass. The flakes from the fallout were like sparkling snowflakes in the desert, and they didn't belong there at all. The heat was more fitting, at its core it radiated, 'tens of millions of degrees centigrade,' making the desert a furnace of death.

When she was little, she was so proud of her father and his work at Trinity in Los Alamos, New Mexico. It was 1945, and he was an Air Force Colonel, in charge of security over the site during the Manhattan Project. At the order of President Franklin D. Roosevelt, all of the brightest minds were gathered there under the direction of theoretical physicist Robert Oppenheimer, to build an atomic bomb. Trinity was the isolated location where the scientists swarmed like locusts under the desert sun to build the atomic bombs that came to be known as, Little Boy, and Fat Man, before they were dropped over, Hiroshima, and Nagasaki, producing the largest explosions ever dropped on humankind, killing an estimated 175,000 Japanese in just two attacks.

Jackie had lost enough of her own family to the radioactive fallout of the bombs that she'd witnessed during her father's service at the Nevada Test Site to understand the power of the bomb. She used to stay up late at night with the questions of an eager child running through her mind. She was only one of hundreds of thousands exposed to radioactive fallout during the experimentation and growth of the nuclear age in the desert sands of Nevada in the 50s and 60s. She often wondered as she grew older, and more bitter, *'How does man save itself from itself?'* She thought it was strange the willingness of people to gamble in this life that they wouldn't have to pay for their sins in the next life. Then the Lord came to her in her late 20s, comforting her, speaking to her the words of freedom and liberation from her pain.

And since that time in the 70s when she discovered the grace of God, she has feared the power of man no more. God is the answer, and there are no more questions that can't be answered under the light of God. For God is almighty and all knowing. If you trust in God, then you don't need any more answers to man's questions, the ones with no real answers anyway. God is the answer, and that's all anyone really needs to know.

Jackie was making pancakes when the doorbell rang. She was surprised because she'd lived in St. John's, Arizona for nearly 20 years, and rarely ever had visitors come all the way out to her quiet ranch, which sat squarely in the middle of nowhere. That was the second time that the doorbell had rung in a week, and she wondered how she'd suddenly become so popular. Her son had bought the ranch for her 6 years ago from the money he received from his father. He was a good son, as a boy he always took care of her and always listened to her preaching. As she scuttled to the door, she wondered if it might be him, surprising her; he was always full of surprises. Since the men from the FBI had come calling, she'd been unable to get him out of her mind.

Through the peephole she saw the two men. "Yes," she answered, opening the door only slightly.

"Good morning," Chase said. "You wouldn't happen to be Ms. Cole, would you? Jackie Cole?"

"I might," she answered, "depends on who's askin'."

"Yes," Chase said, "we're friends of your son, Michael. He was with us in New Mexico and he sort of disappeared. He left a lot of his artwork stored with some of his good friends at the Taos Pueblo, along with some of his personal belongings and we just wanted to find him so we could at least give him his things or see to it that they get to him. We were passing through on our way to Tucson, and thought we'd stop in and see you. He talked about you all the time."

The door flung wide open. "He's a good boy. I miss him so much. Don't know where he is, ya'll likely to have a better fix on his position than me. Always moving around, that boy. Would you fellas like some coffee? I was makin' some pancakes."

Billy and Chase smiled warmly at Jackie. "Coffee sounds good, Ms. Cole," Chase said.

"Yes, I believe I could use a cup as well," Billy said.

"Call me, Jackie," she said. "Have a seat."

They walked into the small log cabin kitchen and sat down at a small metal table with a red Formica top. The kitchen was small but tidy. She had several pots and pans hanging over an island cutting board. Chase and Billy exchanged glances, as they both were having a hard time believing that the monster they were looking for could have her for a mother. She was just a sweet, hospitable little lady.

"So when is the last time you've seen, Michael," Billy asked.

"Oh I guess it was about 2 years ago. He was so skinny. I tried to get him to stay for a while so I could cook for him and beef him up some. I love to cook and he loves my cookin', but he said he had to get movin'. He was always busy, you know. That's how they are when they get all grown up. There's just too much goin' on to hang out with Mama. It's not cool, ya know."

Chase and Billy laughed. "Any thoughts on where he might of gone? He left in a hurry," Chase asked.

"I sure don't," she said, politely. "He used to call, but not so much anymore. Has he got a girl? I figured he might have a girl by now."

"He dated a few girls we know, but nothing seemed to last," Billy said.

Chase frowned at Billy. "What?" Billy said, looking at Chase with a slight grin. "He's my friend, too?"

Chase just shook his head. His buddy Billy thought he was pretty funny, not sticking to the script.

Jackie sat down at the table, as they all sipped their coffee. "I hope you boys don't mind it black, all out of cream."

Chase and Billy nodded politely as they all sat there quietly sharing a moment of the morning. Jackie seemed to disappear into her mind for a spell. The lines of her face betrayed her deep contemplation. She was tanned and her skin was blotched with sun spots, but her green eyes sparkled. There were several pictures of her and Michael on her refrigerator, and she was a good lookin' gal when she was younger. Chase just couldn't believe that she was actually Michael's mother. He was trying to wrap his mind around it, but so far nothing seemed to fit the picture that he had in his mind on the way to her place.

"You all can just leave Michael's' things with me," she finally said. "He'll be around eventually."

"Well, we didn't bring them with us," Billy said. "They're back in storage at the Pueblo."

"Oh," she said, smiling. "In Taos?"

"Yes," Chase answered.

"I met Michael's father in Taos," she said, sipping her coffee with the glimmer of the memory bursting from her eyes. "He was such a handsome man. And we were young. Wow, was I young back then? Didn't know a damn thing. It was the 60s. I went to Taos in 69' after my Mama died from cancer. I was looking to get lost, didn't know that I already was. That's when I met Richard. He was just a college kid then, not the big-shot he is now. He was real smart and all, but I didn't know what he had in him. Never been a good judge of men. I went to college and did well, but when it came to men I was just a country girl. The men I've stayed with have been losers and the men I've left behind have made it rich. Ain't that somethin'?"

Billy smiled. "Maybe Michael went to visit his father?"

Jackie's eyes darted up at Billy, and her eyes furrowed. "So you're friends of Michael, huh?"

"He's a good man," Chase answered.

She turned her stare to Chase. "Where did you say you met him?" she asked.

"We met at the Ranchos de Taos. I was working there and he came along asking a lot of questions about the church and we got to talking. I'm the one that introduced him to Billy."

Jackie relaxed. "He went to the church, huh? I shouldn't have told him about that," she said, her cheeks blushing red.

"Excuse me?" Billy said.

"Oh nothing," she answered. "Yes, I remember the church well. Listen, Michael's father is the Lord, our Father, his Earthly dad never even knew about him until Michael confronted him a few years back.

And that was not my idea. I didn't want anything from him, never did. We were just kids then. Michael grew up wanting to know everything about him. He was fascinated with the man. Boys, I guess, idolize their fathers. It wasn't the money he wanted, it was that connection, you know."

"Money?" Chase asked.

"When Michael finally got up the courage to go meet his father in Seattle, Richard swore he didn't remember me. And that was a lie, of course." she said, smiling. "I know he remembered me. He told Michael that he'd never even been to New Mexico. Michael wanted a paternity test to prove it and Richard refused. He ended up buying Michael off with a large settlement. Michael never told me how much, but it was a lot. He bought me this place and took off, said he had to get back to school. He went to medical school at the University of Arizona, real smart. He had a double major in college, microbiology and geology. I always told him that with his brains, the Lord was going to put them to good use. Did you ever go to Michael's church? He mentioned he'd founded a church where he felt he could exalt in the Lord's scripture."

"I think I know the place you're talking about. A real nice, old Spanish church," Chase said.

"He's a real angel," Billy added.

"An angel," Jackie mused. "That's what I always told Michael, that he was my angel, my miracle baby."

"Miracle baby?" Billy asked.

"I wasn't supposed to be able to have children. That's one of the reasons I was so wild back then, I think. I had numerous ovarian cysts and by the time I was 20 years old, they didn't think I would be able to have children. I've lost a mother to cancer, a father and a sister. I know what those people in LA are going through. Our family's had its share of disease. And it all came from Uncle Sam and his desire to play God. He hit us hard. Michael and I are all that's left."

"Sounds like you all have had some bad luck," Chase said.

"Luck," she said, "there's no such thing. My Daddy was a Colonel in the Air Force. He ran security at Trinity and then also at the Nevada Test Site. Luck had nothing to do with it; it was all proximity to the fallout."

"Are you referring to the -"

"The bomb!" she said, answering Billy. "We used to sit on our rooftops and watch the explosions. Nobody ever said anything about it being dangerous. My Daddy knew all the big-shots and they never said a word to him about dangers, although they all knew it, just didn't talk about it. He stood right next to Oppenheimer and witnessed the first detonation. It was July 16, 1945, the day that evil was born at the hands of a few scientists. My Daddy knew the risks, but he didn't think it could reach our house. Well, he was wrong about that. So Michael was my miracle baby. I always told him that. He was chosen for a special purpose. God had plans for my angel. And man did he ever give him talent!"

"Yes, he's quite the artist," Billy said.

"He absolutely loves it," she said. "I used to buy him a set of paints every time I went into town. His whole room is practically a mural."

"I'd love to see it," Chase said.

"It's back there to the left. Go on and look if you like. Would you all like another cup of coffee?"

"Yes," they said, as they both slipped off to the back hallway to see Michael's room, looking for any clues they could find to his whereabouts.

The room was a sight that weakened their legs. They knew Michael was messed up, but they were stunned by his room, which offered an intense glimpse into the mind of a psychotic. Every square inch of the walls was painted in one giant work of art, depicting many scenes and most of them horrifying. There was a grim reaper hovering over the bed and just out of reach of the reaper's sickle was a giant mushroom cloud, orange colors exploding into red and black smoke and fire. Underneath the text read, "The Manhattan Special, see what man can do!" Then to the right of the explosion began a series of scenes depicting death and suffering for modern society. The first scene was that of a plague, with people lying in hospital beds sick and dying, their skin covered with lesions."

"Look" Chase said, pointing to the scene on the wall. "This scene here is like a plague."

"Small-pox?" Billy asked. "What does the script say underneath?"

"It says, 'In the city of LA'," Chase continued, "'they will fall by the thousands by the wrath of God, and it will have begun.'"

They looked at each other, their eyes exploding like the blast depicted on the wall. "Oh my God," Billy said.

Chase pulled a camera from his light jacket and started snapping pictures of every square inch of the walls, scene be scene, he snapped the photos, like a puzzle, each bowl of wrath was set out before them in a magnificent work of art. Billy quickly shuffled through his chest drawers but there was nothing of any use. Chase knew it didn't matter, the wall was the key. He stopped after taking the last picture and looked at the last scene, the last bowl of wrath. There was a fire, beginning in the Devil's Triangle off the Atlantic coast and it was spreading across the Eastern United States like a wildfire."

"What is it?" Billy asked.

"The last wrath," Chase answered, solemnly. "I saw this in my vision."

They locked eyes. "And?" Billy asked.

"I saw millions of faces burning and melting in a lake of fire. I could smell their-"

"Okay! Okay!" Billy interrupted. "Let's get out of here. This place is filled with bad energy. Michael's -"

"A monster," Chase said.

"Excuse me," Jackie interrupted. "My son is a what?"

Chase tucked the camera into his pocket and turned to the doorway where she was standing. "Sorry, perhaps you misunderstood," he said. "Billy was asking what that was behind the bed. That figure there. And I said, 'Well, it looks like a monster.'"

She looked suspiciously at both of them. "Maybe you all would like to come back into the kitchen and finish your coffee. Don't mean to run you off but -"

"Sure," Billy said, "we'll just be leaving. We're sorry we didn't find Michael. Sure would've loved to have seen him again."

She pierced Chase and Billy with her deep green eyes. "Well, if I speak to him, I'll be sure and mention that you gentlemen stopped by."

Chase and Billy exchanged wild glances and slipped by Jackie, heading quickly for the door. "Thank you," they said uneasily.

"Did the painting on the walls trouble you fellas?"

They turned around to face her. "Why should it trouble us?" Chase asked.

"It's a religious piece and some people don't like religion."

"Do you like religion?" Chase asked.

"I always told, Michael, 'Your job is to bring the truth to the world. You will show the world what God thinks of man's intelligence, of his evil, of his nuclear power. You are the keeper of the truth.' Yes, I told him that, 'The wrath of God would be mightier than if all of the nuclear bombs on Earth exploded at the same time. The wrath of God gives the world a new chance, a start over. Do I like religion? It depends on what the religion is. Is it the religion of war? Is it the religion of love and peace?"

"What about the religion of revenge?" Billy asked.

She smiled. "The creators of evil sew the seeds of evil and evil fruit they shall reap in the great harvest!"

"Harvest?" Chase said.

"The harvest of death by the angels of God. Nuclear energy was only the beginning, not the end, but the end is near. The Lord will not rest until we return to him and the land shall be made desolate. And the human race shall start over. My son, I think you know him, don't you? I can tell that you've looked into his eyes and witnessed his promise. But you still don't yet believe, do you? He is the one. My Michael shall deliver the revelation to the world. It is God's will. Lest we choose more of the wrath of man. What would you choose? The wrath of man or the wrath of God! Oppenheimer and the scientists of the Manhattan Project had great intelligence but no wisdom. Oppenheimer figured it out later, and they made a fool of 'em. The government used them for their knowledge. They were willing to sacrifice the future for the present, which may go down as the most arrogant, ignorant act ever committed. God was watching and with their fission and their plutonium and uranium, they discovered how to make the Beast rise.

"God is always watching. I give a child a gun. Does the child understand the power of the gun? No, but he will fire it anyway. Is the child to blame? No. How 'bout the parent who left the gun in reach of the child? Or, the manufacturer who made the gun and sold it to the dealer? Who is to blame? Does it even matter? Such is nuclear power.

"And maybe that is the great legacy of man: great intelligence, great ignorance, and an inability to strike the balance between the two. We have in a sense tipped the scale on nature, and nature like the atom bomb is imploding every day, eroding the DNA of every living cell in the universe. But do not be afraid, the wrath of God shall take it all back and we will all be gone and the world will start anew. It is the natural evolution of things. Birth and destruction, God knew it! It is written in Revelations! Read your Bible, my friends."

"I'm sorry, but you're just as insane as your son," Chase said, piercing her with his coldest stare. "And when I find him, and I will, he shall not fear the wrath of God more than the wrath of my hands! Justice! Revenge! I'll show him, God! Maybe they did unleash the bomb, but you've unleashed a madman!"

"Who are you to judge my son?" she yelled. "Are you, God?"

"Fuck you lady!" Chase said.

"We are all part of God's universe! We can't control what happens in space and time anymore than we can control what happens in a man's mind! A mind is born by God, just as all things are born by God! My son's destiny is the world's destiny, as we are all apart of each other's! Don't try to stop the wind! Enjoy the cool breeze and embrace it. That's God's will! Ashes to ashes, dust to dust!

"I remember when I was a child and I watched a mushroom cloud explode into the blue sky, the heat blowing downwind was scorching and it burned our skin as we watched. In the bright flash of red light, I saw the Beast. I saw his face, just for a second, but that second has fueled me for a lifetime. His was the face of death. As the wind swept that day through the desert and the sagebrush burnt to a crisp on our ranch, everything in its wake was changed. I swear it was like, it was like a lake of fire, spitting at us from the belly of the Beast.

Chase exchanged a look of dread with Billy. "Lady, I don't give a shit about your religious hocus pocus, I am so sick and tired of that crap! Your son has my brother, and when I catch up with him, he'll wish I was the fucking Beast! I'm afraid that the Beast would be more merciful than I at this point!"

"My," she said, "maybe you are the Beast! I mean who really knows."

"Go to hell, lady!" Chase said.

She smiled. "The way you said that, it's the same way he described his natural father, Richard, speaking to him when they met. If only all men could be like my angel, the world would have been so much better."

"I feel for his father," Chase said. "It must have made him absolutely sick to see what he helped create. His son! The sick, bastard son!"

"Well," she said, "sounds like Richard will have your vote."

"What are you talking about?" Chase asked.

"His father is Richard Novak."

"Richard Novak?" Billy said, wrinkling his long forehead. "As in the presidential candidate -"

"That's right! Before I gave myself to God, one night I gave myself to him! I was a virgin, and on that night I committed a horrible sin in the house of God! I was a whore then! And you are whores now! You are whores to Babylon and the great Beast! You think I'm stupid, don't you? I know why you're here! Do you see what began in LA? Beware the wrath of God is at hand, and there is no shelter from the storm that lies ahead! I pity you and your fear! Now get out of my house!"

CHAPTER 30

GNN.com

U.S. NEWS

Barton Speaks To Nation in Wake of Bio-Terror Attack

President:"We will hunt down those responsible for this attack, and we will bring them to justice. God is on our side in this war on terror."

Friday, September 26, 2007 Posted 8:30 AM EDT

WASHINGTON (GNN) – In an emotional speech, praising the response efforts of health officials and Americans citizens all over the U.S. who have responded to the smallpox attack in Los Angeles, President Barton addressed the nation Thursday night during primetime television in an attempt to calm the growing panic and widespread fear of more attacks. These fears have been promoted heavily in the last few days by the barrage of recent speculation about possible attacks in the near future, largely stemming from the numerous threats received by authorities. "The people of this country," Barton said, "and our freedoms, are the driving force of my inspiration, and the attack that we are now under, which came to us in such a cowardly manner, delivered to us by the hands of evil, shall not deter our spirit, our determination and our will in continuing to live our lives as free people, in a free society, with rights born of God and of our Constitution."

Barton, speaking to the nation for the first time since the outbreak in Los Angeles, delivered a 20-minute statement on the attack, the American response efforts, and the reaction of the global community. Barton made clear that although he could not comment about the investigation that was now underway, he promised that, "The investigation will charge ahead with a full head of steam, and the cooperation of all agencies, state and federal should make all Americans proud." Striking a somewhat controversial chord with many Americans, and the global community, he especially praised the Homeland Security Department's cooperation with local officials across the U.S., in "rounding up potential suspects," downplaying criticism from within the U.S. and abroad that the investigation has focused too narrowly on potential Muslim suspects, without considering possible alternative suspects and motives for an attack of this nature.

Nonetheless, the administration remains under fire for its treatment of Muslims in the U.S. since the smallpox attack in Los Angeles. Barton, however, rejected the notion that people were being suspected as targets merely by the color of their skin, and their Muslim faith, noting that, "We are not a nation that denies freedoms and attacks citizens by the nature of their creed, or their country of origin, but, we cannot, as we learned from the events of 9/11, Somalia, Afghanistan and Iraq, and all over the world, deny that there is a constant threat from radical Muslims against citizens of the U.S.. We, therefore, are not trying to harass our Muslim compatriots, but rather we feel it important for their safety, and for the safety of the U.S., to take all necessary steps to protect America and thoroughly investigate the connections known to our investigators regarding any Islamic connection to this attack."

Other developments:

Muslims protest

Disgusted at the administration's response to the smallpox attack in rounding up mostly Muslim suspects when the evidence thus far has not indicated any Islamic terrorist connection, Muslims began their march in Washington, D.C. today, in the largest gathering of Muslim-Americans ever before witnessed in this country. By the thousands, they marched, showing unity in a peaceful demonstration in front of the White House, and in front of federal buildings across the states. In an outpouring of support, many Americans have joined in what is now being called the Freedom March of Muslim-Americans, calling for an end to the discrimination, which they claim treats all Muslims as terrorists.

One Muslim man, Abdul Saeed, a member of the Center for the Study of Islam, addressed concerns about the direction of the U.S. government. "Ever since 9/11," he states, "whenever something like this happens in this country, it is the Muslims, who come under the eye of the government and not the foreign policy of the government itself. We are Americans, too! I am a businessman, in a free society – I am not a terrorist. Yet, I have to hold my children back from school so that they don't get beat up because they are Muslim. All terrorists are not Muslims, and 99% of Muslims are not terrorists! Why is that so hard for Americans to comprehend? Have they forgotten Timothy McVeigh?"

CHAPTER 31

OCTOBER, 2007 – 3 MONTHS SINCE JIMMY VANISHED

Susan's father, Lake Montera, stood wearily as Chase entered her hospital room at St. Mary's hospital in Tucson, Arizona. Meeting for just the first time, they stood in the center of the small room and shook hands. The room was hot, and Lake explained that the room's vent wasn't working properly and that he'd jumped all over their shit at the front desk and expected it to be fixed shortly.

"She's been asleep for about an hour," Lake said, his tired eyes betraying his steadiness.

"How's she doing?" Chase asked.

Lake grimaced and looked down at Susan as he spoke. "Under the circumstances, I'd say she's doing about as well as can be expected," he said. "Have you found Jimmy?"

"No," Chase said, "not yet."

"Don't give up. Without him, I'm not sure what she'll do. Being pregnant was a saving grace. It was helping her hold onto Jimmy. If it was a boy, she was going to name it after him. I think it was all of the stress that caused it. The doctors said it could have been any number of reasons. Apparently miscarriages are common in early pregnancy."

Chase just nodded and looked down at Susan. She was a beautiful woman. Her dark hair was long and was covering the side of her face while she slept.

"Have a seat," Lake said, pointing to the tan recliner next to the bed, facing the small flat-screen television which hung from the wall. "I'm gonna take off for a while if you don't mind."

"Not a problem. Thank you."

"Thank you, Chase. I'm sorry we had to meet under these circumstances," Lake said, placing his hand on Chase's shoulder and looking him squarely in the eyes. "Jimmy's a good man, like a son to me. This has been real hard on all of us. If there is anything, anything at all that I can do to help you out, please let me know."

"Thank you," Chase said again, "I will."

Chase sat down on the recliner, sinking his head deep into the top cushion. The television was on, tuned to GNN with the volume turned down. He watched the faces come and go on the TV screen and listened to Susan breathe. Tired and worn out from his journey, he closed his eyes and dozed off.

When Chase finally woke up a few hours later, Susan was sitting up in the bed Indian style, wearing a pink hospital robe with a white, linen sheet covering her legs. "You were snoring," she said, her somber eyes focused on him. "Haven't had much sleep lately?" she asked, with a slight smile.

"Hardly any at all," he answered.

"I know that's one of the reasons they wouldn't let me go home. They gave me some pills so I could sleep. I get out of here tomorrow. They said they were keeping me for observation. I think it was due more to the scene that I threw in the emergency room when my father brought me in last night. I was a wreck. They thought I'd lost my mind. I saw a shrink this morning. Isn't that something? I was on the way to UCLA to become a psychiatrist, and now I need one to keep me from flipping out."

"You've been through a lot, Susan. It's understandable after everything that's happened. I just want you to know how sorry I am and-"

"I know," she said. "Thank you for coming." She began crying, and Chase could tell by the way her eyes were dark and swollen that she'd been doing a lot of crying lately. "Any luck finding Jimmy?"

Chase looked up at the ceiling and sighed, the tension in his neck was giving him a pounding headache. "I've got some leads. I won't give up, you know that."

She nodded. "What about that Michael guy?"

Chase looked away. "I'm working on it, Susan. You're going to have to trust me on this because I don't have it all figured out, but this is a religious thing."

"A what?"

"Some kind of a cult."

"Are you kidding me?" she said. "Jimmy's in a cult?"

"Well, believe me, not by choice. We'll get him back. I just -"

"What? A cult? You just what? What?"

"I'm just not sure what he'll be like when we do."

"This is completely insane! I leave him on the side of the road, and he disappears with this freak and-"

"It's a lot to swallow, trust me, I know. I'll let you know if I find out more, but I thought you should know what we're dealing with here. This may take a little time. I just want you to take care of yourself and stop worrying. The good news is that he's alive. We'll get him out of this mess. Keep the faith. I need you to stay strong, to stay strong for Jimmy. Can you do that?"

"I'll try," she answered. "He's all I can ever think about. Him and the baby."

Chase looked down at the floor avoiding her eyes, as she broke down again.

"He's my life," she said, through her tears. "If he doesn't come back safe and okay, I won't be able to live with myself and what I've done to him."

"What you've done! You didn't do this to him! It happened! It's not your fault!"

"You weren't there! I kicked him out of the car in the middle of nowhere and I drove off! I just left him there. It is my fault," she cried. "Oh God, if not for me, he wouldn't be lost. He went on some rant. You know how he does, only this was about not believing in God."

Chase looked up at her, his eyes bulging. "God?" he asked.

"Yes, God!" she said. "I just didn't want to hear it anymore, so I thought I'd teach him a lesson."

Chase swallowed a deep breath, his shirt was nearly soaked from the heat, he looked up at the ceiling shaking his head. *Of all the ironies – God! They were arguing about, God!* Chase reached out and held Susan's hand tightly. "Look at me," he said. "This is not your fault! Do you understand me, Susan?"

"Yes," she answered, with tears rolling down her cheeks. "But it sure feels like it though. I just want him back, Chase. I want this nightmare to end, that's all."

"Me too," Chase said. "Me too."

"So how are you holding up?"

He reflected for a moment before speaking. "Okay, I guess. This has consumed my life. Every day I wake up hoping that we can still get through this."

"You look different," she said. "More than just tired, you look like you've changed. No offense, but that slick lawyer is gone."

Chase laughed. "Just because you're good at something doesn't make you slick."

"Oh, I'm aware of that," she said, rolling her eyes.

"Well, I guess I am different. I'm not sure who I am anymore."

"You're a good man, Chase. That's who you are."

At that moment the TV grabbed their attention when a red "Breaking News" script splashed onto the screen. Chase grabbed the remote on the night-stand and turned up the volume. The reporter, Rob Gallagher, was reporting on the strange note that was discovered at the man's apartment that authorities were investigating for suspected involvement in the LA smallpox attack.

The man was being identified as, Charles Monroe, a former chemical engineer with Dow Corning, originally from Spokane, Washington. He'd been missing for over a year after disappearing while returning from a skiing trip in Colorado. Authorities were asking anyone with information about the movements of this man, or the group that he claimed to have been a part of, *The Church of Seven Angels*, to call an 800 number at the bottom of the screen. Then the reporter read the short note aloud, as a small copy of it was posted for viewing in the top right-hand corner of the screen.

The note was handwritten in black ink, and it read:

Behold, for the glory of the Lamb is at hand! The Beast breathes fire into the new Babylon, but fear not, the bowls of wrath shall be delivered as promised in the Book of Revelations, and our Lord shall return, and all of those who have honored him shall rise with him to the seat of his throne. Prepare for the new order! When the seventh bowl comes, so then shall Armageddon!

The Church of Seven Angels

Chase sat there stunned, as if a bomb had just fallen onto his shoulders, blowing up his hopes and dreams that he could save Jimmy. He couldn't believe what he'd just witnessed. All of his worst fears about Michael and his recruits were just confirmed. Feeling Susan's stare, he tried desperately to contain the wellspring of emotions that he was feeling, not knowing if she could handle anymore than he'd already told her up to that point.

"Are you okay?" she asked. "You look like you're not feeling well. Does that story have-"

"No!" he snapped. "You know, these damn religious fanatics make me ill. That's it. I'm just a little worn out on religion right now."

"How so?"

"I've been reading the *Bible* – *Revelations* – to get a feel for these people, how they think, what their material is, and it's frightening. The *Bible* just may be one of the most dangerous weapons in the world. It's really scary what an ill-intentioned, charismatic person can accomplish with the *Bible*. Hell, even someone that starts out with good intentions can do more harm than good trying to interpret it."

"The world's gone mad, hasn't it, Chase? I find myself getting caught up in all of the negative things that are going on now, too. Since Jimmy disappeared, I think I'm trying to make sense of bad things and bad people."

"Well if you figure that one out, let me know."

"I've been having nightmares," she said. "Lots of them. You and Jimmy are in-"

"Stop!" he said. "Please, I'm having enough difficulty with

everything that's swirling around in my head. If I hear anything else right now, I think I'll just-"

"Freak out!" she said. "End up in a hospital!"

"I'm just on overload, Susan, please."

She nodded, and he slumped back into his chair. "Do you believe in God?" she asked.

Chase covered his face with his hands and wiped his forehead which was dripping profusely with sweat. "I'm not sure why it matters, but, yes, I believe in a higher power. If you want to call that higher power, God, then yes, I believe in God."

"So when you were just talking about the *Bible*, you weren't saying that you don't believe in its contents, you just don't like the way some abuse it."

Chase smiled. "You're going to get me started on a rant here. You know that, don't you?"

"Go ahead," she said. "I want to know what you think. I'm serious. I've had a lot of questions lately about how God fits into all of this stuff that happens, you know?"

"I think the *Bible* is absolutely fascinating," Chase said. "But is it all real? Maybe one day we'll all find out. Some people want to make that happen sooner, rather than later. I mean here's a compilation of writings that were all written at different times, by different writers, in a period of history where religious persecution was rampid. Part of their goal, I believe, was to write in such a way to keep the followers, following out of fear. And to do that you need more than parables, you need the *Book of Revelations*, you need judgment day!"

"Well, whatever happens to us all, Chase, I believe that we're in God's hands."

Chase lifted his shoulders up around his neck, trying to release the tension. "I don't know. This whole situation has forced me to ask myself what I believe. And the first thing I had to admit was that I don't have the answers. And I don't believe anyone alive really knows that much about what's on the other side of life or all the rules of honoring God that apply in this life."

"What do you mean?" she asked.

"If we're in God's hands, what does that mean? Has he placed his faith in us to seek wisdom, to use it in practice and to evolve into a higher level of consciousness? Because if that's the case, there's a learning curve, people are going to make mistakes on the road to enlightenment. Does Allah allow that for Muslims, deviation from the rules? Does he sanction Jihad? What about Christians? If you don't accept Christ as your savior, are you saved by merely being a good man? How do these groups have it all figured out so neatly? Faith?"

"I choose to believe that God is kind, loving and all knowing," she said.

"I do, too," Chase said. "And I believe that God loves without judgment. Judgment is man's idea, and a very simple one at that. To me heaven and hell are an experience of consciousness in life that carries on into the next life. One reaps what they sow. Sew evil, and reap evil. Sew love and good will, and reap love and good will.

"I think that a lot of organized religions prey on fears," he continued. "They want their followers to accept their doctrines as supplying the answers, and they chastise those who don't as non-believers like that is a sin. And they believe that it is. What if they're wrong? They pass judgment on others, and that seems very ungodly to me. What are the answers? If God is truly the Supreme Being, then God has all of the answers. Why should God pass harsh judgment on those who do not?

"Which group should we follow?" he asked. "Which has proof that they are right? I can't find dinosaurs in the *Bible*. Why did God create the T-Rex before man? How did the writers in the *Bible*, with all of their knowledge of God's will, know so little else about this world, still believing it was flat? Through time, our world has evolved from flat to round, yet religion has not evolved from the *Bible*. If it has led to enlightenment of man, then why is there such chaos and conflict in the world?

Chase took a deep breath and then continued. "I question why so many people think they are saved by simply accepting Christ as their savior, and then attending church on Sundays, all the while passing judgment on others in their day to day lives. Why is it that so many people have yet to discover that believing in God is not reserved for a special few in a certain place or time?

"I think it's how you treat other human beings, how you respect our world and the people in it. I refuse to believe that a wise, all-knowing God plays favorites among humankind, which is still ignorant in comparison to the enlightenment of God. I guess some would say, if I'm wrong, I'll burn in hell. What kind of God would burn me in hell for being a good person? When there are hundreds of religions all claiming to have the secret handshake, how can we be held accountable to that standard? Aren't we all children of God? We didn't create ourselves.

"Or, is there only a right way and a wrong way to believe in God, and those on the wrong path, out of the know, are simply damned? I wouldn't want the weight of mankind resting on my shoulders. I don't claim to know the way. I'm just trying to be the best I can be in a very complicated world."

"I'm a devout Catholic," Susan said. "I was raised that way, and until now, this experience, I've never tried to see any other way than what I was taught. You make some very good points. I'm like you though. I wouldn't want to have to save the souls from the fire."

Chase stood from his chair. "Why did you say that?"

"Say what?"

"You said something about saving souls from the fire."

"I don't know," she answered. "Fire has been on my mind lately. I've had a lot of dreams about-"

Chased raised his arm. "Forget it," he said. "Look, I've really had it, Susan. I should get going."

"Okay," she said, "go get some rest, Chase. You look awful."

"Thanks."

"You know what I mean."

He reached down and gave her a hug good-bye. "Take care of yourself, Susan," he said.

"You too, Chase."

He began walking to the door. "Hey," she called out, stopping him, "if it comes to saving souls, choose Jimmy's."

Chase couldn't believe his ears, he stood there not sure whether to respond or just walk out the door. Then finally he turned and looked at her squarely in the eyes. "Of course," he said, "he's my brother."

CHAPTER 32

America adored Jane. She was everywhere! The cover of Newsweek, Time, U.S. News; magazines and periodicals all over the world covered her every move. A reporter no more, she was now the story. Alongside Richard Novak, she'd thrown herself right into the center of the universe where the lights are brightest and scrutiny is always heightened. The religious right had dragged all of her skeletons into the streets and made them public knowledge. She'd slept around in college. She'd been with married men. Her father was a small town preacher, king of fire and brimstone preaching, considered somewhat of a fanatical lunatic by his neighbors. But none of these things seemed to matter to the American people; she was almost omnipresent, untouchable. Her relationship to the people was growing, and she had embraced her role in the campaign.

The sun began going down in the horizon over the dark ocean, sending an orange glowing light that seemed to illuminate everything in its path with a sparkle of gold. Jane sipped her wine, having just made a campaign speech to the students at UC Santa Barbara. She was staying in a beach estate owned by Ted Mitchell. She enjoyed the view and her Bordeaux as she sat outside on the large open veranda, reviewing the itinerary for her next day's scheduled campaign stops.

The campaign trail was burning hot, giving her collection of high heels a workout. She'd already been to 20 states in a blazing two week stretch. Ted was in Florida with Richard. The plan at this point was simple: hit the contested states hard in a late push to seal up enough electors early on election night. She was tired and exhausted, and she longed for the freedom to just live and enjoy the simple pleasures. But, she also longed for power. And she knew how to use all of her skills to get what she wanted. After all, as Richard was fond of saying, "Every vote counts in an election year." She was simply doing her best to weather the campaign challenges so as to not come off like an absolute rookie.

Ted's maid, Anita, escorted young Norm Stewart, the sterling reporter from the LA Times out to the patio table where Jane was seated. She was accustomed to giving several interviews a week, so she didn't even prepare anymore.

Jane stood to greet the tall man in the blue coat and silk green tie. "Sorry to push this thing back so late," she said, "but it's been a busy evening."

"No problem," he said. "I came in early and took in your speech."

"What'd you think?"

"It was good."

"Just good?"

"Hey, I'm trying to remain unbiased here," he said, smiling.

"Oh screw that," she said. "When you leave, you'll be on my team. One vote at a time – take no prisoners."

He laughed, shaking his head.

"Have you eaten," she asked.

He nodded. "I stopped and had some dinner and some wine. I love the wine in this area."

"Me too. Ted has a really nice collection, can I offer you something?"

"Just whatever you're having."

Jane reached for the intercom button behind where she was sitting on the stucco wall.

"Can I help you, Ms. Tierney?"

"Anita, please bring Mr. Stewart a glass of the Bordeaux I'm drinking."

"Certainly, Madam, be right out."

Jane turned to Norm. "If I get you drunk will you handle me with kid gloves in this interview?"

He smiled. "You're a reporter, you know what to expect."

She peered deep into his eyes. "Exactly, it's so boring talking about myself – be gentle, won't you?"

"This shouldn't be too painful," he said.

"Pain is good sometimes," she said, smiling.

"I'm just here as an unbiased reporter, to get the story," he stammered.

"The story is a hot one," she said. "Think you can handle it?"

She removed her feet from her heels and began tracing up his legs underneath the table.

"It'll be very presidential," he stammered. "I mean, vice-presidential. The article."

"Sure," she answered. "Sure." She just looked at him smiling, as she backed away for a moment to let the poor fellow catch his breath. There was nothing he could do. He was just prey.

"Well let's talk about your early years. Did you grow up wanting to be in politics?"

"No!" she said. "Oh, God no! I grew up wanting to be a reporter, like you. Politics, from this perspective of being a politician is still very new to me. I think that's why people connect with me so well. I'm not an insider. I'm normal. My family has never produced a politician."

"What did your parents do?"

"Well, my mother is deceased. She died when I was born so I never knew her. My father raised me. He's a good man, but it was tough. I always had work to do around the house since my mother was gone, and that was a lot. My father was a farmer by day and a fire and brimstone preacher by night."

"A preacher?"

"That's right."

"Wow, so what was that like growing up with a preacher?"

"Well, I didn't know any different so I just went with it. He didn't preach so much to me. He knew he didn't have to. It was the other way around. I preached more to him about religion and things. I kept him in line. He thought he had all the answers, until he talked to me."

Norm laughed. "So who won those battles?" he asked.

"I did, of course," she smiled.

"And how'd you do in school?"

"I was class president in high school, and valedictorian. I set the curve. I was always a good student. My father always knew I'd do something special."

"Well, running for vice president is certainly that."

"Sure, but I can do more than that."

"And what's that?"

"Win! Richard Novak and I are going to win this election."

"And then what, take over the world?"

She smiled. "We'll see," she said. "Right now we're just concentrating on one vote at a time."

"So what kind of a preacher was your father? Baptist or -"

"He was somewhat nondenominational," she interrupted. "A hell cat, ya know? Spirited. Revelations was his focus and he took it very seriously."

Norm smiled wide.

Jane slid off her heels again under the table and started massaging his leg with her foot. "Yeah, you can laugh," she said. "A lot of people thought my old man was a nut! He was a ranter and a raver! What can I say? He never bothered me one bit. He was my protector. He kept me safe. Sure, he was intense at times, but I always had my own take on things and he never misunderstood my purpose."

"Your purpose?"

"Let's just say that he knew who I was. He respected me for who and what I am, and I respected him for who he was. It was mutual, and still is."

"Care to elaborate on that?"

"Not really. I don't think that everyone needs to know me like my father knows me. The past is over. People need to know who I am, and I understand that, but it takes time. And I promise in time, everyone will know who I am, but in time."

"What about Mr. Novak – have you clashed with him over religion, given your background?"

"You don't really know much about my religion."

"True," he said, "but have you -"

"No," she answered, sharply. "I respect his views. His atheism is not a concern of mine."

"It doesn't conflict with your views?"

"Maybe. Maybe not. What difference would it make? We're all different with different backgrounds. Some are from Heaven. Some are from Hell. Some are in between, some are indifferent and some just don't have a clue that there's a difference."

"What do you mean?"

"Oh God, was I ranting. I'm sorry, I'm tired." Her foot now reached the zone ordinarily reserved for his wife.

He was silent for a moment.

"What do you believe," she asked. "Do you believe in God?"

His eyes were closed now as he settled into the massage.

"I do," he said, softly, "but it's so easy to get lost."

Jane leaned up to his ear. "How 'bout," she said, "we go inside and fill the tub with wine and lose our souls together for a spell? Does that sound good to you?"

With that he submitted to her seduction and they disappeared into the house. Hours later, he emerged from the house a changed man. Driving down Pacific Coast Highway along the coastline, he wondered what to tell his wife about the trails of markings on his back from Jane's fingernails. The thoughts left him feeling shallow and empty, damned by his lack of will to walk away from Jane, he now felt miserable. The story was due for submission in just a few hours and he was hopelessly lost in his own despair. *Goddamn whore! Shit, what have I done! What have I done!*

CHAPTER 33

The holidays were hard on Susan, she hadn't heard from Chase in several weeks and she was worried. Chase sounded despondent and depressed the last few times she'd spoken to him. He was so obsessed with finding Jimmy that he'd begun to fall into a deep despair. Susan had known Chase to be driven, no matter what he'd done in life. Jimmy had always said that Chase would lose himself in it to the point of forgetting about everyone and anything else. But this was different. This thing had the power to destroy him completely.

While Susan tried to lay low and think positive and remain hopeful about Jimmy, Chase was immersing himself into a new world. He spent several weeks at the pueblo with Billy and was learning a lot about their people and their struggles from Red Hawk and Billy. Billy and Chase were bonded by their experiences searching for Jimmy, and they'd developed a strong friendship that was keeping them going.

Chase had also been on Larry King Live, Good Morning America and all the cable shows. He'd made Jimmy's disappearance a national story without ever once mentioning Michael or connecting him to the angels. His strategy was to try not to get Jimmy in trouble with the law, and even though he knew that was a huge risk, he wanted to keep Jimmy from doing anything else to ruin his life. Chase figured that with Jimmy's face recognizable, Michael would be less inclined to get Jimmy to attempt a public crime. Chase was torn, he just didn't want to find Jimmy, but he wanted to be able to save him from the disgrace and backlash of being connected to Michael. He was thinking like a lawyer, building Jimmy's case in the best way that he knew how.

Still the months and days passed and eventually Jimmy's disappearance became old news with the networks. The search for Jimmy was a long and winding road of loose ends and bad leads. It had been a long and difficult year for Chase and Susan. The nation too had suffered. The small-pox attack that rocked Los Angeles had shaken the country from its moorings and launched a period of introspection the likes that the world had never seen.

Susan remained living with her father in Tucson, and received periodic updates from Chase, who was still out there on the trail of Michael and the angels, giving every ounce of his energy to find his brother. He was dejected, and he had become a man obsessed, but it didn't matter anymore, he wasn't about to give up looking for his brother. He would keep looking until he found him. And if he didn't find him, he'd die trying to find him. There was no other way for him now. This was his life.

CHAPTER 34

FEBRUARY, 2008 – THE ELECTION STORM BREWS

Months had passed since the death of Mayor Roberto Gonzalez in the smallpox attack in Los Angeles, but the holy war that it began was beginning to take center stage in America. With the power of a thunderous explosion, the focus of the 2008 presidential election in the United States had shifted to terrorism and religious fanaticism.

Rising like an inferno through the eye of the storm was no other than, Richard Novak, the candidate of the newly formed party of Socrateans, a party named for those who seek enlightenment through knowledge, wisdom, science and the advancement of technology. Richard was fast becoming an American Icon. The whole world was watching with great interest as America became embattled in a great political debate that threatened to explode into a revolution of the likes that the modern world had ever witnessed.

Richard wanted to lead the revolution and was doing everything in his power to promote the idea that if America wanted a better world then the U.S. needed to finally put religion into its proper perspective. He provoked outrage and hatred from many religious fundamentalists, and honest curiosity from others who were undecided on what to make of his politics and orthodox, or lack of one, and then, of course, there were those who supported him with a fervor that seemed to catch everyone, religious or not, off-guard.

The timing of the smallpox attack had helped launch his campaign. And, Ted Mitchell, brilliantly seized control of the airwaves with ads that brought the issues of religious fanaticism and technology to the forefront of discussion in every American household. The ads were everywhere, on billboards, on the sides of public transportation, on TV, on the radio, anywhere and everywhere where they could reach the voters.

Richard Novak, dubbed the "Enlightened One" by his supporters, said it was his, "Personal mission to take away the pain and bloodshed brought to the world by religious fanatics." With his message, he'd caught the world by surprise. The Republicans and the Democrats had dismissed him. And yet there he was everywhere they turned, stealing the headlines and dominating the press' attention. For some reason, people found him fascinating. There was a charm and an intellectual substance to his mantra that made him admirable to Americans who seemed tired of being preached to by their politicians that, "God is on our side."

Richard's message, over and over, was that he was not advocating religious fanaticism, and that he was not saying that religion was all bad, but he believed that it was religious intolerance that causes terrorism, wars, genocide, and that all religions and governments have been guilty of allowing the intolerant fundamentalists to continually wreak havoc on enlightenment and the promotion of modern society. At the heart of his message was the complete separation of church and state, not just in America, but he made it clear that America, should promote the idea, not of theocracy that the fundamentalist Christians secretly desired, but of democracy, with at its core, true separation of church and state. He argued that government needs moral men, not necessarily Christians or Muslims, or any other creed, but moral individuals to lead its citizens consistent with moral laws that promote prosperity and enlightenment for all.

Most organized religions denounced Richard Novak for focusing on religion as being responsible for terrorism. The Muslims had marched and protested during his speeches and political rallies. The Christians, infuriated about the accusations now coming forth that the smallpox attack may have come from one of their own radical fundamentalists, also marched and protested throughout the campaign stops of Richard

Novak and Jane Tierney. And the media loved every minute of it because it all made for a fireball of a story.

Richard publicly declared the smallpox terrorist act as a religious crime in the vein of 9/11, where fanatics, who themselves are religiously intolerant seek to get their message out by killing innocent people. His campaign ads posed the questions, "Can religion bring the world peace?" and, "Is religion the great plague of modern society?" Richard, for his part, claimed he knew the answers and spent millions upon millions of his dollars on television and radio ads, flooding the airwaves across America, saying that not only was fanatical religion the great plague of modern society, but vehemently setting forth the proposition that the great religions of the world, all of them, not one in particular, were preventing the enlightenment of the world by allowing fanatics to thrive. While he advocated religious tolerance, he also argued that religion was like a disease, slowing the advancement of modern technology and science, and that in the end religion could be the world's great undoing. "The world is threatened by terrorists," he said in one ad, "who want to use the world's technology to destroy modern society for it is their delusion that they will advance their position with their God or Allah in the next life."

In another prominent ad, Richard contended that, "But for religion there would be no terrorism." The Republican incumbent, President Barton, and his supporters were beside themselves and had even actually cooperated with the Democrats to jointly fund and launch a series of attack ads which blasted Richard Novak as a man without faith and as a man whose vision of America and the world would lead modern society not to enlightenment, but to destruction and anarchy. The ads, however, backfired and actually increased the attention paid to Novak.

While the two politically entrenched parties wanted to overlook Novak, they were instead being forced to focus on him. The Gallup polls actually had Richard Novak winning the election, as voters split 51% for Novak, while the Republican incumbent President Barton garnered 36%, and the Democrat, Samuel Jacobson logged in with 13%. So the stage was set early in 2008 – Richard Novak, had masterfully turned the election into a discussion of all of the issues that he wanted to talk about. And he was not only out front early leading the race, but he was taking the old two party system by storm. He had raised a national and world debate about the place of religion in modern society, and everyone had an opinion, and everyone was listening.

CHAPTER 35

OCTOBER 19, 2008 – THE PRESIDENTIAL DEBATE

The months had flown by, and ever since the small pox attacks in LA, Richard Novak's campaign had been riding high in America. By all accounts it had been a breakout year for Novak and his candidacy for the highest office in the land was going full steam.

With the presidential debate at hand, the public wanted to hear more from him and the candidates. They wanted insight and perspective as to the place and the effect of religion in the present and future of modern society, at least as told from the perspective of the three candidates from the United States running for president in the election of 2008.

The citizens of the U.S. wanted the debate, needed the debate and in the ensuing days leading up to the debate, had demanded it as their right. It was as if they truly expected the debate to bring them freedom from their fears, that the problems of the world could be solved, that the great debate would be a salve in a time of fear and that all would come away saved.

While most politicians wanted the religious issues to subside, Novak's campaign, masterminded by Ted Mitchell, had made religion the number one issue. Richard himself had argued that the terrorists of religion would not stop and would not be satisfied until they brought Armageddon to the world. And frankly, even moderate Muslims, Christians, and peoples of all faiths, believed that if there was even a kernel of truth to that proposition, given the nuclear technology of mankind, that they should at least hear what the candidates had to say about the issue that was now the thorn of not just the election, but as Richard Novak noted, modernization and modern society throughout the world.

Due to major security concerns after the smallpox attack, the usual public format for the presidential debates had been scrapped, and there was now only going to be one debate that would be limited to a live broadcast, and would take place at the U.S. Capitol building on Capitol Hill under heavy security in the Old Senate Chamber.

The stakes of the debate were high. The presidency was at stake, as well as the confidence of the American people, not to mention the rest of the world.

Darkness began to set in as Richard's motorcade passed through the first of several armed blockades leading up to the Capitol. He peered out the window at the large, heavily armed contingent of soldiers and FBI lining the streets. He wondered if the soldiers and agents understood that their new leader had arrived. He felt the power of the moment stirring deep inside of him as he engulfed the view. Even in the twilight, the U.S. Capitol building in Washington, D.C., stood boldly as an architectural achievement. Combining Roman and Greek styles, from any side, the grandly lit dome was omnipotent, evoking images of Rome during the height of the Roman Empire.

The Capitol stood at the eastern end of the National Mall, a monument to free government and a testament to the wealth and grandiose idealism of the nation's founding fathers. First construction began in 1793, and through that time the building had seen many changes, and many legends of politics' past had walked through its majestic Rotunda and filled its Senate and House floors with free speech and democratic debate.

In one sense, Richard relished the idea of this turning point in American history, transpiring in that same place where others had come in critical times to take on the establishment. In the same manner as former President Abraham Lincoln had once done, then as the unabashed lone Whig Party representative from Illinois. Richard understood what it meant to take on the establishment, and he also understood the enormous power of the American government. The United States, in its short history, had achieved greatness and wealth, but it had also survived through many wars, including the War of 1812, when British troops took hold of D. C., and set fire to the Capitol on August 24, 1814. Still, America survived only to build the Capitol bigger and stronger.

Richard Novak, blanketed by secret service agents, dashed quickly through the rotunda, where like a spiritual presence hovering, he could feel the power of the American government. Richard wanted that power to be his alone. He wanted to take hold of the American government and to guide it into the new age of technology as the leader of the free world, making it the grandest empire of all time. The Dog Star had arrived, this was his destiny, and no one could stop him now.

Richard charged into the camera lights in the small, but grand Old Senate Chamber ready to take on the two party system. Seeing himself as the champion of change, long desired and desperately needed change, for the American people, the American government, and the world, he strode confidently, with purpose. He felt prepared, having spent numerous days, mock-debating with all of the greatest political minds his money could buy. In many ways he knew that the debate would either make or break his campaign. He knew the world was watching. He knew the American voters wanted to know if he was the real deal or if he was another fade-out new guy that was more money and talk than ideas. The public wanted to know whether he was truly an enlightened man, one who could help bring peace to the world or whether he was just a rich madman that was only making things worse with his attacks on religion, as the Democrats and Republicans had asserted in their multi-million dollar anti-Novak offensive.

The Old Senate Chamber is typically a tourist attraction, a place where visitors come to see where some of America's greatest orators, such as Henry Clay and Daniel Webster, gave their famous speeches on slavery in the 1800s, leading up to the Civil War. What they find is an elegant, stately room that boasts early American furnishings and a stunning portrait of George Washington. They also find a room that is small in stature, and grand in design, much like the roots of the small nation whose 32 Senators came there long ago to fight for their constituents and debated at length and often for days on the best interests of the Union.

The moderator of the debate, the elder and highly regarded Norm Ebert, a longtime anchor with the Independent Broadcasting Service, made his way over to Richard and shook his hand firmly and then led him over to the podium on the left side of the room. President Barton and Samuel Jacobson were already there. The three briefly exchanged handshakes and warm greetings, and then took their places behind their respective podiums which were placed in a semi-circle about ten feet apart in front of the old vice president's desk and shrouded by the red drapery back-drop, looking out toward the mahogany lift-top desks.

The room was cool, and Richard could smell foul cologne lingering in the air. Richard mused to himself that the cheap cologne he smelt must have belonged to President Barton, and for a moment he snickered to himself and wondered how the President would react if he asked him if it was his, "Brute-Cologne that he smelled."

Richard felt relaxed. He'd been waiting for this moment his whole life and he wondered if the world would praise him or lynch him after the camera lights finally shut down. There was no turning back, he was on a collision course with his destiny and he knew the great storm was only getting started. He took a deep breath and looked up at the balcony. The dance of the serpents was soon to begin, and Richard saw himself as the King Cobra, guided by the brightest star in the northern sky, born for greatness and destined to win the ceremonial dance of candidates.

After a few moments the clock finally hit 9 PM, and Norm Ebert began the show by going through the rules for the debate. All of it was negotiated and agreed to by the candidates prior to the debates and most of it was fairly standard. The final format chosen was simple: Norm Ebert, as the moderator would ask direct questions to each candidate, allowing each a response time of two minutes, and when he felt it was necessary, at his discretion he would allow for a 30 second rebuttal. The candidates were not allowed to address questions to each other, and Norm Ebert, as moderator, chose the questions that were meant to be an honest attempt to address the pertinent issues of the campaign.

The first question went to President Barton. "Mr. President, your administration has recently taken some heat in campaign ads by Mr. Novak's newly formed Socratean party for allowing your faith and religion to dictate how you rule and lead the nation. They say that your constant insistence that, "God is on our side in the war on terrorism," has done nothing but add fuel to the terrorists, who also believe that God, Allah is on their side. How do you reconcile, Mr. President, the fact that when we present our position and follow it with our own statement that, "God is on our side," that we may be making this exactly what the terrorists want – a holy war, where the battlefield is all over the world and the soldiers are all fighting in the name of God!"

"Well," President Barton, shot back, stiffening at the podium. "Would you suggest that God is on the terrorist's side? Mr. Ebert, the American people understand that evil lies in the hands and cold hearts of the monsters out there that relentlessly attack the innocents of the free world in their jihad. These people are evil at their core, and we must defeat them. Yes, I am a religious man, and I believe in my heart that terrorists are the face of evil, and I guess if the face of evil lies somewhere else then we'll fight it wherever it lies because this is America, and we do not give up on freedom and we don't let hooligans and thugs tell us how to live. I pray for peace everyday! And I also pray for victory against the terrorists, and so help me God we will get our victory."

"Mr. Novak, I see that you are chomping at the bit over there. Would you like to respond to the question?"

Richard took a quick drink of water and flashed a sheepish grin. "I most certainly would, Mr. Ebert, Thank you. But First, I want to thank the American people for allowing me to attend this most important debate for the nation's highest office."

President Barton slumped a little at the knees as Richard spoke, realizing that in his haste to answer the question, he had not spoken the traditional courtesies to the people watching the debate. *Damn!*

"I do not take lightly this invitation," Richard continued, "for as you well know the President and Mr. Jacobson didn't want me to be here. They didn't want you to hear my voice, even though my campaign has gotten on the ballot in every state, including some landmark legal battles to get it done. Still, they didn't want me here. And why not? Because when God is on your side, there is no need for the voice of reason and logic!"

Richard's dark eye's burned with fire as he spoke. "Hear me now as that voice, the voice that they did not want you to hear. I am the voice that says we can fight the war on terrorism but we can never win it the way that we are now fighting it!

"Now, I recognize the futility of that statement because we cannot lay down our arms or we will surely suffer a heavy defeat. But we cannot win such a war where the enemy is born anew every day in cities all over the world, lifted fresh from the womb into their mother's and father's arms. The mothers and fathers that hate America, that hate the country whose children grow up rich in a foreign and unfamiliar culture and who also claim to have God on their side. These terrorists, the mothers and fathers of even more terrorists have nothing to live for, and yet the promise of the afterlife offers them the riches of the universe.

"So, why wouldn't they fight to get there? What do they have here to make life more than a painful passing to the next? If we want to fight terrorism we need to first recognize that the countries that are producing and supporting terrorists are those that keep all of the wealth, mostly from oil, in the hands of the ruling elite. They do this at the expense of their people. They do this while accepting the propaganda that is preached about the evil of America and Western society. As long as their people are fighting the evil of America and Israel and the Western world, they aren't trying to overthrow the very governments that are holding them down.

"These people, the terrorists, are starving for recognition. And they don't know the power of democracy; they only know the power of religion. It fills their void for power. It is the vacuum used by these countries and terrorists to control their societies, or to at least point their weapons at the Westerners. We need to lead the world in helping us fight the economic crisis that is creating these fanatics. The terrorists claim to fight in the name of Allah, and what they are really saying is I am just as worthy as you to the riches and the love of God. And their hope is that by killing the enemy they will benefit in their next life.

This is the most desperate, depraved kind of hope that there is among humankind. And that is how bad this crisis has now become.

"But they are wrong and they are ignorant. Their leaders want them that way – those same wealthy elite that spend their holidays in Europe and the U.S. buying thoroughbreds and getting educated. And we have not learned that if you fight hate with hate, surely you will only sow hate, not end it. That's all they have done with their murderous attacks, and that's all we've done with our tanks, and our guns and our bombs. We have sewn hate and it has grown into a strong back-draft that is now a cancer to the free world, sucking us into their world instead of enlightening them to ours.

"I beg you all, please look closely into your hearts and you will see that this is not like other wars before it! This war is not for land! This war is not for wealth! This war is for equality, whether it be in the eyes of God or in the eyes of the world. People want to be acknowledged.

"And the rich, here and abroad, all over the world want to turn their eyes away from the real problems because they don't want to share what they have. If you want real leadership in this war to fight the root causes of this epidemic, which is more about economics and the desperate starvation for power and recognition, than God, then elect me, and we can work together to apply reason and logic to this madness that has pervaded the world for centuries. I will not say that, "God is on our side," because I do not believe any loving God would take sides against people, who have not only lost their way, but were born in darkness from the beginning. We should focus on bringing them into the light! Let all people be on each other's side, and then all sides will cease to exist!

"What I am saying is that we need to bring our brothers and sisters in the Middle East into the fold. We must use our might, reasonably and logically, to encourage their leaders to change from within and to open their societies to freedom, technology and development, and to share their wealth.

"The problem with Islam is not with the religion, but with those who would turn it into a means to achieve evil and to control people, rather than to liberate them with freedom and peace. If you want to control people, then religion has proven time and time again to be the best means for achieving control, it's even better than military might. However, if you want to free people and to liberate societies and to bring them into the modern world, then you do not conquer them with military might or religion, you conquer them with your culture. And if the people do not desire your culture, then you can never conquer them, not even if you achieve a military victory.

"And what if the leadership in the Middle East will not work with us? What if they say we don't want what you have to offer? Do we invade them when they send out terrorists to attack us? We will certainly defend ourselves, but how do we win the peace? We must win it with our culture! We can never win the peace, uninvited in a foreign land with guns alone! We can sanction them, which we must! We can cut their governments off, if they won't cooperate, which we must! But the only way that we can win the propaganda war is with action! We can bring them exposure to who we are, our culture, by dropping the people food, clothes, medical supplies, water, books, movies, and giving them the supplies they need to survive.

"In the end, if we are well intentioned, we can win the hearts of the majority of the people. But if they want democracy, we can help them fight for it, but we cannot, in my opinion, force it upon these countries militarily. We've had our own bloody revolution, and our own bloody civil war. Freedom must be born from the struggle within! We cannot bring them freedom unless they want it enough to fight for it themselves against the real enemy! Please, for more on my position and my plan on transforming the Middle East into a modern region of the world, please check out www.RichardNovak.com. But, don't be naïve – these are long term plans, very long term. We cannot bring peace to this region and end terrorism over night, but in the long run it can be done if we are willing to share more than our military might."

"Thank you, Mr. Novak. Mr. Jacobson, you look like you have something to add on this issue, I'll allow you two minutes as well."

"Thank you, Mr. Ebert," Samuel Jacobson said. "I also want to thank the American people and the audience around the world for tuning into this debate. And I would like to respond to Mr. Novak directly. My campaign has never challenged your attendance at these debates as you are well aware. It was the Republicans who did not want you here. I believe in a debate that shares all views.

"However, I must admit that I do not understand yours. You talk of terrorism as if it can be fixed with a few billion dollars and some loafs of bread, and that is simply not the case. If we cannot win the war on terrorism by killing and catching the bad guys and bringing them to justice, then we can never bring peace to the world. I believe that winning the fight is possible, and we must strive for a military victory! We must win! Our allies in Israel are surrounded by enemies in the Middle East and they have not fallen-

"Yes, and nor are they free!" Novak interrupted.

"Freedom is relative!" Jacobson shot back, looking squarely at Novak. "Israel is a democracy; they live and fight for peace and freedom for their people!"

"Yes, and maybe when they die," Novak said, "peace will be theirs! But in this world, they live in a war zone where there will never be a lasting peace as long as they seek a military victory! You can conquer the world with culture and technology, but not with force!"

"I strongly disagree, Mr. Novak, and frankly although your brand of politics may sound brash and new, I find it quite scary and I hope the American people are paying close attention to you."

Richard smiled warmly. "Yes, and I hope that the people will see that what we have here are two parties who no longer have any solutions and-"

"Mr. Novak, I must interrupt you, and I must remind each of the candidates that this debate is to be led by me, and that I will ask the questions and direct them to each candidate. My, gentleman, you three are like a herd of bulls! I must do my service to the American people and rein you in so that we can have a fair, orderly and focused debate."

The candidates laughed and chuckled.

Then the lights suddenly flickered inside the Old Senate Chamber, and the cameramen struggled to hold onto their cameras as the walls shook slightly. The loud boom echoed from outside somewhere in the city. The Secret Service scurried about the back of the room on walkie talkies and cell phones, desperately seeking an explanation from outside. The moderator went to a quick commercial and at that moment a Secret Service agent rushed to the podium, whispering in the moderator's ears a message that caused his face to shrink in horror.

All in the room could feel the tension, knowing that something terrible had just taken place.

The candidates were ushered out of the corridors of the Old Senate Chambers surrounded by the Secret Service. In the Chaos, President Barton, a few feet away from Richard, shot him a quirky smile. "Mr. Novak," he said. "Can you feel the terror? The American people can feel it, and they won't elect a man that says we cannot win this war! Nor will they elect a man who does not believe in God!"

"Thank you, Mr. President, for expressing your fear," Richard said.

The president smirked, and then said, "And what do you fear, Mr. Novak?"

Richard's dark eyes narrowed in on the presidents'. "I fear men who rage holy wars and pray for victory, claiming God is on their side! That's what I fear!"

"Maybe you just fear that God is not on your side, Mr. Novak?"

Richard smiled. "God is the myth of fools, and the tool of people like you to hold power over the weak. I intend to expose you. I shall bring them the light of wisdom to the world – not God!"

"You just sound bound for hell to me," President Barton said. "As a Christian I think-"

"Hitler was once a Christian, too," Richard interrupted. "It's just a word. How you are, how you act – that's what separates men and defines them!"

President Barton couldn't believe his ears, he stared blankly back at Richard for a moment, completely stunned, before he was whisked away down a shiny corridor in the opposite direction.

CHAPTER 36

GNN.com

BREAKING NEWS

Bomb Explodes on Metrobus
in D.C. Kills 17; Presidential
Debate Canceled Amid Security
Concerns

Tuesday, October 19, 2008 Posted 11:00 PM EDT

WASHINGTON, D.C. (GNN) – Early this evening
at approximately 9:45 PM, and in the midst of the live
presidential debate being televised all over the world, a
loud explosion shook D.C. and the nation. In an instant,
the debate that was touching upon the social issues that are
dividing our country was silenced, as the candidates were
led under heavy security from the Old Senate Chamber in
the U.S. Capitol to unknown locations for their safety.

The explosion took place inside a Metrobus in downtown Washington, D.C., near the National Academy of Sciences building on Constitution Avenue. All passengers riding inside the Metrobus were killed. In the ensuing aftermath of the explosion, the investigators, including the FBI, the Secret Service, and the CIA, along with local law enforcement officials continue to work in a multi-coordinated effort, sifting through the rubble and the charred remains of its 17 victims searching for answers to the madness.

It is too early to determine if there are any suspects, but one survivor who apparently was let off the bus a block before the explosion took place described one of the passengers, "as a nervous, young Arab man," with a briefcase sitting on his lap. We must caution that this witness was quickly swept away by investigators. Officially, at this time, no one individual or group has claimed responsibility for the attack.

Stay tuned to GNN. As this story develops, we will keep you posted.

═══ CHAPTER 37 ═══

LATE OCTOBER, 2008

In a dark warehouse in Arlington, Virginia, shadows danced mysteriously in the flickering light of a raging fire that burned from an open hearth in the corner of a large, open room. The air was crisp and cold, the fire providing the only heat on that dark morning. A refrigerator hummed in the opposite corner of the room, and three black suitcases sat on top of a stainless-steel table across from a makeshift laboratory.

In the center of the large room, the archangel Michael, with his willowy locks and electrifying presence, was holding the last ceremony for his angels. The angels sat on the floor gathered around him in a small circle, as he held court. They were all there. And oh how they loved Michael. He was so beautiful, so full of God's love. They simply found him mesmerizing, and his glowing enthusiasm for the Lord's work was contagious just like the smell of sweet tulips in the spring.

The time had come for Gabriel to accept the brand of God. He had waited ever so patiently for this moment. Michael had promised him special things were to come, and he was so right. Gabriel was to be the deliverer of God's message, the angel of angels, in a world that had so few. Gabriel was chosen, as they all had been. He was honored to be in Michael's presence, and ready to serve the Lamb.

The number of the Lord is seven, and the seal of God is a crest of angels encircled by crossing sevens and emblazoned in a sun of light.

The brand, designed by the archangel Michael, was called the *Circle of the Lamb*. All of the angels had accepted the brand of the Lamb. The brand is given to them in what is known as the *Ceremony of Passage*. The ceremony frees them from the pain of this world, where although they retain their physical bodies, their minds are freed to roam on the other side. They go to the place where the angels sing songs of resurrection and the children of days past play in the reigning sunlight of the Lord.

Gabriel was ushered to the center of the circle by Michael.

Only in dreams could Gabriel recall his past life. Even then it was only flashes, for most of it was buried so deep into his psyche that when he woke he actually believed that he had dreamed about another man, not himself, but a lonely man who longed for something in his heart that he was never able to find. He felt the deepest sorrow for that man. The dreams only strengthened his unity with the Lamb.

Gabriel bent over the wooden stool and Michael pulled the white linen cloak up and over his opaque shoulders. Michael then walked to the fire, pulling the scorching brand from its flames.

Then the chant began, "Behold the glory of the Lamb! Behold the glory of the Lamb!"

Then Michael put the scolding brand to Gabriel's back, and Gabriel's finger nails sank into the wood of the chair as he screamed from the bowls of his soul, as if molten lava had just been poured onto his skin and he was melting away. The chant of the angels grew louder, almost to a shout, filling the room, as Gabriel writhed with pain. Filled with the love of the Lamb, Gabriel cried violently, and then Michael lowered the white cloak over his freshly sealed back. His flesh was burned and the smell of his charred skin filled the room, but so did the love of the Lamb.

Michael's eyes glowed intensely like an inferno as he picked up the *Bible* that had been sitting on the small wooden table next to the burning fire. The wooden floor creaked as he walked back to the angels, taking center stage once again, he commanded their attention.

"It is written here in this great book, the prophecy which now unfolds!" he said. "We have been chosen for this task to bring to the children of God their reward by separating them now from those who worship the Beast. Now let me read to you from the great book, the promise of God." He paused and cleared his throat and then spoke out with feverish enthusiasm. *"And I heard a voice from the sanctuary shouting to the seven angels, 'Go and empty the seven bowls of God's anger over the Earth!'"*

Michael locked onto the eyes of each and every angel and smiled upon them. They were so lovely and so deserving of God's praise, and so ready for his word. *"The first angel went and emptied his bowl over the Earth ... there came disgusting and virulent sores."* Michael's bright eyes beamed, and he continued. "I think we now know my angels that this prophecy has come true, and that the sores are killing many, the many who have fornicated with the Beast and swallowed his vile.

"And we are told, *'The second angel emptied his bowl over the sea, and it turned to blood, like the blood of a corpse, and every living creature in the sea died. The second angel emptied his bowl into the rivers and water springs and they turned to blood. Then I heard the angel of water say, "You are the holy He-Is-and-He-Was, the Just One, and this is a just punishment: they spilled the blood of the saints and the prophets, and blood is what you have given them to drink; it is what they deserve." And I heard the altar itself say, "Truly, Lord God Almighty, the punishments you give are true and just." The fourth angel emptied his bowl over the sun and it was made to scorch people with its flames; but though people were scorched by the fierce heat of it, they cursed the name of God who had the power to cause such plagues, and they would not repent and praise him. The fifth angel emptied his bowl over the throne of the beast and its whole empire was plunged into darkness. Men were biting their tongues for pain, but instead of repenting for what they had done, they cursed the God of heaven because of their pains and sores. The sixth angel emptied his bowl over the great river....*"

"In *Revelations*," Michael spoke, "They say the great river is Euphrates, but we now understand that all of these prophecies, Armageddon, and the plagues all take place in a world far removed from the world of the times in which this prophecy was written. God has brought to me the gift and the power of his voice, and the ability to interpret this prophecy for us, the angels of revelation." He paused just for a moment and they all looked upon him with great reverence. Then all at once the Holy Spirit lifted his aura and they felt his energy rise. "Behold!" Michael yelled out, raising his arms out wide and lifting them up, as if he were Moses dividing the Red Sea, "You have been given your instructions, and these are the word of God!"

"Behold the glory of the Lamb!" They chanted in unison. "Behold the glory of the Lamb! Behold the glory of the Lamb!"

At that moment, Michael leaned over to the angel Gabriel, and kneeled before him touching him gently on the cheek and peering deep into his eyes with a paternal love. Gabriel was the special one, the one who would bring the last bowl of wrath to the new Babylon. "And then there was the seventh," Michael said, proudly. "*The seventh angel emptied his bowl ... and there were flashes of lightning and peals of thunder and the most violent Earthquake that anyone has ever seen since there have been men on the Earth. The Great City was split into three parts and the cities of the world collapsed; Babylon the Great was not forgotten: God made her drink the full wine cup of his anger. Every island vanished and the mountains disappeared; and hail, with great hailstones weighing a talent each, fell from the sky on the people. They cursed God ... it was the most terrible plague.*"

Michael rose, speaking to the group. "It is this promise," Michael said, "this great prophecy, that we bring to the world! Remember, although these words were written in a different time, by applying this text to the modern world of sin through my visions from God, we can now understand the true messages and we now know what plagues shall fill the seven bowls, and how they are meant to be delivered by us, the seven angels. This book was a work of art, and we are the seven painters of God! The message is clear, we bring the wrath of God to Earth, and the new Babylon shall fall! Now let us each us fulfill our promise before the eyes of the Almighty! Glory be to God for his blessings, his power and his wrath! For we unite like molten steel and we are the might of his sword, slashing through the whispering wind upon the lost souls of mankind we cannot lose. Like locusts we shall fall upon the Earth, until it is done!"

"Behold the glory of the coming of the Lamb," they chanted.

"Yes, behold," Michael yelled out, "for the Beast, the Red Dragon of ten horns and seven heads has risen, and with the wrath of God, he shall fall back into the splinters of hell, deep into the great lake of fire!"

CHAPTER 38

"Ask, and it shall be given you; seek, and ye shall find; knock, and it shall be opened unto you."

Matthew 7:7

OCTOBER 30, 2008

Chase was lost inside himself at the posh Fairmont Olympic Hotel, in Seattle, staring at the photographs he'd taken of Michael's wall at his mother's home. He'd been staring at the pictures for days in his suite, trying to put the puzzle together before his meeting with Ted Mitchell. Chase believed that the pictures were Michael's blueprint for his master plan, and he'd finally managed to convince Novak's people that a meeting with him was not only necessary, but of vital importance to national security.

So the meeting was set. Chase was to go to Red Diadem Tower at 8 PM, for an evening meeting with Mr. Mitchell, which he hoped would lead to a meeting with Richard Novak, and ultimately add valuable resources to their search for the angels. With Richard's connections and security resources, Chase was sure that it would be much easier to track the whereabouts of the angels and to foil their plans. He just wished that he had more insight about their plans to take to the meeting.

While the images on the dark-painted mural were disturbing, they were also very difficult to make any geographic sense out of because there were very few landmarks and the clues were hidden in jumbled religious text. After days of study and deliberation with Billy, they had both begun to see the big picture, and it was quite scary.

If the images in Michael's artwork depicted the seven plagues that the angels planned to carry out, then thousands, maybe hundreds of thousands or even millions of people were going to die horrible deaths. The angels were responsible for the massive smallpox attack in Los Angeles, and the death toll from that attack alone was still climbing.

For the angels, the smallpox attack was the first plague; it was the beginning of the Apocalypse. And they were far from finished. Michael was orchestrating the end of times, and he had proven his capability to carry out his heinous crimes. He'd also proven deft and elusive, the master planner, always several steps ahead of his enemies.

In the *Book of Revelations* there were seven plagues. On one of Michael's paintings on the mural, he took directly from revelations and the words echoed in Chase's mind. He was haunted by those words. The words bore an unmistakable imagery and similarity to his vision-quest, or what he knew more clearly as his nightmare. "*And the beast was taken, and with him the false prophet that wrought miracles before him, with which he deceived them that had received the mark of the beast, and them that worshipped his image. These both were cast alive into a lake of fire burning with brimstone.*"

Where is, Jimmy? How do we stop this madness?

Chase and Billy had become very good friends, bonded by their unique ordeal in the desert at the angel's ranch and by their continued search for Jimmy and the angels. Billy had saved Chase's life. Without Billy escaping at the ranch, Chase knew that he'd already be dead and the search for Jimmy would be over. He felt fortunate to have Billy's aid, and he wondered how he could possibly ever repay him for all of his help. He hoped, however, that maybe the reward would lie in the good that they might achieve by stopping Michael and his angels from doing any further harm to anyone else.

While Chase wanted to free his brother, he knew that there was much more at stake than saving Jimmy alone – mankind was at stake. On the last picture in the mural, there is a mushroom cloud rising up out of a large body of water, possibly the ocean, and the aftermath is nothing but death and darkness. If the picture was accurate in setting forth the angel's plans, then Chase feared that they possessed a nuclear weapon among their most unholy arsenal. And so far nothing he'd learned about Michael and the angels gave him any cause to believe that they wouldn't use it. In fact, he was quite confident that they would.

That's why he desperately needed Novak's help. And he figured Novak had more at stake than anyone if the story were to get out that all of the madness of the smallpox attack in LA was designed by his son. A story like that would kill any chance that Novak had at winning the White House, and frankly all of the money in the world couldn't free a man from that kind of publicity.

Billy had argued that going to Novak was a bad idea, and had really wanted to go to the authorities. So, they struck a deal. If Novak wasn't interested in helping them bring an end to the madness, then they would go to the authorities and tell them everything that they knew and warn them as to what they now believed was coming. Chase no longer knew if he could save Jimmy, but he knew that his only shot at saving innocent lives from the plagues was to let the world know what they intended to do. He had to give the people a chance.

Susan, for her part, had also begged Chase to go to the authorities and she had promised him that if anything happened to him that she would carry the torch. Susan was prepared to alert the authorities and inform the media about everything that she knew if it appeared to her that Chase was gone, even if there was no longer a prayer of saving her beloved Jimmy.

Like Billy, the idea of a meeting with Novak didn't seem like such a good idea to her, but Chase was a persuasive trial lawyer and he'd won that battle. She was worried about Chase just as much as she was worried about Jimmy. She feared that they had done all that they could to find Jimmy, and that maybe it was time to seek help and just pray that he somehow could find his way back to the light. When they last spoke, Chase had told her, "If anything happens to me, the first thing that you do is go to the media, and then the police." And she had of course agreed.

Chase had set the meeting with Ted Mitchell days earlier and with the hour of the meeting at hand, he was growing nervous and considered canceling and just going straight to the authorities. Still, having lost his brother, he felt as if he owed Novak a little warning about his bastard son and his sociopathic deeds. But if Novak wouldn't help him, then the plan was to let the reigns go to the story that he'd been holding onto so tightly.

The complexity of the pictures and the enormity of the suffering on the faces had brought it home to both of them that this thing was bigger than they had even imagined, and after the smallpox attack, and remembering everything in the lab at the ranch, they knew that it was all within the realm of possibility. And that very reality scared the shit out of both of them. *How do you save the world from a monster like Michael – a hell bent, religious nut that will stop at nothing until he brings suffering to all?*

Billy was packing his things when Chase entered his adjoining suite. Billy nodded at Chase with a warm smile, as Chase plopped down into a small suede sofa next to a window on the west side of the room.

"We've come a long way, Billy, haven't we?"

"I wish I could have been more help. I wish we would have found him by now," Billy said.

"Me too," Chase said. "You've been a great friend to me; you saved my life."

"Well, I try to save a white man's life at least once a year," Billy said.

Together, they laughed under the soft lighting in the room, and for a moment they were just two friends sharing a laugh. Finally, Chase interrupted, "Don't get too full of yourself, Tonto! I think a lot of people are going to die."

Billy's grim face fell to the floor. "What does your vision-quest tell you?" he asked.

"What?" Chase said. "Billy, you know we-"

"What does it tell you when you close your eyes at night, Chase?"

Chase slumped down into the chair. "I see thousands of people, maybe more, they're screaming, and many are burning. It's as if the sea has exploded into a pit of death, and those people, men, women and children of all ages are being swept away right into it – right into the center of hell. And it just keeps going. When I close my eyes I see them and they're dying, and they're not just dying, they're suffering badly.

"I've let them down, haven't I, Billy?"

"What is that white expression again? 'It ain't over till the fat lady sings'" Billy said.

"Man, you're too much!" Chase said.

Billy smiled wide. "Well we haven't quit! This is just too big! If these people have a chance, it lies with you."

"Stop saying that!"

"I'm serious, Chase, and besides, you already know that, don't you. You are the one that can save these people. That's why I've been helping you. Your vision was a sign! You are a warrior of God!"

"All right, that's enough!"

"He has sent you here to us for this purpose," Billy continued. "There is a question, and there is an answer. How do we save the people? You hold the answer to that question!"

"I think you're expecting more from me than I can possibly give, Billy. My nightmare, vision, whatever you want to call it, hasn't answered anything. I haven't got a solution to this madness!"

"Not yet," Billy said, "but you must keep your faith. The great eagle follows you, and when it is time the eagle will deliver the message to you, just like when it led you up the mountain to Blue Lake at the pueblo."

"I hope you're right, I'd listen to an eagle right now if I thought it would help. What does that make me, Tonto – crazy like a fox?"

"Nah," Billy answered, "that makes you a searcher, a wise soul!"

They both started laughing again, this time the laughter completely filling the room. Every once and a while their conversations were so strange that it could be hard to remain serious. But, Billy wasn't joking. He was there because he believed that stopping the angels was the counterbalance necessary to save Mother Earth. Without it there could be no peace, and no harmony among the universe. Chase couldn't see it in himself, but Billy knew that he was special, a great man that could help deliver the world from its madness. Billy's intuition told him that that time was approaching fast, and as Chase so often said, "Time is of the essence!" They both knew that was true now more than ever.

It was 8 PM, just a little over a few days away from the presidential election, and Ted Mitchell was sitting in his office atop Red Diadem Tower when his guard informed him that Chase had arrived and was waiting in the large conference room. This meeting had Ted nervous, and he didn't like it at all. He quickly picked up the phone from his desk and dialed Richard.

"He's here," he said, "are you sure you want to do it this way?"

"Yes, Ted," Richard said, confidently, "stick with the plan. Trust me."

"Well, if something goes wrong, and we blow this election -"

"Just do it!" Richard shot back, agitatedly.

"Fine!" Ted said, hanging up the phone. "Fine, it's done!"

Chase stood in front of the floor to ceiling windows,

staring down at the Seattle streetlights in the glowing orange twilight. He could see for miles and miles. The view was stunning, but what caught his eye was the small black bird that landed on the ledge outside the window. The bird was sleek, its feathers silvery and dark, and it almost seemed to be peering in through the thick glass directly at Chase. A chill crept up his spine, and he felt as if a message had just been delivered. But it was no eagle delivering the message. Something bad was about to happen, Chase could sense it in the stillness of the air. His stomach was churning, just as it does prior to presenting closing arguments at trial. He tried to calm himself and turned away from the window.

At that moment, the glass conference doors swung over and Ted Mitchell entered the room throwing a sharp glance at Chase. He walked to the long mahogany table and slammed his briefcase down.

"Have a seat," he said. "Haven't got much time. This campaign has worn my old ass out." Ted went to a cabinet next to the plasma display screen at the front of the room and pulled out a half-full bottle a cognac. "Like some?" he asked.

"Sure," Chase answered. "Look, Mr. Mitchell-"

"Call me, Ted!"

"Ted, look I know you're very busy right now, but I am sure that you will want to hear what I have to say."

Ted sat down across from Chase, studying his face and his eyes. "Then let's get right to it," he said. "You said on the phone, if I understood you correctly, that Mr. Novak's campaign was going to fall amidst a huge scandal that will destroy him. Is that right?"

"Yes," Chase answered. "That's absolutely right!"

"So, then, you tell me how is this going to happen when I am running this campaign and I have the best intelligence in the world, and I don't know anything about this, except that your persistence and threat to run to the media has forced me to meet with you?"

Chase felt Ted's scowl, but he wasn't intimidated. "Look, there's been a change in plans," he said.

"There has?" Ted asked.

"Yes," Chase said, "I came here thinking that maybe we could help each other. I figured I could help you out."

"And now?"

"Now, I think that you and Mr. Novak can just go fuck yourselves, that's what I think."

Ted smiled. "Well, thank you for your sincerity. Now tell me what you came here for! What was so goddamn important that you've been harassing me for all these weeks to set this fuckin' meeting?"

Chase looked away. What he wanted at that moment was to grab Ted by the neck and give him a southern whipping, but the two guards that searched him before entering stood by the entrance to the conference room, making that impossible.

"Look, you like sincerity, huh? Well, in all sincerity," Chase snapped, "I don't give a fuck about you or Mr. Novak! His son, Michael, has kidnapped my brother and I believe his cult, or whatever the hell it is, is mobilizing right now as we speak to unleash what they believe to be the seven plagues of Revelations, killing thousands, maybe millions of people!"

Ted broke out into coarse laughter. "Sounds credible," he said.

"I know," Chase said, "that kind of publicity, once it gets to the media, that won't shake Novak's world at all, will it? Do you think people want that kind of 'old man' to be their man in the White House?"

"So what do you want?" Ted asked.

"Nothing!"

"What do you mean nothing?"

"I told you there's been a change of plans. I can't work with you or Novak; I'm going straight to the media and then to the authorities."

Ted's laughter filled the room. His voice was like listening to irons scraping over coals. Finally, he stopped and lit a cigar, and then looked dead into the center of Chase's eyes. "If you break the story, Chase, we'll kill you, okay. End of story! Who do you think we are, Chase, amateurs? You're way out of your league! You don't have a fucking clue of who or what you're dealing with, do you? You don't think that we don't already know everything there is to know about you. You're a good lawyer, but this whole thing has been bigger than you from the start, hasn't it? Give it a rest! Let it go, before more people get killed."

The words hit Chase hard, and he looked around planning his escape. Finally, he said, "If you kill me, people will know I'm missing and they have-"

"Only two," Ted interrupted, "and one is already dead." Ted looked at his watch. "Or close to it," he said, "and soon both will be gone."

Chase had heard enough, and he stood to leave. "Sit down," Ted ordered, "let's watch a little home movie, shall we?"

At that moment, Ted picked up the remote control that was sitting near him on top of the table and pushed a few buttons. The screen lit up, and instantly the struggle for life filled the room. All Chase could do was turn away as Billy engulfed his last breath of air, gurgling and choking on the blood.

"Do you hear me now? Do you hear what I'm telling you?" Ted snapped at Chase.

Chase started to back up, making his way around the table as Ted walked toward him. The two guards burst through the glass doors at Ted's command. The screams of Billy were deafening in Chase's mind, and he felt at that moment as if he were going crazy. As the guard brandished the gun at his chest, Chase locked eyes with Ted. Ted's eyes pierced him from a deep, hollow place where the wit of men knows no laughter, only the solemn despair of their soul begging for mercy when there is none to come.

CHAPTER 39

They came at night to her father's ranch in Tucson on the eve of Halloween. There were two of them. Susan had tried to wait up for Chase's call after his meeting with Ted Mitchell, but she finally fell asleep when the call never came. The creaking floor gave them away. She opened her eyes in the dark room, and tried hard not to move, holding her breath, frozen in fear.

From the couch where she was lying, she could see the man enter the room. Her poetry book slipped behind her back as she moved slightly. He moved closer, and then finally stopped right in front of her. Slowly, he began to move his fingers across her face as she pretended to sleep. In her mind, she counted to three and then without hesitation she rose up and sank the ink pen deep into his foot. He screamed violently, writhing in pain he lost all control and knocked her to the floor with a clinched fist. Then as he tried to remove the pen that had gone all the way through his foot, Susan grabbed a letter opener from her father's desk and stabbed it into his back.

The man dropped to the floor this time like a bag of bricks, and moved no more.

For a second after, all was quiet, and then she heard the struggle going on upstairs coming from her father's room. Quickly, she crept past the stairwell on the creaking hardwood floor, and walked over to the fireplace and grabbed a shotgun off the shelf and loaded a shell.

She was scared and she was shaking wildly. She heard her father's cries, and she ran up the staircase and headed straight to his room with the shotgun in her hands. Lake was a big man, but the intruder he was fighting seemed twice his size, and he had somehow managed to get a rope around Lake's neck. Susan fired the gun, sending a blast right into the intruder's back, dropping him to the floor buckled over at his waist. The shot echoed throughout the house, and Susan couldn't hear anything for a moment. The smell of gunpowder filled the room. Sensing the intruder was still breathing, she grabbed a Tiffany lamp off of the night-stand and hit him as hard as she could over the head.

Her father was lying on the floor semi-unconscious, but he still had a pulse and was moving slightly.

Susan was in shock, and didn't know what to do. Frantically, she called 911, and she was beginning to administer CPR when her father lunged forward for a burst of air.

"Susan," he asked, barely audible, "did that-"

"I'm okay," she answered. "Just rest. The ambulance is on its way."

"You have to go, Susan."

"No way, I'm not leaving you."

"Susan, you remember what you promised, Chase?"

"I can't do it."

"You're going to have to do it. You have to leave now."

Susan began crying, and her father put his hand on her shoulder. "Susan, you have to go now. Go downstairs and take the .38 from my desk. There's some ammo in the drawer – take it with you. Keep it on you at all times."

"Okay," she said, with tears streaming from her brown eyes. "I love you."

"I love you, too," he said. "I love you, too."

Susan took one last look at the dead man lying across the room sprawled out next to the bed. She could see the white skin of his wrists, but he was wearing leather gloves and a mask. *Why? Why is this happening?*

"I don't know what's going on, Daddy," she said. "They may come back. Don't stay here."

"You just take care of yourself," he answered. "If anything happens to you that would kill me for sure."

CHAPTER 40

The red Bell 407 helicopter landed aboard Red Trinity in the midst of a violent storm. Waves were crashing up against the yacht, making the landing a challenge. But the orders were clear. There was precious cargo to unload.

Chase was still unconscious when the burly guard pulled him from the chopper. The man put his arms under Chase's shoulders and dragged him into the galley, and then through a series of doors.

Several hours passed before Chase began to stir, the injection they'd given him made him groggy and his head was pounding from the fight with the guards. He rubbed his temples and remembered the hell he'd been through. He remembered Billy. And then he wondered why he was still alive. He rose from the bed in the dark room and clung to the walls like a blind man searching for the light. When he finally found the light-switch and the soft lights lit the room, he finally discovered that the swells going on in his stomach were partly due to the fact that he was on a boat. He'd wondered if his nausea was related to the pounding in his head, but to his surprise, he was on a goddamn boat.

As he rolled his eyes around the room, looking closely at the Victorian antiquities and the grand Mahogany ceiling and wall to wall crown moldings and the furnishings all covered in rich, red velvet cloth, he realized that he was not just on an ordinary boat. He was on a yacht!

Novak's yacht!

He walked to the large double-door and wasn't at all surprised to find it locked with a deadbolt. His quarters were an interior room, and there were no windows, only a bed, a sitting area with a television, a small bathroom and a wet-bar. Seeing no escape, and growing sicker by the moment, he laid back down on the high framed bed, trying his best not to move.

When the doors opened, it happened so fast and swift that Chase had no time to prepare himself for an attempted escape. He simply sat up on the side of his bed, expecting the worst, and hoping to get it over with quickly without any torture.

With an air of executive confidence, Richard strode into the room like a brush fire, instantly devouring all of the energy the room had to offer. Chase simply stood, studying his clean shaven visitor that was casually dressed in jeans and a white oxford, looking completely refreshed and vibrant.

"Chase Davidson – the heroic lawyer!" Richard said, extending his hand which Chase shook only lightly. "It's a pleasure to finally meet you.

"I apologize for the conditions that brought you here, but I prefer to see it simply as the stars aligning with perfect symmetry, organizing a meeting between us. This is fate."

"Fate?" Chase said. "You're holding me here. You killed my friend. It seems the stars have aligned in your favor, not mine."

Richard slightly smiled and looked at Chase, his dark eyes narrowing in on Chase's, before he sank down into a soft chair in front of the bed. "You're not a prisoner, Chase," he said.

"Can I leave?" Chase asked.

"Soon, in time you can, but first we need to talk. Please try to relax; your life isn't in jeopardy here. No one is going to harm you. You're safe."

"Why did you kill, Billy?"

"I didn't."

Chase's eyes peered deep into Richard's with disbelief. "Your men killed him, I saw it."

"What did you see? You saw him get beat up, and you saw him go unconscious. That's all that you saw."

"Let me see him!"

"Chase," he said, "I wouldn't lie to you. I don't have to. Billy is alive and he's okay. He's been sent home to his pueblo, to his family. I have never had the need or the desire to kill either Billy or you."

Chase was perplexed; the enormity of the moment left him dazed. "Why should I believe you?"

"You're alive, aren't you?"

Chase was quiet for a moment, collecting his thoughts. He realized that no matter what Richard said, he wouldn't believe Billy was alive until he saw him with his own eyes.

He looked up at Richard. "What do you want with me?" he asked.

Richard stood and walked over to the wet-bar and pulled out two bottles of water from the small refrigerator, handing one to Chase. Then he sat back down in the red lounge chair in front of the bed.

Finally, Richard answered, "You and I have something in common."

"Yeah," Chase said, sharply. "And what the fuck is that?"

"We both know the pain of losing someone to religious fanaticism."

"What are you talking about?" Chase asked.

"Don't be coy, Chase. I know what you've been doing. I know where you've been."

"Then you know about your son, Michael?"

Richard withdrew a deep breath. "Yes," he said, looking distant. "It's unfortunate, you know, I barely knew his mother. I guess she found religion," he said, smiling. "She messed Michael up, what can I say?" He threw up his hands and looked at Chase, as if seeking commiseration.

"Well," Chase said, "I guess the apple didn't fall too far from the tree, just far enough to rot to hell."

"How's that?" Richard asked.

"You're both kidnappers!"

Richard smiled. "I'm sorry about all of this. I told you that, but I needed to meet you."

"You know they plan to unleash the seven plagues of Revelations upon society. Michael sees America as the new Babylon. He's intent on bringing Armageddon to the world."

"Yeah," Richard said, "he's a sick kid."

"How much money did you give him?"

"Enough for him to go away and live his life and not have to worry about money."

"Well, he's spent it like a terrorist!" Chase said. "The smallpox attack in LA, they did that! And that's nothing compared to what's coming!"

Richard sighed. "I know," he said, "they're going to kill a whole lot of people."

"Then let's stop them!"

"Richard leaned over and sat his water down on the coffee table. He picked up a large, black remote control, and hit the power switch, surfing through the stations to the TV that hung on the wall. Finally, he left it on a channel where the dark shadow of a man could be seen sleeping on a bed in what appeared to be an old, worn down hotel room. A black suitcase lay next to him on a small table. With the push of a few buttons on the remote, Richard was able to pan in for a close-up of the man's face.

"Oh my God," Chase said, "It's Jimmy! This is incredible, you've found him!"

Richard sat back in his chair, and studied Chase carefully. "It's not exactly what you think, Chase," he said. "Yes, that's Jimmy. And yes, I know exactly where each of the angels is right now at this very moment. I know their every movement. When they go to the bathroom, I know about it. It's the beauty of technology, and interactive TV. Amazing, isn't it! I'm still amazed at the things that we've been able to do and I started it all. I'm very proud and yet very fortunate. I've been following, Michael, ever since he came to me. I knew then from his hard-core religious banter that I had to keep an eye on him. And obviously I had the resources to do it. I don't know if you like reality TV, but let me tell you something, the networks haven't seen anything like this one. The Church of Seven Angels are a really scary bunch. They represent the worst of religion, and its destructive powers. And I have no intent to stop them."

"Why?" Chase begged.

"I didn't know what to make of Michael at first. I didn't know how to use him. And then one day, it just dawned on me that what he was doing was perfect for me. Without trying to sound too Machiavellian, let's just say that for me, the end justifies the existence of the angels. Their plans and my future are for the moment, intertwined. They're going to get me elected. With their madness, I am able to rise from the inferno as the voice of reason. The American people will understand that I am the one that will put these fanatics into their proper place in our world."

"But not before thousands, maybe millions die!"

"Survival of the fittest is a law of life. It's a lot like chess; sometimes the pawns must be sacrificed for the sake of the king. Nature is cruel. Life isn't fair. Have you ever heard that saying people sometimes use when something bad happens to someone, 'There but for the grace of God, go I.'

"Nature is God!

"Think about it, Chase. There are over 6 billion people living in the world. Last year alone, 5 million children died of hunger and malnutrition. Do you realize how many people that is? There are about 3.8 million people living in LA – that's how many children died. Where were you? What did you do to help those kids? Nobody cares about them, really! Did you send any of your attorney's fees to help those kids? Over 30 million people have died from AIDS, and there are over 60 million HIV positive living in primarily developing countries right now.

"Those people are going to die," Richard continued, piercing Chase with his dark eyes. "Let's face it, every day people in developing countries are dying of preventable diseases. So I ask you, what difference does it make if a few millions Americans die?

"Are we more deserving? Are we better? If you haven't ever bothered saving anyone else before, then what difference does it make to you now?"

"Because this is different!" Chase said. "We're Americans! These people could be our family, our friends!"

"Exactly," Richard said, with a sheepish grin, pointing to the TV. "Let's talk about what you really want to talk about – you want to save him. You want to save your brother!"

Chase shook his head in disgust. "Yeah, you're right! I want to get my brother out of this fucking mess! But I can't let innocent people die if I can stop it!"

"Did you miss my point?" Richard said. "Every day you're letting innocent people die, and you aren't doing anything to stop it! Just because you can't see that child that's sitting next to his mother in sub-Saharan Africa who just died of starvation, and the brother next to him with a bloated belly and a dry mouth full of dirt, doesn't mean they don't exist! You're half awake! The reality you see every day is only half the truth! That kid's being swarmed by flies and maggots are ready to prey on his flesh when he too, dies, without notice to you that he ever lived. He's starving and he's sick. There's no food in his belly, and none to come.

"He's still real, Chase! He's real, and he's still going to die and it will be a slow and painful death! And don't get me wrong, I'm not picking on you! Everyone does it! We don't give a fuck about the people that we don't see – the people we don't know!"

"That's not true!" Chase exclaimed.

"It is true!" Richard followed. "You're lying to yourself so you can sleep at night! We all do it! And then what do we do, we go to church and we pray that the people in the world will live on Earth as in Heaven! It really is hypocrisy," Richard said, smiling. "We pray to God to save those that we won't lift a finger to save! Look at the war on terrorism. We've spent over $700 billion on the war on Iraq. Toss in the billions that we've spent chasing Bin Laden in Afghanistan, and elsewhere in the world, and so we're nearing in on the trillions of dollars spent. Sure, the terrorists have killed thousands of Americans, but poverty and hunger kill 12 million people a year, every year, but we could care less! So why is it any different with the people that might die at the hands of Michael and his angels? We don't know these people personally! The world is overpopulated, so can't we spare a few for the sake of a better world? Everybody has to die sometime, Chase! Their deaths will pave the way for something better!"

"You're really sick!" Chase said.

"I am going to use this tragedy to shine the spotlight on the dangers and the consequences of religious fanaticism. And in the long run it will save a hell of a lot more lives! Sometimes you need to sacrifice a lamb to save the flock! That's nature; that's life. And life can be cruel."

"Well, I've heard some great rationalizations as a lawyer from my clients, but you take the cake! So why are you telling me all of this, anyway?"

Richard smiled, his brown eyes sparkling. He was having a good time, and it showed. "Because you're in a very unique position," Richard said.

"How's that?"

Richard turned the channel, using the remote to find his library of recordings. With the push of a few buttons, Chase saw himself appear on the screen as Billy cut him down from the altar. Chase dropped to his knees. He couldn't believe what he was seeing! The blood of the lamb was everywhere, and Chase and Billy were both drenched in the blood. And Richard had watched it all!

"Chase, I feel like I know you," he said. "I've seen your soul cry. You are my kind of guy. You're not hiding anything. You'd be great on my team. When I win this election, fighting these religious zealots is going to be one of my top priorities and I'm going to want people in my cabinet who understand the issues we're facing. Who understands these issues better than you and I?"

"No! It won't happen," Chase said.

"Of course, I knew you'd say that. I'm not stupid. How do you think I got to where I am in life? I don't ever ask the question until I know the answer. And I am always right.

"Here's your dilemma – your choice: You can get your brother and stop him from going any further in this madness. My people will eradicate any evidence that he was ever with them."

"At what price?"

Richard smiled. "Nothing's ever free, is it?" he said. "The other plagues will go on as planned by the angels without interference. Then when I am elected president, you'll work for me. And together we'll fight to end fanaticism, saving more lives than would have ever been possible by stopping Michael and his angels."

"And what if I just say, 'Fuck you!', and that, 'I think you're a fucking nut case?'"

"You won't!"

"How do you know?"

"Because Jimmy's your brother, and he means more to you than a bunch of people that you've never met before."

"Innocent people!" Chase said.

"Yes, innocent people! But like the people in the Sudan aren't innocent! Like the 12 million who die of starvation every year aren't innocent. He's your brother and that makes all of the difference in the world and you know it!"

"And if I say, no! You haven't answered that question."

"I thought I did," he said, his eyes glowing wildly. "You won't say no! But hypothetically speaking, if you did, the plagues will happen anyway. Jimmy will do his part. And then you, Jimmy, and Susan and anyone with any knowledge of what's really happened will join those innocent children who die of starvation every year. End of story!"

"You drive a hard bargain," Chase said, glumly staring down at the floor.

Richard smiled warmly. "Look, I like you, Chase. If I didn't, you wouldn't be getting this opportunity in the first place. We can achieve great things together, or not! At this point, whether we ever work together is completely up to you."

"No pressure," Chase responded sharply.

"That's right," Richard said, "no pressure at all. The election is this coming Tuesday, that's four days from now. I think the angels are planning to act soon, all signs indicate as much. You're safe here. I'll give you a few days to think about all of this." He held up the remote in his hand and pointed it at the TV on the wall. "The video recordings of everything that the angels did to Jimmy are all right here on channel 63. I'm confident you can figure it out. I want you to see what they did to your little brother. Then when I get back you can tell me whether or not you're willing to give Jimmy a second chance at life."

CHAPTER 41

NOVEMBER 3, 2008

Susan was early for her meeting with Jane Tierney, the political correspondent turned vice presidential candidate, running mate to Richard Novak, the wealthiest TV and technology magnate in the entire world. Susan was freaking out. She'd been running scared and she was tired, weary of always looking behind her back around every street corner. After hours of research in a public library, she'd called nearly every television producer in the U.S., and they all thought she was just another nut-case when she told them her story.

All but one.

Max Weinberg was skeptical at first, like the rest, but he listened and promised her that he would get back to her after he had a chance to check out some of the details of her story. Three days passed before the phone rang, and she knew she'd struck gold when she heard his voice. Max was suddenly very nervous. He knew something. Something she'd told him had checked out. Otherwise, she knew he would have never set up the meeting with Jane Tierney.

Chase had asked Susan to provide anyone who would listen in the news industry with the story about Novak and Michael and the angels. He wanted her to connect them to the smallpox attacks, and to tell them that the FBI had investigated Michael as a suspect. He wanted her to tell the world that more attacks were imminent. And he wanted the world to listen.

Susan understood why Max was so nervous. But Susan was also nervous as hell. After all, Richard Novak, owned GNN, and Jane was his running mate. Max had assured her that she could trust Jane, and that nothing she said would get back to Richard. Susan didn't know whether she could trust her or not, and she knew that if she was wrong the cost could be her life.

Still, there was too much at stake not to try.

Max set up the meeting to take place in a small privately leased jet in a small hanger at Columbus International Airport, where Jane was campaigning nearby. Typically, Ohio figured to be a hotly contested state in the coming election. The meeting was to be completely clandestine. In fact, the only people that were to know about it were Susan, Max and Jane. At least Susan hoped that was the case.

Susan sat at a small table on the plane. She was nervous, and smoking, something that she'd never done before the past week. She wondered if Jimmy would ever forgive her. He'd always hated smoking. The thought of Jimmy made her smile, and it also brought tears to her eyes. She prayed that both Chase and Jimmy were alive. She prayed that she survived the day. She'd tried to be cautious, but she was just an ordinary girl trying to manage her emotions, let alone suddenly have the survival skills necessary to elude whoever was looking for her.

Jane finally arrived and quickly introduced herself. Her dark, short hair was windblown, and her smile was warm and friendly. Susan instantly felt at ease with Jane. That was Jane's gift. And it had always worked like a charm, and it had given Jane more than one great story, but never anything like this one.

"Susan," she said, "you seem very bright, and you're very beautiful. How'd you get mixed up in this mess? Max told me your story. He checked some things out that are very interesting. You have our attention. What kind of proof do you have that these people may be planning more attacks?"

Susan pulled the pictures that Chase had given her from her purse. "This is Michael's room," she said, "at his mother's house. These are the pictures I was telling Max about on the phone. If you look at the pictures in order, starting next to the doorframe, you'll see the first plague. That stadium there, we now believe is Dodger Stadium, it was first disseminated to the public in LA. The people there lying on the ground, their scars are symptomatic of small-pox. The rest of the pictures identify the next 6 plagues, but the clues aren't easy to discern, just like with the stadium, it could have been any stadium. It's difficult to-"

"It's very thin, Susan," Jane said.

Susan sighed deeply. "What did Max find out? He found out something or you wouldn't be here. He wanted proof, and he took his time getting back to me! And he came back nervous!"

Jane studied Susan quietly, and she didn't see anything that showed anything other than complete sincerity and concern. Finally, she said, "He traced a large transfer of money to Michael several years ago to offshore accounts. The source is unidentified, it's possible it was Richard, but we can't prove it. It tends to corroborate the meeting that you said took place between Michael and Richard."

"Anything else," Susan asked.

"That's it," Jane answered.

"You're lying," Susan said. "I can tell by your eyes."

Jane blushed. "There is something else," she said, "but it really doesn't prove anything."

Susan smiled slightly. "What is it?"

"Michael's birth certificate, his father was identified as Richard Novak by Michael's mother. That was back in the 60s. All it proves is that Michael's mother claimed that Richard was Michael's father, and it might explain-"

"But Richard wasn't famous or rich back then was he?"

"No, not to my knowledge," Jane answered.

"So why would she lie?" Susan asked. "Maybe it's the truth!"

"If it's the truth, then we have one hell of a story to tell the world, don't we? That's why I'm here, I might be an old, salty politician, but I still love a good story."

"The story of all time!" Susan said.

"If we're wrong," Jane said, "we'll ruin lives. I have to let Max do his homework on this so that we can get it right. We can't move too fast and get it wrong. I want to help you, and I am sorry about Jimmy and your -"

"Well," Susan said, "move too slow and millions of people might die! Can you live with that, Jane? The cruel murder of millions!"

Jane was cold silent. She had no words to offer Susan.

CHAPTER 42

Chase had been watching video of Jimmy's torture for what seemed like days. He began to understand the systematic breakdown of Jimmy, and exactly how it happened. From his own experience with Billy, he knew Jimmy's torture had to have been bad, but what he discovered was that Michael had completely erased Jimmy's identity. He simply wasn't Jimmy anymore; Jimmy was gone. Chase could only hope that somewhere deep down in the recesses of Jimmy's brain, his identity was buried, and when prodded by professionals, he would reemerge. But, there were no guarantees that even with the best help that science and money could offer that Jimmy would ever be the same or even close to the man that he was before he was taken to the ranch and became Gabriel.

When he could watch no more, Chase finally turned off the TV. He just couldn't stand to watch his brother suffering, knowing he was helpless to help him. Chase looked for a way out of the locked room, but there was none. The only escape possible would have to be made through the locked double-doors, but he knew that they were heavily guarded by armed guards. Without the TV on, he could hear them talking and exchanging jokes. He was trapped, emotionally and physically in a floating prison.

The enormity of Richard Novak, his power, and his plans, began to sink in and it left Chase wondering how anyone could ever stop him. In all of his life, he had never seen a man so charged by his own power that he was willing to let massive-scale murder take place in order to clear the way to the top of the food chain. Chase believed that Richard would succeed in being elected the President of the United States. After all, Richard was leading in all of the polls, and it seemed that people had really bought into his message. Chase also knew that Richard had been right in his assessment of the American people, the smallpox attack in LA, and extreme acts by fanatics played right into his campaign's hands.

Richard had the world by the balls. And at the moment, he had Chase's locked into a vice-grip, as he turned the lever just a little more every hour.

Hours earlier, Chase watched as Jimmy carried a suitcase along his side and walked to McDonald's to eat, and then went back to his hotel room, where he sat in the darkness in isolation from the real world. He was in Miami; Chase gleaned that information from the *Pink Flamingo* sign that flickered with cheap fluorescent lights at the roadside motel. In the room, Chase could see where Jimmy had broken out the glass to the two mirrors in the room, the one above the dresser and the other above the sink. His eyes appeared dead, like a bird's eyes, they were dark and showed only a glint of life.

Chase clung to the hope that a spec of life was still alive inside of Jimmy. He could tell that Jimmy was in really dire straits. His condition was that of a terribly depressed human being. *If there be a God, then how could this have happened?*

He wanted so badly to help his brother survive. He wanted to free him from his nightmare. But then he was also in a nightmare of his own, and when he closed his eyes he could see the faces of people burning – their skin was melting and they were reaching out to Chase for help. He felt completely helpless. He wondered if he could save Jimmy at the expense of thousands, possibly millions of lives. And then he thought about Susan. Her words still haunted him. "If it comes to saving souls, save Jimmy's," she'd said.

After several more hours of going back and forth over everything in his mind and praying for guidance, Chase finally fell over on his back and went to sleep. Then he began to dream, but this was a different dream than the one he'd been having.

In this one, he found himself running at full speed in a dark and vast forest. His heart was pounding and he felt the fear of being lost propelling him forward, deeper into the forest. He ran through trees, trampling through the thick brush with leaves falling all around him and twigs cracking under his feet as he barreled into the woods. Finally the tree canopy closed and darkness fell all around him.

But he kept running, tripping now over everything in his way because he couldn't see anything in front of him. He felt his arm banging against the trunks of tress, and felt thorns dig into his hands. His body was taking a beating, but he just kept running. He was running from everything, from all of his promise, and from all of his promises. He was running from his fears, running to escape the pain. He was running from everyone, and running to no one.

He could hear the maddening roar of the suffering souls he was leaving behind, howling like the wind, demons blowing at his back, their screams filling the forest. And so he ran, and he kept running, and he didn't stop until his soul began to cry like the lamb that was slaughtered by Michael at the ranch, crying out for mercy. Finally, he tripped over a dead branch and fell to the forest floor. He closed his eyes, breathing heavily, trying to rest.

Then he awoke. He was lying in a green field. The glorious sun was shining in his face. Hummingbirds were echoing in the nearby trees. And as he sat up and looked around, he realized that the golden valley was surrounded on all sides, by the towering trees of the forest. And so he lay there all day, not knowing which way to go, afraid to move. And then the night came again. It seemed as if he'd not found the light at all, but only lost himself in eternal darkness.

When Chase finally awoke from his dream, he had no idea what time it was so he turned on the TV, his only connection to the outside world. He flicked through the stations until he found the news, and when he did he saw the horror of the plagues unfolding before his eyes.

History was being made.

People were being killed. And it was devastating, and very dark. Fear and outrage were everywhere.

He turned the channels and the same story was on every station.

The angels had been very busy. They were executing their plan.

All hell was breaking loose in America – the new Babylon. Mysterious bacteria and microorganisms had been detected in the water supply in New York, LA and Atlanta. Already people had flooded the hospitals and clinics with flu-like symptoms that quickly digressed into symptoms mimicking the Ebola virus.

Virologists and health professionals worked as fast as they could to identify the parasitic virus and its genome that was allowing it to inhabit the host cells in its human victims. The authorities were too far behind to catch up to the damage that had already been done, but if they couldn't identify the virus, they couldn't try to fight it effectively. Even the scientists panicked, as the victims filled the waiting rooms across the land, they saw the future, and it was filled with death. And it scared the hell out of them. Their worst fears had come true, and it had happened in such rapid succession they couldn't keep up.

People were dying all across America.

Some were bleeding through their own skin, dying a painful, gruesome death. Officials estimated that thousands had been infected, and the outbreak spread like wildfire.

The CDC placed all hospitals and clinics under quarantine – no one could leave once they checked in for care. And all hospital staff were required to stay until the outbreak was brought under control, which authorities were estimating could take days, even weeks or longer given the enormity of the outbreak and the gravity of the virus.

Then, only hours later, the second story broke.

Chase sat there on the edge of the bed in horror, as he watched his nightmare become America's reality. Hundreds of cases of Mad Cow disease were cropping up all over the Midwestern states. St. Louis, Kansas City and Chicago were hit hard. Authorities had been quick to respond, but they believed a large shipment of contaminated beef was responsible for the outbreak. They were investigating the outbreak as fast as they could. And the people kept showing up at the already overwhelmed hospitals. The Authorities were simply losing control. Doctors were breaking down in news conferences, as the feeling of utter helplessness swept the country. No one could explain how the strict U.S. regulations had been broken so badly, allowing for the Mad Cow disease outbreak to happen.

The outbreaks were spreading all across the country and it was simply too much for the government to handle. They had never prepared for such a massive attack on its citizens. The scope of this nightmare was beyond comprehension. This had the power to kill off millions. This had the power to change the world and send America into anarchy and it was all man-made madness brought to the world by a group of merciless fanatics.

People, hundreds of them, were getting very sick from the meat that they had digested only hours before their first symptoms hit. The virus was breaking them down. Their bodies were fighting a battle they couldn't win. They were fighting a virus, a super- virus that had made them super sick. They were going crazy; they were losing their minds, as the virus rapidly attacked their systems.

The doctors knew the infected were all going to die. They knew there was no treatment for Mad Cow disease, and that its victims had little hope of surviving.

The new Babylon was in complete chaos. The angels had staged a multifaceted, monstrous attack. And it was all done too easily. The government had failed to protect its citizens. People were angry and they were frightened, and with good reason. The angels weren't finished. Michael had been studying and planning and preparing for this attack for years.

To Michael, the wrath of God was being unveiled one plague at a time.

He was a madman, a sociopath, and a charismatic leader who had tortured and brainwashed his angels and turned them into slaves of evil. They believed that the last plague would tip the scales on the sins of Babylon, and according to Michael's prophecy, unleash Armageddon.

Chase sat there stunned, as the news continued to cover the horror that had struck America. Only a few hours later, the bowls of hell poured out yet another plague onto another American city street.

The angels had struck in Dallas, Texas. Hundreds of people reported to hospitals with symptoms of a strange stomach virus. The symptoms were striking its victims so fast that it had quickly begun to overwhelm local emergency officials in Dallas. The patients were exhibiting symptoms of dysentery, extreme nausea and vomiting, and the cause, of course, was unknown, but was suspected to be a highly fast spreading, infectious bacteria that was possibly airborne or spread person to person. There had been no reported cases of death, but people were very sick and the bacteria did not appear to be responding to antibiotic treatment. The residents of the city were frightened and a mass evacuation flooded the streets, threatening the containment of the virus. Authorities weren't ruling out any possibilities, testing the water supply, food from local establishments and groceries, and even taking air samples. However, they had not yet identified the root cause of the outbreak.

In Houston, authorities at local hospitals reported that there had been 13 deaths within the day. They were all attributed to the lethal bacteria, vancomycin-resistant staphylococcus aureus (VSRA). The city limits of Houston had been closed – with no one going in, and no one permitted to leave. Again, as in Dallas, the exact cause of the outbreak had not yet been identified. However, officials were worried that more cases would arise if it were not contained quickly. There was no known cure or treatment for the bacteria, as it has been highly effective at outmaneuvering the most powerful antibiotics known to the modern world.

Chase was so sick to his stomach that he was about to turn off the TV, and then another big revelation hit!

All across the U.S., computers began crashing, as if an avalanche was pouring down a mountain devouring every computer in sight. This was not the typical computer virus or worm; this was a super-virus, designed to infect and destroy all computer operated equipment. The damage was estimated in the multi-billions, and the government was going to take the biggest hit of all. Major functions of the government were crippled instantly. All major electronic security systems were computer operated and were infected with the virus. NASA was shut down. NORAD was shut down. The NSA system was completely disabled. Medical equipment was being rendered useless. Airlines were unable to move their customers from city to city, as their computers were all shut down.

The super-virus quickly was spreading across the seas, with the capacity to bring the modern world to a halt all over the globe in the most pervasive and destructive computer attack ever seen.

Chase was in shock and he couldn't believe what he was seeing on the TV.

America was under attack!

The angels had coordinated a massive attack, orchestrated by a genius with stuffed pockets, who believed he was the archangel Michael, preparing the way for the Lamb. He was Richard Novak's son. He was the son of the man who'd been waging a war against modern religion and the religious right, and the man who was closing in on the presidency of the United States.

Has the world gone mad! How is this happening? Why?

Chase turned the channel back to Jimmy. He was still sitting there in the dark, breathing slowly in a small hotel room in Miami. Chase watched and wondered what was going on in Jimmy's mind.

What is he planning to do? What is he thinking?

Jimmy hadn't moved in hours, and it seemed as if he was lost in a trance. Chase prayed that his mind wasn't completely gone. He prayed that his brother would not go through with the seventh plague. By Chase's estimation, Jimmy was the only angel left with work to do. He wondered if any of the others were still alive. The perpetrator of the smallpox attack had died of smallpox, but the plagues' victims were still mounting in LA. Chase figured that was all part of the plan: hit, then self-destruct, leaving as little evidence behind as possible.

Chase wanted so badly to save Jimmy, and as he watched the news unfold he became even more frightened of what Jimmy might do. What crime was he going to commit against humanity? How many people was he going to kill? How many children?

Chase prayed over and over that Jimmy wouldn't do it and he felt completely helpless to stop it from happening.

The world had simply gone mad.

Victims were everywhere, helpless, and dying.

The violence and the despair that the angels had brought to America was eating like a cancer at Chase's soul, and yet he was locked away in that *goddamn room*. "Please God," he begged, from the core of his being. "Please!" he cried. "Help me stop this nightmare! Help me stop, Jimmy!"

He picked up a chair and turned it over, running at full speed he smashed its legs into the TV that was mounted on the wall. The wooden legs penetrated the screen and the TV went dead.

The show was over. He dropped to his knees.

Then he heard the lock to the door turning, and someone began to open the double-doors.

CHAPTER 43

GNN.com

BREAKING NEWS
Violent Religious Riots Erupt in Cities across America

Monday, November 3, 2008 Posted 11:00 AM EST

(GNN) – Reports today that, The Church of Seven Angels, the same group investigated for their involvement in the deadly Los Angeles smallpox attack, is also involved in the recent bio-terror attacks across the nation that has spawned religious attacks among Muslims and Christians nationwide. The tension has spread from the privacy of homes, and has now rolled like a violent river into the city streets.

Around 4 AM the fires began. At the First Baptist Church in Indianapolis, Indiana, the first reported church fire began with giant flames spewing out of the stained glass windows, reducing the church to ash and burnt timber. The response was immediate, in what has become an eye for an eye war among American Muslims and Christians. Almost immediately following the fire at the First Baptist Church, Christians responded by torching a mosque, the Nur-Allah Islamic Center in Indianapolis, creating a nightmare scenario for citizens and authorities alike.

With the news of the fires hitting the airwaves, people all across major cities in America took to the streets in the most horrific rioting this country has ever witnessed. Authorities estimate that over a 1000 people have been killed since the riots began early this morning, with several thousand reporting to hospitals with injuries ranging from minor scrapes to severe life threatening wounds.

Coming on the eve of elections, and just on the heels of the worst bio-terrorism attacks ever unleashed in the U.S., the National Guard and all police agencies have been called up to restore order to a nation that appears to be boiling over with rage and grief.

If it seems the world has gone mad, one thing is clear: The Muslims are blaming the Christians for the recent bio-terror attacks that have made them prisoners in America. And the Christians are angry that they have been singled out for the radical acts of a single-minded terrorist organization.

While officials work to quell the violent eruptions, some officials are wondering if the presidential election will be postponed, something that would be an unprecedented event, the first postponement of a presidential election in American history.

Stay tuned for more as the story continues to develop.

CHAPTER 44

NOVEMBER 4, 2008 – ELECTION NIGHT

In the European decor, stately presidential suite high atop Seattle at the luxurious Alexis Hotel, America's prince stood in the center of the room with a drink in his hand and surrounded by his people. This was the command center for the final night of the campaign – election night. It seemed to all of the scholars and stars in attendance that everything had played into their hands, and to those gathered before their prince, the world's new brightest star, it was as if he had been ordained to the moment long ago.

The voting booths in the east were closed and results were already pouring in from across the country. The East Coast states were falling first: New York, Connecticut, Virginia and Georgia – all to Novak. The election began as a sweep. The excitement energized everyone in the room. All across the country, the plagues had killed scores of thousands, and taken their toll on President Barton and his campaign. People had lost faith in his message. They just didn't want a leader telling them that, "God was on their side," after learning firsthand the kind of violence and rage that remarks like that can incite among fanatics.

Americans had suffered and died painful deaths from deadly viruses and many still lay sick and dying, but Richard Novak was feeling great; he was on top of the world. He was after all, the Dog Star, the brightest star in the northern sky, and he was truly shining brighter than ever. Everything had gone according to his plan. Now it was his time to take center stage. He wanted it all, and now nothing and no one stood in his way. He was going to build the greatest empire the world had ever seen.

Jane was sitting in the corner of the room sipping a glass of Chardonnay, and talking intently with Ted Mitchell when she saw the two guards at the door escort Max into the room.

A huge smile enveloped his face when he saw her. "My you're beautiful," he said, extending his arm down to Jane. "Do you mind if I steal her from you for a moment, Mr. Mitchell?"

Ted smiled. "You can have her," Ted said, as he stood and walked to the bar.

Jane stood and walked with Max to a door. "Let's step inside here," she said, opening the door.

The room was a small office with a sitting area. Jane sat behind the large 18th century desk. The party raged on next door in the main room, with occasional knocks against the wall.

"How do you like me being in charge behind this desk?" Jane asked. "Are you threatened by women in power?"

Max laughed. "No," he said, "only men who seek it so desperately. They drink of it and never come down from the intoxication. You, on the other hand, are smarter than them. You let them drink, and take advantage of their intoxication. You could get away with murder if you wanted. They'd never see you coming."

Like a harpsichord, Jane played the tune with Max perfectly. "And what about, Richard? Will he get away with it?"

"Not if I have anything to do with it." Max replied, almost obediently.

"What do you need me to do, Max?"

"Nothing!" he said, his eyes glowing with fiery intent.

"Stay out of the fire! Whatever happens, no one needs to know that you knew anything, do you understand what I'm saying?"

"I think so," she answered.

"Some people, my darling, have no civility," he said. "They're so full of themselves that you are forced to knock them down. Promise me that you will never let your power make you forget who you are and where you came from."

"Oh," Jane said, smiling wide, "I won't. You can count on that!"

"You're special, Jane. Don't ever forget it!"

"Max, are we breaking up?"

"The story, if it comes out," he said, "I'm afraid it could ruin you and I am not about to let that happen. I'm your protector, remember."

"I remember," she said, looking deeply into his eyes, studying him carefully. "Max," she said, "You've been a great friend to me. I have always loved you, and you will be rewarded by all of this, you know that?"

"Yes."

She stood and walked to the door. "I have always known that a day like this would come," she said. "I think we both know what you have to do, Max. Don't be afraid. It will be okay."

He nodded and she walked back into the crowded room.

Around 8 PM the presidential suite at Alexis Hotel really began to rock. The anointed one, Richard Novak, celebrated with his family and friends, a sweeping victory. He'd taken the country by storm. The plagues had killed thousands, and those deaths and the growing number of sick, swayed the votes of millions, sealing the deal for Richard Novak. The grand master was ready to take his place among the great pantheon of kings, the golden halo shining all around him, this was his night and he loved every minute of it.

Jane was standing with Richard, holding his right arm high above their heads in victory, proclaiming him the champ, the victor and the spoiler. His white oxford was drenched in champagne, as if he'd just won the Super Bowl. Fire burned deep in the core of his eyes.

Max was smiling graciously, as Jane called him over to meet Richard. They shook hands, and Jane whispered in Max's ears. "Do it now," she said.

Max pulled the letter opener that he'd removed from the desktop in the sitting room and sank it deep into Richard's chest. Richard screamed but the room was so loud that only those close to him heard his scream. And only those that saw Max, stabbing him violently over and over understood what was happening. Quickly, they spread out like scared wolves, as Max's eyes rolled back into his head and he kept stabbing and stabbing and stabbing and stabbing until finally he was tackled by security guards.

Richard dropped to his knees, holding onto Max's legs as he slid to the floor. Blood gurgled from his open mouth. Jane was holding Richard, screaming for help. Richard's white oxford was drenched in blood. The fire in his eyes was gone.

Richard Novak, the newly elected President of the United States of America, was dead.

CHAPTER 45

GNN.com

BREAKING NEWS

President-Elect Richard Novak Assassinated

Tuesday, November 4, 2004 Posted EST 11:45 PM

(GNN) – In a chaotic scene at Alexis Hotel in Seattle, Washington, at approximately 8 PM this evening, the nation's newly elected President, Richard Novak, was stabbed repeatedly as he stood victorious among his supporters. Witnesses at the gathering in the presidential suite report that Mr. Novak was sharing a moment with Jane Tierney, his running mate and vice president elect, when Max Weinstein, a longtime GNN producer, charged and stabbed Mr. Novak several times in the chest prior to being restrained by security guards at the scene.

While many questions remain yet to be answered in the days that follow, what is certain is that the president-elect, at the age of 45 years old, on the eve of the greatest moment of his life, has been killed. And now a nation that has seen so much recent tragedy and heartache must find a way within itself to grieve yet another tragic loss.

Stay tuned to GNN as the story develops.

CHAPTER 46

The day following the election and assassination of president-elect, Richard Novak, in so many ways, was a day of mourning for America and the world. The crowd at Miami International Airport was barely recognizable, as people solemnly and quietly went about their business in the Delta terminal.

As Chase walked through the doors with the other passengers unloading from the Atlanta flight, he saw a familiar face in the crowd, and tears were streaming down her beautiful face. Susan ran to Chase, nearly tackling him in front of everyone, embracing him with everything she had. Susan lost control, sobbing and squeezing her arms tightly around Chase, sending a sharp pain through his arm.

"It's okay," he whispered. "It's okay."

"I thought you were dead," she said. "When you called, it was like an angel from heaven, I couldn't believe it."

"I'm lucky to be alive. My temper saved me," he said. "I turned into a madman." Tears welled up in his eyes. "I killed two men, Susan, I-"

"Stop," she said. "Stop it! You had no choice. Whatever you did, you had to do it!" She pulled back and looked into his eyes. "I'm just so glad you're here."

He smiled, wondering just for a moment what it would be like to kiss her. He quickly erased the thought, knowing it was wrong. "Yes, I'm still here," he said. "Now, let's go get Jimmy."

With that they took off toward the rental car that Susan left in short-term parking. Chase stopped along the way and called the front desk of the Pink Flamingo Hotel, getting detailed directions from the airport, and then he also bought a map of Miami. He'd traveled all over with his practice, but never to Miami. As Chase drove, Susan plotted the fastest way there using the directions and the map. They had no idea if Jimmy would still be there at the hotel. It had been three days since Chase last saw Jimmy from the video feed on Richard's yacht. A lot had happened since that time. Chase and Susan both feared that Jimmy was either dead or just flat-out gone.

Chase raced through the sun-drenched streets of Miami, trying his best to contain his emotions and not get pulled over by the police. Security all over America was at an all time high. A national curfew of 10 PM had been imposed, as authorities all over the U.S. were working together to restore order.

But order was difficult to come by. Hospitals were still busting at the seams with victims of the plagues, and the riots across America had caused thousands of deaths and billions of dollars in damage. Miami, for its part, had done well. The people in Miami didn't riot, their peaceful protests were passionate, but never turned violent. But then they had not experienced the violence firsthand that many others had witnessed: the loss of their children, of brothers and sisters, family and friends. When the loss is personal, the rage is more likely to follow. Miami had been spared, so far.

Jimmy was sitting on the floor in his small, dim hotel room when he heard the first knock on the door. He was startled and jumped to his feet, quickly putting on his shoes.

"Jimmy," Susan called out. "Jimmy, are you in there?"

"Jimmy," Chase followed. "It's Chase. You're safe. If you're in there, please open the door."

Jimmy stood there for a moment in shock. Then he quickly grabbed the black suitcase from the table and placed it in the shower in the bathroom, closing the curtain to hide it. He walked to the door, and began to unlock the deadbolt.

Susan pushed through the door. She threw her arms around Jimmy. He'd lost about 40 pounds, and his eyes were so dark and tired, and lonely. Jimmy was gone. He appeared gone. She didn't care; she hugged him and kissed him on the cheeks and squeezed him tight. But he didn't flinch. He didn't respond to her touch. He didn't even acknowledge her emotion. He was just gone. After a moment he pulled back from her and stepped away.

She stood there in disbelief and in horror. "Jimmy," she said, "it's me!"

"It's okay," Chase said, walking toward Jimmy, who again stepped back a step. "I know what they did to you. We can help you. We're here to help you. You can still have a life."

"A life," Jimmy said his voice shaky and strained. "There is but one life, and that is the universal life of the Lamb! You, me, we don't really exist!"

"Yes we do!" Susan cried. "Yes we do. You do!" She dropped to her knees sobbing. "Jimmy, please come with us! Leave this place!"

"Behold," Jimmy said, "The end has come. Soon the Lamb will be among us. And when the Lamb comes, she shall bring with her Armageddon!"

"What did they do to you?" Susan cried. She reached toward him and he backed away and ran to the bathroom and locked the door behind him.

Susan turned to Chase, who was just standing there in shock. He couldn't believe his eyes, and yet he'd seen Jimmy before at the ranch, it was just so horrible to see it in person. Chase gathered himself, and charged the locked bathroom. Recognizing that Jimmy wasn't about to open the door, he stepped back and threw his weight into his left leg and kicked in the door.

A light ocean breeze blew through the window. Jimmy was gone. Chase looked out the window and saw Jimmy running down a sidewalk. He climbed through the window and took off after him. Jimmy was carrying a suitcase, and had lost a step since his days playing high school football, but he was still faster than Chase. Chase was cursing the whole way as his knees began to kill him. He was lagging behind at least 50 yards when he saw Jimmy turn left into a small bay, running to a small boat dock to a row of moored motor boats. Jimmy reached a medium size motor boat and untied the line to the dock and sped away out into the blue bay out toward the dark waters of the Atlantic. All Chase could do was stand there and watch as Jimmy disappeared into the sun.

Susan was sitting on the steps to the office of the Pink Flamingo as Chase finally walked up.

"He's gone," he said, breathing heavily.

"I know," she answered, still crying. "He was lost before we got here."

"I know," he said. "I know."

"We have to call the police. We have to try to stop-"

"I know," Chase said, his eyes filling with tears. "I know. Let's go get this over with."

CHAPTER 47

The citizens of Miami had the perfect view and they looked east when the bomb exploded off the coast, close to the Bermuda Triangle, also known as the Devil's Triangle. The force of the 8-kiloton bomb produced a mushroom cloud that rose faster and higher into the blue sky than any other explosion ever produced by man has gone.

The technology of the Russians had worked to perfection.

The blast produced a horrific sky of red that erupted into a large mushroom. Then it was like sunshine, only brighter, and flashing and followed by an intense heat blast that literally melted the skin from people's bodies. Everywhere fire burned, and people were either dead or dying.

And then the giant waves came.

The explosion unleashed a torrent of hell towards the East Coast. Miami took a direct hit. The mega-tsunami was like nothing the world had ever witnessed. Others Tsunamis paled in comparison to this giant beast, a beast that brought with it the greatest plague of all, a giant exploding, rolling sea of fire and water, barreling towards land and destroying everything in its path.

Nothing like it has ever been witnessed by man, the magnitude an proportion defy logic and reason. On that day, hell was born in the Devil's Triangle.

One man, a survivor, interviewed days later affectionately called it, "A lake of fire." The man said he looked up into the sky and, "It was a giant beast, like a red dragon with horns spreading across the sea, coming right at us."

The blast was so intense and deep that it thundered magnificently into the core of the sea shelf, penetrating deep into the ocean floor and right smack into large pockets of methane gas that had built up over thousands of years. The same methane gas deposits that some say account for the mysteries of the Bermuda Triangle. When the forces of the bomb hit the gases, multiple explosions under the water erupted on the ocean's floor and the disturbance shifted the Earth in multiple locations under the sea. And what followed was a series of waves, fast and swift, the fiery 150 foot blast waves of methane gases were sent out in all directions. The most fearsome Tsunami ever witnessed by mankind was born, and the lake of fire of Revelations became reality for millions of people.

The Bermuda islands were hit hard. The Miami coast was burned up just as fast, as if it were all made of straw and someone had set a match to it, the flames spread out across the city like wildfire. The waves ripped all the way up the East Coast and swallowed up the land and the people with the might of something so powerful and devastating, that one caught in its path could only feel that the end of times had come.

The location of the blast was exactly where the archangel Michael had planned for it to be all along. A geologist as an undergrad, he was always fascinated by the mysteries of the Triangle, and believed that the methane gases buried there underneath the ocean's floor would add to the intensity of a nuclear detonation and create giant waves of fire. And he was right.

The result was the greatest disaster the world had ever witnessed, a man-made quake that sent tsunami-size waves of breathing fire barreling towards all land in its path.

And so Jimmy's plague was set forth upon the land. And Babylon was shaken from its very core. Although the actual plan had called for the detonation to occur on Inauguration Day, with simultaneous detonations in New York and D.C., ripping Babylon into three pieces, the actual result was far greater than even Michael had dreamed possible.

For as it is written in Revelations, *"The seventh angel emptied his bowl into the air, and a voice shouted from a sanctuary, 'The end has* come.' *Then there were flashes of lightning and peals of thunder and the most violent Earthquake that anyone has ever seen since man has been on Earth. The Great City was split into three parts and the cities of the world collapsed; Babylon the Great was not forgotten: God made her drink the full wine cup of his anger. Every island vanished and the mountains disappeared: and hail, with great hailstones weighing a talent each, fell from the sky on the people. They cursed God for sending a plague of hail; it was the most terrible plague."*

And so the East Coast of the United States was drowned in giant waves of fire. Millions were left dead. Burned corpses floated aimlessly among the trash and charred debris. Countless others washed out to sea where their spirits would swim in eternity in the images of the horror of that day. And the people of America watched in complete shock, as yet again, their faith and their spirits' were put to a great test. And although the hand that Jimmy dealt America was not the actual design that the archangel Michael had envisioned, it was nonetheless, in terms of hands, a Royal Flush.

Over the years the Bermuda Triangle had notoriously and mysteriously swallowed hundreds of vessels and aircraft. Stories of the Triangle's powers were plentiful by merchants in the old days, and often exaggerated for heightened effect, but what the world witnessed on that day pouring into Miami was so extreme as to be unimaginable.

Over and over, the survivors recounted the same tale: The red cloud rose like a rocket into the air, illuminating the sky so bright that it seemed as if the sun had fallen into Earth's atmosphere. Then the thunder came. And then the wave of burning heat. And then the came the giant walls of water, filled with fire from the exploding methane under the ocean's floor.

And if they were still alive after all of that, they were in a deep state of shock.

The explosions were so powerful that they were felt all the way across the U.S., but it was those in its path that saw the evil grow and become death. People and cars and buildings and souls were being swept away into the ocean which had become a giant lake of fire. People were dying, they were burning and they were screaming out in great pain.

Those that survived stood helpless, many with their skin falling off of their bodies, their eyes bearing the irreversible damage to their being. Some were completely charred where they stood. Others had escaped to buildings, only to be crushed and burned. Few survived the monstrous walls of water and fire, and those that did were scarred for life, physically and emotionally. Babylon was drowning from its sins, the cities on the East Coast were destroyed, their dense populations devastated. This was truly the worst plague of all. People all across Babylon were dying from the scourge of the plagues.

Chase hid under the desk of the Dade County Sheriff wondering how a religious fanatic could spread such a cancer to the world, only to serve the one he claimed to be fighting.

"How much hell can one man bring to Earth?" Chase asked aloud, as the walls came crashing down in flames around him.

"This much!" Susan said, choking on the smoke that was enveloping the air.

"And the *Bible*," Chase screamed, pulling Susan to her feet. "Look at how these nuts use it to kill!"

"I don't want to die," she cried out.

"We've got to try to get out of here, Susan. Don't let go of my hand"

They ran through a flaming door-frame. Darkness was all around them, except for the flames all they could see was thick, black smoke. They ran into a hallway where they could hear the screams of people dying, of people burning, but they couldn't see them. They searched through the thick smoke for a way out of the building, but they couldn't see anything. Their lungs were quickly filling with smoke, and without help they were just a few breaths away from finding out what lies on the other side of life, answering the eternal questions that have brought mankind religion. They slumped to the floor. Chase was still holding onto Susan's hand, and then darkness came as his eye's closed. He felt her squeeze his hand tightly, and he thought of her beautiful face. That was his last thought before he passed out in the smoke.

CHAPTER 48

GNN.com

BREAKING NEWS

Deadly Nuclear Attack Explodes in the Bermuda Triangle – Giant Waves of Fire Unleashed Upon East Coast – Millions Feared Dead; 'Church of Seven Angels' Suspect Arrested in Washington, D.C.

Wednesday, November 5, 2004 Posted EST 5:09 PM

(GNN) – A nuclear explosion today near the Bermuda Triangle off the coast of Miami has once again brought a nation under attack to its knees. Besieged by a wall of fiery waves from methane gas released from the ocean's floor near the Bermuda Triangle, the East Coast has been devastated. The loss of life is expected to be in the millions.

Fires are burning all over Miami and there are no fire departments left to attempt to fight the enormous, sweeping blaze that has unleashed hell upon a city completely taken by surprise. Yes, without warning the fiery waves hit, washing people from where they stood off into the sea of rushing water.

While the scene draws to mind images from *Dante's Inferno* of Dante Alighieri's, *The Divine Comedy*, this horrific, criminal attack against mankind is best called, a divine tragedy.

But America is responding in the only way it can after all of this madness – unity. People from all across the nation are headed to the area to help the victims of this horrendous crime against humanity in anyway they can.

Other news: Suspect Arrested in Washington D.C.

Authorities arrested a yet to be identified man near the Washington Monument, and word has quickly spread that he is considered a prime suspect in the plagues that have been unleashed upon the citizens and cities of America.

Sources of GNN are claiming that this man is Michael Novak, the religious leader of the Church of Seven Angels, the man authorities have been seeking for several weeks.

Stay tuned to GNN as the story develops.

CHAPTER 49

Billy's condition remained the same all throughout November. He was in a coma. The blunt trauma to the head nearly killed him and his brain had to be drilled in order to relieve the swelling. Even if he woke up the doctors had no idea what to expect.

Red Hawk was sitting vigil by his side. He had heard it all from the doctors at Harborview Medical Center in Seattle, and he was growing tired of the white man's medicine. To Red Hawk the white man's medicine lacked faith and spiritual prayer, which is why he never left Billy's side. He believed that Billy would return to the world, triumphant, a new warrior. The elders had always called him "Redwood," and Red Hawk believed that Billy's skull must be as hard as Redwood or he would have been dead already.

The police had been by and wanted to speak to Billy if he woke up. They didn't really care about what had happened; it was simply a duty call. Red Hawk knew that it was only by the grace of God that Billy was still breathing. He sat by his side for hours and hours, and prayed to the Great Spirit for a healing. After several days of prayer with nothing changing in Billy's condition, he felt as if there was nothing to lose anymore so in the middle of the night, Red Hawk and Billy's younger brother, Dan Aranjo, snuck him out of the hospital. Typical for Seattle, it was raining that night, and although their vision was blurred in the old Ford Bronco with the broken windshield wipers, they headed south toward the Sangre de Christo mountain range. They were going home to the pueblo where they could properly administer Indian medicine in the hopes that their tribal rituals would succeed where the white man's medicine had failed.

Billy looked grim, the spirits of death were nearby. Red Hawk knew that they would be coming soon to take him if he could not rescue his spirit. He believed that any healing must first begin with Billy's soul. His internal spirit could be revived and it would heal his body from the inside out. With enough prayer and ritual, Red Hawk believed that Billy would recover fully and completely. And his faith never wavered.

Dan wasn't so sure if that would be the case, but he wasn't about to challenge his grandfather, a respected elder, still holding firm to his traditional belief in the life and energy of everything. But Red Hawk was not disillusioned; he was wise in the ways of the spiritual world. The time for conventional wisdom had passed, and all that remained was Billy's spirit.

Neither of them knew what had really happened to Billy, or who exactly had cracked his skull. They feared the absence of Chase meant that he was probably dead or near death in the hands of the same evil doers.

When they arrived at the pueblo after driving straight through, a 23 hour trip, they placed Billy in a small carriage and headed off on horseback up the mountain to Blue Lake. Once they arrived at their camp site next to the lake, they covered Billy from head to toe with bandages cut from a cottonwood tree and dipped in sacred medicinal roots. An owl could be heard a short click away, watching them as they danced and sang over his body to the steady, low beat of the pueblo drum. The rituals were continual and seemed to go on for days in the cool December air. At night the campfire billowed smoke into the sky, as chants and prayers to the Great Spirit were sung in the native tongue, Tiwa.

Over time, the swelling in Billy's brain began to subside. While his body remained still, on the inside, doors were opening in his mind, and a light was appearing, and deep inside the light was a dance of two snakes. He walked closer and closer until he became an Eagle and took flight into the light, landing upon a cliff overlooking a small path. He was a warrior, the Eagle, and he was hunting. The two snakes were equal in size. Billy recognized them as Western Diamondbacks, indigenous to the desert and armed with deadly venom. These snakes, however, were different than the indigenous snakes of the region; they had come from deep within the caverns of Hell, and with deadly venom. Yet, between the two, one was more deadly than the other.

This snake the Eagle dubbed the "King Snake." This snake bore blue, exotic eyes unlike any snake Billy had ever seen. The snake with the blue eyes carried within its fangs, the venom of evil, with enough toxins to bring damnation to the entire world. The other snake, while extraordinarily deadly, carried only enough venom to kill those who would cross its path. Billy could sense that both snakes were evil, but the extent of the evil and the power between the two was vastly different.

His spirit vision, dark and blurry at first, only became clearer as Billy began to come around. He could see the deceit in the snakes' eyes. He could feel the heat of the desert and sense the fire of their venom, and ever so slowly he began to regain consciousness.

Red Hawk was still by his side. At first their interactions were sporadic, lasting for only seconds at a time. As time wore on they were lengthening and becoming more frequent and Billy's eyes were becoming more lucid. Clearly, a healing was taking place, just as Red Hawk knew that it would. For in his great Indian spirit, he knew that the civilized, white man's world had discovered no medicine better than faith. And his faith burned brighter than the elements of the sun.

CHAPTER 50

January 20th, 2008

INAUGURATION DAY, WASHINGTON, D.C.

Millions of people gathered in front of televisions across America and around the world watching with great anticipation the inauguration ceremony of America's newly elected 44th president, Jane Tierney. She was only running for vice-president, along side Richard Novak, but his assassination made her next in line and so she was there to serve the people.

She was born of humble beginnings in Alabama. Her father was a small town preacher. She grew up the bad girl, and as preacher's daughters often do, she embarked out into the world with a mission to find out who she was and what she wanted in life.

In college at Georgetown University she discovered something about herself that she'd kept a secret from all but a few special people. She knew them as her protectors. Max was one of them. But there were others, always watching, always ensuring her safety.

She was chosen. She was the whore of Babylon, and the world would fornicate with her. But, while some believe they are chosen, some really are. And Jane was one of those. The dreams she'd had as a child had followed her into her adult life, but she was no longer scared of them. Life is a journey, and even for her it remained somewhat of a mystery. She always knew what to do at the right time, but never too soon before its arrival.

Jane stood nervously in her black business suit and high heels, as Supreme Court Chief Justice Robertson administered the oath of office outside the nation's Capitol Building. When Jane spoke, her words echoed across the country. She was America's sweetheart once, and now she was going to be their President. While the sun was buried behind the clouds, Jane planned to bring the people sunshine, if only for a moment.

"I do solemnly swear," she said, "that I will faithfully execute the Office of President of the United States, and will try to the best of my ability, to preserve, protect and defend, the Constitution of the United States."

Missing from the end of her oath were the words, "So help me God," a statement first uttered by George Washington back in 1789.

Following tradition, Jane stepped up to the podium in front of the bullet-proof security glass to give her first inaugural address to the nation. The entire modern world was watching every move she made and every breath that she took. The crowd gathered for the inauguration was at least two million strong. Many had camped out on the lawn near the Washington Monument. The American people desperately needed a message of healing. The broadcast was expected to draw the largest audience ever for any live television event.

This was a day when history was being made on many levels. Not only was a woman being sworn into office as President of the United States, but she was the first female president the U.S. had ever seen. And her ascent to the highest office in the land had come at a time when the nation and the world were under the greatest test it had ever faced.

The events of the past year had rocked the foundations and the core beliefs of all Americans, and all citizens of the world felt caught up in America's quest for freedom from the chains of religious zealots gone mad. The Church of Seven Angels, with their crimes and their fervor had divided a nation and then sought to destroy it, but the nation and the world were rebounding with words and acts of greater tolerance and freedom.

Jane had written the speech herself. She'd written several drafts before finally settling on the draft she would present to the world.

She took a deep, long breath, clicking her heels nervously. "I address this speech to all citizens of Earth, whether you be Muslim, Christian, Jewish, a Palestinian or an Irish Protestant, a Hindu, an Atheist or Catholic, or whatever your creed, whatever your nationality, I address this speech and this proposal to you.

"We have all been under attack," she said, as the sun broke free of the clouds above her. "Yes, maybe the attacks did not occur everywhere, but surely they were heard and felt everywhere. The attacks represent an explosion of our differences. To each other we are all foreigners, we are all strangers, are we not?

"But what unites us also makes us the same, and what inspires us, I believe can make sunshine of rain.

"Can you hear it? Can you hear my message to you?

"Who are we to judge and condemn our neighbor? What can we agree upon that will keep this from happening again? I propose a contract of unity, a treaty to be signed among all nations of the world, by representatives of every tribe and every creed and every nationality. This will be our contract to each other, and if it cannot be signed by all nations, then it is not binding. But if we all sign it then we must hold one another to it. Those who do not sign will not benefit from our trade and our goodwill shall no longer shine upon them. For we can govern ourselves with different laws, but there is one thing that we can no longer do. We can no longer allow people to attack people because they are different, and have different beliefs, especially when it comes to the existence of a God, and the commandments of that God.

"Throwing buckets of water at the rain to stop the rain from falling just makes the puddles of water larger, but it does not stop the rain from falling. It cannot. For water can no more stop water, than violence can stop violence.

"The war against terrorism omits the fact that war is terrorism.

"If we want peace, we must offer our hands in peace.

"If we want war, then we must use our weapons against each other without mercy.

"But as long as we practice an 'eye for an eye' against our neighbors, we shall only reap that which we have sewn.

"If we want a harvest of peace, we must begin now to plant the seeds of peace and we must nurture it until our bond is strong, until we can truly call ourselves united.

"For we have a common interest to protect, and we have common ground.

"We are all citizens of Earth.

"This has been a gift to us all regardless of creed or nationality. We should not let our religion destroy us. We come to our own religion in so many ways. Most are born into their creed, for others it was their choosing by way of their own spiritual journey, but however you come to it, and even if you do not, do not let it make you judge another's faith as evil, lest you yourself become evil.

"Do not seek to make your religion the only religion, lest you become a martyr for the abyss. If we do not find acceptance and tolerance of other religions in this world, then we will not find heaven, paradise or enlightenment.

"To the terrorists who follow jihad, I ask you, who made you God so that you have all of the answers and so that you could bestow your uneven judgment upon the citizens of Earth?

"Is it the fear of death and what lies beyond this world that makes us so quick to accept a belief system that on its face provides us with all of the answers? Our divinely inspired books of God, the *Koran*, the *Bible*, the many writings of the Eastern religions, and the philosophies, and all of the others, do not condone murder.

"Yes, maybe to pardon and to forgive murder is of the highest divinity but to pursue it in any form, for any reason, where is the justification? The bomber of the abortion clinic, who made him more justified in his homicide than those he has decided to judge himself?

"If we cannot live in a world of laws respected by all men and women, and a world of faiths accepted by all men and women, than we shall not prevail as a global community.

"For those who believe in Christ as their savior, was not his message to turn the other cheek when he said, 'For you among us who has not sinned, cast the first stone.'

"For those of you who follow Mohammed, does Mohammed really sanction murder?

"Let me propose to you, not answers, nor a doctrine of how the world shall come to an end, but a proposal as to how we can all come together to write a new history for our world. Let us show history that we had the wisdom to learn from our mistakes, that we understood that our neighbor's lives were just as valuable as our own.

"For those who believe in God, show that you wish to follow by example in making the world a community in which all people treat others as they themselves would have others treat them. Show each other and show God that we can use the brains and the intelligence that we have been so blessed with to live in peace and in harmony with one another and to take care of the Earth that is our home. Peace on Earth should not be a mystery; it should be a way of life.

"I say to you now that the greatest test on Earth for all people is not how you treat those of your faith and of your likeness and belief system, but how you treat the other children of the Earth who are different from you. How big of a mistake would it be to kill or harm another on a false belief that you were better than the other, or that they were somehow less than you, or that you were indifferent to their value as a human being altogether?

"What if you did kill another and then one day you died yourself, only to find that your God was not approving of your actions and felt that you should reap as you have sewn? Are you prepared for that wrath?

"What is the risk, on the other hand, of being accepting of others? What is the harm of caring for others? What do we lose by treating all people, men and women alike of all faiths, creeds and nationalities, as equals?

"Let me rephrase that question, what is the risk of being good and noble versus the risk of being right about a belief that may or may not be true, a belief taken on faith alone?

"And don't misinterpret me for ill gotten gain, faith, I believe, is good if it promotes goodness and acceptance, but not if it promotes a pious adherence to tenets that say, 'I am right, so therefore you are wrong! I am good, so therefore you are evil!'"

"We love the books of divine inspiration because they tell us in black and white how to live, but the gray part is that nowhere is it written whether to apply these books literally or as stories to support a way of life that is moral and just.

"I say to you who may be too zealous in your convictions, be more afraid of being wrong, than being right, and then maybe you will add some reason to balance your convictions that may just promote a more peaceful and loving world. And how could any loving God ever fault that?

"As one who chooses to believe in God, let me now share with you what I believe so that you understand that it won't affect my rule in a negative way. So that you know that I am a uniter and not a divider. I believe that finding religion is about knowing God, and you can't find religion if you don't know your own heart. Look inside yourself, what do you see? How do you feel? You must feel something when another person suffers. I believe if you have met with sorrow and loss, you have met with God. Through your suffering, he is with you, by your bedside and by the bedside of all people, as all people are worthy of God.

"There is no more of a right way to follow God than to follow your heart. That will provide you with more than enough sacrifice, more than enough love. And by doing so, you will know God.

"And God will know you.

"Be not afraid of what you do not know, but fear those who do not know and say that they do. For there is no right or wrong way to follow God if you are following a loving heart that believes in love and prosperity for all people. And I believe that how well you follow your heart is how well you follow God's will.

"The word of God, the first, the middle and the last, should tell you nothing more and nothing less than to follow your heart and to love one another the best that you can.

"For that is the test of man – can they learn to follow their hearts?

"If you follow your heart, you should never have to worry about what lies on the other side of life.

"Your focus must be here in this world on what good you can do with your life.

"So now I ask you, will you help me make this a better world?

"This question, whether you believe in God or not, still applies to each and every one of you. And how you act and the choices that you make, will answer the question for you.

"Give the children of the Earth your love and the world will give it back to you. Give me your heart, and together we will make the Earth

the Promised Land. Give me your heart and I will not lead you astray.
Give me your heart and together, we shall unite the world."

With those final words Jane turned and left the podium, promptly
surrounded by her security detail she turned to embrace her family
and friends. Ted Mitchell, her newly appointed chief of staff had been
standing off to the side of the platform during her speech, and waited
for her in the presidential limousine.

"Do you think they bought it?" she asked him, as she stepped
inside.

"Of course they did?" Ted said, as he smiled from ear to ear. He
was so excited, so full of energy. "You're the Great One," he said. "The
Book of Revelations was always the code of the Beast, written as the
plan for the One. And now the world is yours for the taking. Richard
Novak, he was the prophet of the campaign, but he was also just a
puppet in a game he never really understood."

Jane smiled as the words soaked into her skin. "It's a cool day," she
said, "a great day!"

"A great day indeed!" he answered.

"It was a great book, wasn't it – *Revelations*?" she asked.

"Greatest book ever written!" he said.

Jane smiled. "Always loved the ending, the ambiguity is absolute
perfection."

"That's right," he said, beaming. "Never judge a book by its
cover!"

"The devil's in the details!" she said. "Isn't that what Richard always
said?"

"Your father taught you that, too. Didn't he?"

"Of course," Jane said. "He was a preacher, a fiery one."

"Wasn't on God's team, was he?" Ted asked, smiling, knowing the
answer.

"Nope! He was on my team! Never was much of a fan of God,"
she answered, "but he just loved the fire of *Revelations*. Absolutely
loved every word of it!"

At that time, Jane felt a sudden uneasiness and she looked out the
window, scanning the crowd of people lining the streets. She was struck
by a tall Indian man standing by a fire hydrant, he was old with long
flowing gray hair, and next to him was another Indian with his head

bandaged around his forehead. The old Indian seemed to be looking right into the limousine, and Jane felt as if he could see through to the darkness of her soul, and for a moment she felt naked and revealed. The old Indian and his comrade were wearing war paint on their faces, and Jane knew that they were there for her. For the first time, she had seen the face of the real enemy and she had seen no fear.

Jane looked at Ted. "That Indian man, with that lawyer in Seattle that-"

"Yes," Ted answered sharply. "What about him?"

"Are you sure he was taken care of?"

"Sort of?" Ted smiled.

"What do you mean sort of?"

"Well if he ever wakes up from the coma he was in, he'll be jabbering like a one year old."

"Ted, I don't need to remind you that we have enemies. I think he's alive. I think I just saw him back there!"

Ted turned violently, looking out the back window. "Where?"

"In the crowd by the fire hydrant," Jane said, pointing to the spot.

"I don't see any Indian," Ted scowled.

"There were two," she answered. "They were just there."

"Well they're gone now. Jane, I seriously do not believe for a moment that that was him. He was barely alive!"

"But he was alive! Next time, get it right!" she said. "No more fucking comas! What about the lawyer?"

Ted's neck tightened. "He's dead! He took a flight to Miami, apparently not a good choice of destination. He's gone."

"Gone is not dead!"

Ted turned to face Jane. "Look, Ms. President, you let me worry about these things. You have enough to worry about already. If they're not dead, it's a fucking mistake on their parts."

Jane shook her head. "No, Ted, it's a fucking mistake on your part. And I hate to tell you but I think they're alive. This has only just begun you know," she said, her brow stiffening in disgust. "The Revelation Wars have begun!"